ORPHAN STAR

ORPHAN STAR
Alan Dean Foster

NEW ENGLISH LIBRARY/TIMES MIRROR

For Joe and Sherry Hirschhorn, and their
Three Princesses,
Renee, Bonnie, and Janice,
Who would grace any fairy tale,
With love from Alan . . .

First published in the USA in 1977 by
Del/Rey Ballantine Books.
© 1977 by Alan Dean Foster

FIRST NEL PAPERBACK EDITION JUNE 1979

NEL Books are published by
New English Library Limited from
Barnard's Inn, Holborn,
London EC1N 2JR.
Made and printed in Great Britain by
William Collins Sons & Co Ltd, Glasgow

45004271 5

CHAPTER ONE

'Watch where you're going, *qwot*!'

The merchant glared down at the slim, olive-skinned youth and made a show of readjusting his barely rumpled clothing.

'Your pardon, noble sir,' the youngster replied politely. 'I did not see you in the press of the crowd.' This was at once truth and lie. Flinx hadn't *seen* the overbearing entrepreneur, but he had sensed the man's belligerence seconds before the latter had swerved intentionally to cause the collision.

Although his still poorly understood talents had been immensely enriched several months ago by his encounter with the Krang – that awesome semisentient weapon of the now-vanished masters of the galaxy, the Tar-Aiym – they were as inconsistent as ever. The experience of acting as an organic catalyst for the colossal device had almost killed both him and Pip. But they had survived and he, at least, had been changed in ways as yet uncomprehended.

Lately he had found that at one moment he could detect the thoughts of the King himself off in Drallar's palace, while in the next even the minds of those standing in close proximity stayed shut tight as a miser's purse. This made for numerous uncertainties, and oftentimes Flinx found himself cursing the gift, as its capriciousness kept him in a constant state of mental imbalance. He was like a child clinging desperately to the mane of a rampaging devilope, struggling to hang on at the same time he was fighting to master the bucking mount.

He shifted to go around the lavishly clad bulk, but the man moved to block his path. 'Children need to learn how to mind their betters,' he smirked, obviously unwilling, like Flinx, to let the incident pass.

Flinx could sense the frustration in the man's mind, and

sought deeper. He detected fuzzy hints of a large business transaction that had failed just this morning. That would explain the man's frustration, and his apparent desire to find someone to take it out on. As Flinx considered this development, the man was making a great show of rolling up his sleeves to reveal massive arms. His frustration faded beneath the curious stares of the shifting crowd of traders, hawkers, beggars, and craftsmen who were slowing and beginning to form a small eddy of humanity in the round-the-clock hurricane of the Drallarian marketplace.

'I said I was sorry,' Flinx repeated tensely.

A blocky fist started to rise.

'Sorry indeed. I think I'm going to have to teach you . . .' The merchant halted in his stride, the threatening fist abruptly frozen in midair. His face rapidly turned pale and his eyes seemed fixed on Flinx's far shoulder.

A head had somehow emerged from beneath the loose folds of the youth's cape. Now it regarded the merchant with a steady, unblinking gaze that held the quality of otherworld death, the flavour of frozen methane and frostbite. In itself the skull was tiny and unimpressive, scaled and unabashedly reptilian. Then more of the creature emerged, revealing that the head was attached to a long cylindrical body. A set of pleated membranous wings opened, beat lazily at the air.

'Sorry,' the merchant found himself mumbling, 'it was all a mistake . . . my fault, really.' He smiled sickly, looked from left to right. The eyes of the small gathering stared back dispassionately.

It was interesting how the man seemed to shrink into the wall of watchers. They swallowed him up as neat and clean as a grouper would an ambling angelfish. That done, the motionless ranks blended back into the moving stream of humanity.

Flinx relaxed and reached up to scratch the flying snake under its leathery snout. 'Easy there, Pip,' he whispered, thinking warm relaxing thoughts at his pet. 'It's nothing, settle down now.'

Reassured, the minidrag hissed sibilantly and slid back beneath the cape folds, its pleated wings collapsing flat against its body. The merchant had quickly recognized the reptile. A well-travelled individual, he knew that there was no known antidote for the poison of the Alaspin miniature dragon.

'Maybe he learned whatever lesson he had in mind to give us,' Flinx said. 'What say we go over to Small Symm's for a beer and some pretzels for you. Would you like that, summm?'

The snake summmed back at him.

Nearby, buried within the mob, an obese, unlovely gentleman thanked a gratified goldsmith as he pocketed a purchase indifferently made. This transaction had served the purpose of occupying time and covering up his true focus of attention, which had not been the just-bought bauble.

Two men flanked him. One was short and sleek, with an expression like a wet weasel. The other showed a torso like a galvanized boiler, and half a face. His one eye twitched persistently as he stared after the retreating figure of Flinx, while his small companion eagerly addressed the purchaser of the tiny gold-and-pearl piano.

'Did you see the look on that guy's face, Challis?' he asked the plump man. 'That snake's a hot death. Nothin' was said to us about anything like that. That big idiot not only saved his own life, but mine and Nanger's too.'

The one-eye nodded.

'Ya, you're goin' to have to find someone else for this bit of dirty stuff.' His short companion looked adamant.

The fat merchant remained calm, scratched at one of his many chins. 'Have I been ungenerous? Since you both are on permanent retainer to me, I technically owe you nothing for this task.' He shrugged. 'But if it is a question of more money . . .'

The sleek weasel shook his head. 'You can buy my service, Challis, but not my life. Do you know what happens if that snake's venom hits you in the eyes? No antivenom known will keep you alive for more than sixty seconds.' He kicked at the gravel and dirt underfoot, still moist from the regular morning rain. 'No, this isn't for me and not for Nanger neither.'

'Indeed,' the man with half a face agreed solemnly. He sniffed and nodded in the direction of the now departed youth. 'What's your obsession with the boy, anyway? He's not strong, he's not rich, and he's not particularly pretty.'

'It's his head I'm interested in, not his body,' sighed

Challis, 'though this is a matter of my pleasure.' Puffing like a leaky pillow, he led them through the bustling, shouting crowd. Humans, thranx, and representatives of a dozen other commercial races slid easily around and past them as though oiled, all intent on errands of importance.

'It's my Janus jewel. It bores me.'

The smaller man looked disgusted. 'How can anyone rich enough to own a Janus jewel be bored?'

'Oh, but I am, Nolly-dear, I am.'

Nanger made a half-smirk. 'What's the trouble, Challis? Your imagination failing you?' He laughed, short, stentorian barks.

Challis grinned back at him. 'Hardly that, Nanger, but it seems that I have not the right type of mind to produce the kind of fine, detailed resolution the jewel is capable of. I need help for that. So I've been at work these past months looking for a suitable mental adept, trying to find a surrogate mind of the proper type to aid in operating the jewel. I've paid a lot of money for the right information,' he finished, nodding at a tall Osirian he knew. The avian clacked its beak back at him and made a gesture with its graceful, ostrichlike neck, its periscope form weaving confidently through the crowd.

Nanger paused to buy a thisk cake, and Challis continued his explanation as they walked on.

'So you see why I need that boy.'

Nolly was irritated now. 'Why not just hire him? See if he'll participate willingly?'

Challis looked doubtful. 'No, I don't think that would work out, Nolly-dear. You're familiar with some of my fantasies and likes?' His voice had turned inhumanly calm and empty. 'Would you participate voluntarily?'

Nolly looked away from suddenly frightening pupils. In spite of his background, he shuddered. 'No,' he barely whispered, 'no, I don't guess that I would . . .'

'Hello, lad,' boomed Small Symm – the giant was incapable of conversing in less than a shout. 'What of your life and what do you hear from Malaika?'

Flinx sat on one of the stools lined up before the curving bar, ordered spiced beer for himself and a bowl of pretzels for Pip. The flying snake slid gracefully from Flinx's

8

shoulder and worked his way into the wooden bowl of trapezoidal dough. This action was noted by a pair of wide-eyed unsavoury types nearby, who promptly vacated their seats and hastily made for the rearmost booths.

'I've had no contact with Malaika for quite a while, Symm. I've heard he's attending to business outsystem.'

Flinx's wealthy merchant friend had enabled him to quit performing his personal sideshow, having provided him with a substantial sum for his aid in exploring the Tar-Aiym world of the Krang. Much of the money had gone to set up Flinx's adoptive mother, Mother Mastiff, in a well-stocked shop in one of Drallar's better market districts. Muttering at her capriciousness, the old woman had rescued Flinx as a child from the slave-seller's block, and had raised him. She was the only parent he had ever known. She muttered still, but with affection.

'As a matter of fact,' he went on, sipping at the peppery brew, 'Malaika wanted me to go with him. But while I respect the old hedonist, he'd eventually get ideas about putting me in a starched suit, slicking my hair back, and teaching me diction.' Flinx shuddered visibly. 'I couldn't stand that. I'd go back to juggling and audience guessing games first. What about you, father of oafs? I've heard that the municipal troops have been harassing you again.'

The owner of the bar leaned his two-and-a half-meter-tall, one-hundred-seventy-five-kilo frame on to the absorbent wood-plastic counter, which creaked in protest, 'Apparently the marketplace commissioner took it as a personal affront when I ejected the first group of officious do-gooders he sent round to close me down. Maybe I shouldn't have broken their vehicle. Now they are trying to be more subtle. I had one in just this week, who claimed to have observed me serving borderline minors certain hallucinogenic liquids.'

'Obviously you deserve to be strung up by your ex-tremities,' commented Flinx with mock solemnity. He, too, was underage for much of what Symm served him.

'Anyway,' the giant went on, 'this heckster flies out of a back booth, flashes his municipal peace card, and tried to tell me I'm under arrest. He was going to take me in, and I had best come along quietly.' Small Symm shook his massive head mournfully as Flinx downed several swallows.

9

'What did you do?' He licked liquid from the corners of his mouth.

'I really don't want any more trouble, certainly not another assault charge. I thought an inferential demonstration of a mildly physical nature might be effective in persuading the gentleman to change his opinion. It was, and he left quietly,' Symm gestured at Flinx's now empty mug. 'Refill?'

'Sure. What did you do?' he repeated.

'I ate his peace card. Here's you beer.' He slid a second mug alongside the first.

Flinx understood Small Symm's gratification. He had his reputation to uphold. His was one of the few places in Drallar where a person could go at night with a guarantee of not being assaulted or otherwise set upon by rambunctious rovers. This was because Small Symm dealt impartially with all such disturbers of the peace.

'Be back in a minute,' Flinx told his friend. He slid off the stool and headed for the one room whose design and function had changed little in the past several hundred years. As soon as he stepped inside he was overwhelmed by a plethora of rich smells and sensations: stale beer, hard liquor, anxiety, tension, old water, dampness, fearful expectation. The combination of thick thoughts and airborne odours nearly overpowered him.

Looking to his left, where the combination was strongest, he noticed a small twitch of a man watching him anxiously. Flinx observed the man's outward calm and felt his internal panic. He was holding an osmotic syringe in one hand, his finger coiled about it as if it were a weapon. As Flinx started to yell for help, his rising cry was blanketed by the descent of something dark and heavy over his head. A mental cry was aborted by the cool efficiency of the syringe . . .

He awoke to find himself staring at a jumbled panoply of lights. They were spread out before and below him, viewed as they were through a wall and floor of transparent plastic.

Slowly he struggled to a sitting position, which was accomplished with some difficulty since his wrists were manacled together by two chromed metal cuffs. A long tube of flexible metal ran off from them and disappeared among rich furniture. The chain meandered through the thick transparent carpet like a mirror-backed worm.

Looking out, Flinx could see the lights that were the city-pulse of Drallar, dominated by the glowing spires of the King's palace off to the left. The view enabled him to orient himself. Combining the position of the palace with the pattern of lower lights and the knowledge that he was several storeys above ground indicated that he was being held captive in one of the four sealed inurbs of the city. These guarded, restrictive enclaves held the homes of the upper classes, of those native to Drallar and those off-worlders who had commerce here. His assailants, then, were more than gutter thieves.

He was unable to pick up any impressions nearby. At the moment the only alien sensation he could detect was a slight throbbing in the muscles of his upper right arm, where the syringe had struck home. A different kind of sensation was inspired by his own anger, anger directed at himself for not detecting the inimical emanations his attackers must have been putting out before he entered the bathroom.

Suddenly he noticed another sensation missing, too. The comfortable weight of Pip was absent from his shoulders.

'Hello,' ventured a tiny, silvery voice.

Spinning, Flinx found himself eye-to-eye with an angel. He relaxed, swung his feet off the couch, and regarded her in surprise. She could not have been more than nine or ten years old, was clad in a powder blue-and-green fringed pantsuit with long sleeves of some transparent lacy material. Long blonde hair fell in manicured ripples to the backs of her thighs. Baby-blue eyes looked out at him from the high-boned face of a sophisticated cherub.

'My name's Mahnahmi,' she informed him softly, her voice running up and down like a piccolo trill, 'what's yours?'

'Everybody calls me Flinx.'

'Flinx.' She was sucking on the knuckle of her big finger. 'That's a funny name, but nice.' A smile showed perfect pearly teeth. 'Want to see what my daddy brought me?'

'Daddy,' Flinx echoed, looking around the room. It was dominated by the great curve of the transparent wall and balcony and the sparkling panorama laid out below. It was night outside . . . but was it that same night? How long had he lain unconscious? No way to tell . . . yet.

11

The room was furnished in late Siberade: lush cushions, chairs and divan mounted on pencil-thin struts of duralloy, with everything else suspended from the ceiling by duralloy wires so thin that the rest of the furniture appeared to be floating in air. A massive spray of luminescent spodumene and kunzite crystals dominated the domed roof. They were surrounded by circular skylights now open to the star-filled night sky. Climatic adjusters kept the evening rain from falling into the room.

His captor was a very wealthy person.

Petulant-rich with nonattention, the girlish voice interrupted his inspection. 'Do you want to see it or not?'

Flinx wished the throb in his upper arm would subside. 'Sure,' he said absently.

The smile returned as the girl reached into a suit pocket. She moved closer, proudly opened her fist to reveal something in the palm of her hand. Flinx saw that it was a miniature piano, fashioned entirely from filigree gold and real pearls.

'It really plays,' she told him excitedly. She touched the tiny keys and Flinx listened to the almost invisible notes. 'It's for my dolly.'

'It's very pretty,' Flinx complimented, remembering when such a toy would have cost him more credit than he ever thought he would possess. He glanced anxiously past her. 'Where is your daddy right now?'

'Over here.'

Flinx turned to the source of those simple, yet somehow threatening words.

'No, I already know you're called Flinx,' the man said, with a wave of one ring-laden hand. 'I already know a good deal about you.'

Two men emerged from the globular shadow. One had a sunk-in skull half melted away by some tremendous heat and only crudely reconstructed by medical engineers. His smaller companion exhibited more composure now than he had when he'd held the syringe on Flinx in the bathroom at Symm's.

The merchant was talking again. 'My name is Conda Challis. You have perhaps heard of me?'

Flinx nodded slowly. 'I know of your company.'

'Good,' Challis replied. 'It's always gratifying to be

recognized, and it saves certain explanations.' The uncomfortable pulsing in Flinx's shoulder was beginning to subside as the man settled his bulk in a waiting chair. A round, flat table of metal and plastic separated him from Flinx. The half-faced man and his stunted shadow made themselves comfortable – but not too comfortable, Flinx noted – nearby.

'Mahnahmi, I see you've been entertaining our guest,' Challis said to the girl. 'Now go somewhere and play like a good child.'

'No, I want to stay and watch.'

'Watch?' Flinx tensed. 'Watch what?'

'He's going to use the jewel. I know he is!' She turned to Challis. 'Please let me stay and watch, Daddy! I won't say a word, I promise.'

'Sorry, child. Not this time.'

'Not this time, not this time,' she repeated. 'You never let me watch. Never, never, never!' As quick as a sun shower turns bright, her face broke into a wide smile. 'Oh all right, but a least let me say good-bye.'

When Challis impatiently nodded his approval she all but jumped into Flinx's arms. Much to his distress, she wrapped herself around him, gave him a wet smack on one cheek, and whispered into his right ear in a lilting, immature soprano, 'Better do what he tells you to, Flinx, or he'll rip out your guts.'

Somehow he managed to keep a neutral expression on his face as she pulled away with a disarmingly innocent smile.

'Bye-bye. Maybe Daddy will let us play later.' Turning, she skipped from the room, exiting through a doorway in the far wall.

'An . . . interesting little girl,' Flinx commented swallowing.

'Isn't she charming,' Challis agreed. 'Her mother was exceptionally beautiful.'

'You're married, then? You don't strike me as the type.'

The merchant appeared truly shocked. 'Me, life-mated? My dear boy! Her mother was purchased right here in Drallar, a number of years ago. Her pedigree claimed she possessed exceptional talents. They turned out to be of a very minor nature, suitable for parlour tricks but little else.

'However, she could perform certain other functions, so I

13

didn't feel the money wholly wasted. The only drawback was the birth of that infant, resulting from my failure to report on time for a standard debiojection. I didn't think the delay would be significant.' He shrugged. 'But I was wrong. The mother pleased me, so I permitted her to have the child . . . I tend to be hard on my property, however. The mother did not live long thereafter. At times I feel the child has inherited her mother's minuscule talents, but every attempt to prove so has met with failure.'

'Yet despite this, you keep her,' Flinx noted curiously. For a second Challis appeared almost confused, a sensation which passed rapidly.

'It is not so puzzling, really. Considering the manner of the mother's death, of which the child is unaware, I feel some small sense of responsibility for her. While I have no particular love for infants, she obeys with an alacrity her older counterparts could emulate.' He grinned broadly and Flinx had the impression of a naked white skull filled with broken icicles.

'She's old enough to know that if she doesn't, I'll simply sell her.' Challis leaned forward, wheezing with the effort of folding his chest over his protruding belly. 'However, you were not brought here to discuss the details of my domestic life.'

'Then why was I brought here? I heard something about a jewel. I know a little about good stones, but I'm certainly no expert.'

'A jewel, yes.' Challis declined further oral explanation; instead, he manipulated several switches concealed by the far overhang of the table between them. The lights dimmed and Challis's pair of ominous attendants disappeared, though Flinx could sense their alert presence nearby. They were between him and the only clearly defined door.

Flinx's attention was quickly diverted by a soft humming. As the top of the table slid to one side, he could see the construction involved. The table was a thick safe. Something rose from the central hollow, a sculpture of glowing components encircled by a spiderweb of thin wiring. At the sculpture's centre was a transparent globe of glassalloy. It contained something that looked like a clear natural crystal about the size of a man's head. It glowed with a strange inner light. At first glance it resembled quartz, but longer inspection showed that here was a most unique silicate.

The centre of the crystal was hollow and irregular in outline. It was filled with maroon and green particles which drifted with dreamy slowness in a clear viscous fluid. The particles were fine as dust motes. In places they nearly reached to the edges of the crystal walls, though they tended to remain compacted near its middle. Occasionally the velvety motes would jerk and dart about sharply, as if prodded by some unseen force. Flinx stared into its shifting depths as if mesmerized . . .

On Earth lived a wealthy man named Endrickson, who recently seemed to be walking about in a daze. His family was fond of him and he was well liked by his friends. He also held the grudging admiration of his competitors. Endrickson, though he looked anything but sharp at the moment, was one of those peculiar geniuses who possesses no creative ability of his own, but who instead exhibits the rare power to marshal and direct the talents of those more gifted than himself.

At 5.30 on the evening of the 25th of Fifth Month, Endrickson moved more slowly than usual through the heavily guarded corridors of The Plant. The Plant had no name – a precaution insisted on by nervous men whose occupation it was to worry about such things – and was built into the western slope of the Andes.

As he passed the men and women and insectoid thranx who laboured in The Plant, Endrickson nodded his greetings and was always gratified with respectful replies. They were all moving in the opposite direction, since the work day had ended for them. They were on their way – these many, many-talented beings – to their homes in Santiago and Lima and New Delhi and New York, as well as to the Terran thranx colonies in the Amazon basin.

One who was not yet off duty came stiffly to attention as Endrickson turned a corner in a last, shielded passageway. On seeing that the visitor was not his immediate superior – a gentleman who wore irritation, like his underwear, outside his trousers – the well-armed guard relaxed. Endrickson, he knew, was everyone's friend.

'Hello . . . Davis,' the boss said slowly.

The men saluted, then studied him intently, disturbed at his appearance.

'Good evening, sir. Are you sure you're all right?'

'Yes, thank you, Davis,' Endrickson replied. 'I had a last-minute thought . . . won't be long.' He seemed to be staring at something irregular and shiny that he held cupped in one palm. 'Do you want my identity card?'

The guard smiled, processed the necessary slip of treated plastic, and admitted Endrickson to the chamber beyond which contained the shop, a vast cavern made even vaster by precision engineering and necessity. This was the heart of The Plant.

Moving with assurance, Endrickson walked down the ramp to the sealed floor of the enlarged cavern, passing enormous machines, long benches, and great constructs of metal and other materials. The workshop was deserted now. It would remain so until the early-morning shift came on five hours later.

One-third of the way across the floor he halted before an imposing door of dun-coloured metal, the only break in a solid wall of the same material that closed off a spacious section of the cavern. Using his free hand while still staring at the thing in his other hand, he pulled out a small ring that held several metal cylinders. He selected a cylinder, pressed his thumb into the recessed area at one end of it, then inserted the other into a small hole in the door and shoved forward. A complex series of radiations was produced and absorbed by the doorway mechanism. These passed judgement on both the cylinder and the person holding it.

Satisfied that the cylinder was coded properly and that its owner was of a stable frame of mind, the door sang soft acquiescence and shrank into the floor. Endrickson passed through and the door noted his passage, then rose to close the gap behind him.

A not quite finished device loomed ahead, nearly filling this part of the cavern. It was surrounded by an attending army of instruments: monitoring devices, tools in repose, checkout panels and endless crates of assorted components.

Endrickson ignored this familiar collage as he headed purposefully for a single black panel. He thoughtfully eyed the switches and controls thereon, then used another of his ring cylinders to bring the board to life. Lights came on obediently and gauges registered for his inspection.

The vast bulk of the unfinished KK-drive starship engine loomed above him. Final completion would and could take place only in free space, since the activated posigravity field of the drive interacting with a planet's gravitational field would produce a series of quakes and tectonic adjustments of cataclysmic proportions.

But that fact didn't concern Endrickson just now. A far more intriguing thought had overwhelmed him. Was the drive unit complete enough to function? he wondered. Why not observe the interesting possibilities first-hand?

He glanced at the beauty in his palm, then used a second cylinder to unlock a tightly sealed box at one end of the black board. Beneath the box were several switches, all enamelled a bright crimson. Endrickson heard a klaxon yell shrilly somewhere, but he ignored the alarm as he pressed switches in proper order. His anticipation was enormous. With the fluid-state switches activated, instructions began flowing through the glass-plastic-metal monolith. Far off on the other side of the locked door, Endrickson could hear people shouting, running. Meanwhile the drive's thermonuclear spark was activated and Endrickson saw full engagement register on the appropriate monitors.

He nodded with satisfaction. Final relays interlocked, communicated with the computermind built into the engine. For a brief second the Kurita-Kita field was brought into existence. Momentarily the thought flashed through Endrickson's mind that this was something that should never be done except in the deep reaches of free space.

But his last thoughts were reserved for the exquisite loveliness and strange words locked within the object he held in his hand . . .

Had the unit been finished there might have been a major disaster. But it was not complete, and so the field collapsed quickly, unable to sustain itself and to expand to its full, propulsive diameter.

So, although windows were shattered and a few older buildings toppled and the Church of Santa Avila de Seville's ancient steeple cracked six hundred kilometers away in downtown Valparaiso, only a few things in the immediate vicinity showed any significant alteration.

17

However, Endrickson, The Plant, and the nearby techno-
logic community of Santa Rosa de Cristóbal (pop. 3200)
vanished. The 13,352-kilometer-high mountain at whose base
the town had risen and in whose bowels The Plant had been
carved was replaced by a 1200-kilometre-deep crater lined
with molten glass.

But since logic insisted the event could have been nothing
other than an accident, it was so ruled by the experts called
upon to produce an explanation – experts who did not have
access to the same beauty which had so totally bedazzled the
now-vapourized Endrickson . . .

Flinx blinked, awakening from the Janus jewel's tantalizing
loveliness. It continued to pulse with its steady, natural
yellow luminescence.

'Did you ever see one before?' Challis inquired.

'No. I've heard of them, though. I know enough to
recognize one.'

Challis must have touched another concealed switch
because a low-intensity light sprang to life at the table's edge.
Fumbling with a drawer built into the table, the merchant
then produced a small boxy affair which resembled an
abstract carving of a bird in flight, its wings on the down-
beat. It was designed to fit on a human head. A few exposed
wires and modules broke the device's otherwise smooth
lines.

'Do you know what this is?' the merchant asked.

Flinx confessed he did not.

'It's the operator's headset,' Challis explained slowly,
placing it over his stringy hair. 'The headset and the
machinery encapsulated in that table transcribe the thoughts
of the human mind and convey them to the jewel. The jewel
has a certain property.'

Challis intoned 'property' with the sort of spiritual
reverence most men would reserve for describing their gods
or mistresses.

The merchant ceased fumbling with unseen controls and
with the headset. He folded his hands before his squeezed
out paunch and stared at the crystal. 'I'm concentrating on
something now,' he told his absorbed listener softly. 'It
takes a little training, though some can do without it.'

As Flinx watched raptly, the particles in the jewel's

18

centre began to rearrange themselves. Their motion was no longer random, and it was clear that Challis's thoughts were directing the realignment. Here was something about which rumour abounded, but which few except the very rich and privileged had actually seen.

'The larger the crystal,' Challis continued, obviously straining to produce some as yet unknown result, 'the more colours present in the colloid and the more valuable the stone. A single colour is the general rule. This stone contains two and is one of the largest and finest in existence, though even small stones are rare.

'There are stones with impurities present which create three and four-colour displays, and one stone of five-colour content is known. You would not believe who owns it, or what is done with it.'

Flinx watched as the colours within the crystal's centre began to assume semisolid shape and form at Challis's direction. 'No one,' the merchant continued, 'has been able to synthesize the oleaginous liquid in which the coloured particulate matter drifts suspended. Once a crystal is broken, it is impossible to repair. Nor can the colloid be transferred in whole or in part to a new container. A break in the intricate crystal-liquid formation destroys the stone's individual pizeoelectric potential. Fortunately the crystal is as hard as corundum, though nowhere near as strong as artificials like duralloy.'

Though the outlines shifted and trembled constantly, never quite firmly fixed, they took on the recognizable shapes of several persons. One appeared to be an exaggeratedly Junoesque woman. Of the others, one was a humanoid male and the third something wholly alien. A two-sided chamber rose around them and was filled with strange objects that never held their form for more than a few seconds. Although their consistency fluctuated, the impression they conveyed did not. Flinx saw quite enough to turn his stomach before everthing within the crystal dissolved once again to a cloud of glowing dust.

Looking up and across from the crystal he observed that the merchant had removed the headpiece and was wiping the perspiration from his high forehead with a perfumed cloth. Illuminated by the subdued light concealed in the table edge below, his face became that of an unscrupulous imp.

'Easy to begin,' he murmured with exhaustion, 'but a devilishly difficult reaction to sustain. When your attention moves from one figure, the others begin to collapse. And when the play involves complex actions performed by several such creations, it is nigh impossible, especially when one tends to become so . . . involved with the action.'

'What's all this got to do with me?' Flinx broke in. Although the question was directed at Challis, Flinx's attention was riveted on those two half-sensed figures guarding the exit. Neither Nolly nor Nanger had stirred, but that didn't mean they had relaxed their watch, either. And the door they guarded was hardly likely to be unlocked. Flinx could see several openings in the floor-to-ceiling glassalloy wall which overlooked the city, but he knew it was a sheer drop of at least fifty metres to the private street below.

'You see,' Challis told him, 'while I'm not ashamed to admit that I've inherited a most successful family business in the Challis Company, neither do I count myself a dilettante. I have improved the company through the addition of people with many diverse talents.' He gestured towards the door. 'Nolly-dear and Nanger there are two such examples. I'm hoping that you, dear boy, will be yet another.'

'I'm still not sure I understand,' Flinx said slowly, stalling.

'That can be easily rectified.' Challis steepled his fingers. 'To hold the suspended particles of the Janus jewels, to manipulate the particulate clay, requires a special kind of mind. Though my mental scenarios are complex, to enjoy them fully I require a surrogate mind. *Yours!* I shall instruct you in what is desired and you will execute my designs within the jewel.'

Flinx thought back to what he had glimpsed a few moments ago in the incomplete playlet, to what Challis had wrought within the tiny god-world of the jewel. In many ways he was mature far beyond his seventeen years, and he had seen a great many things in his time. Though some of them would have sickened the stomach of an experienced soldier, most of them had been harmless perversions. But beneath all the superficial cordiality and the polite requests for co-operation that Challis had expressed, there bubbled a

20

deep lake of untreated sewage, and Flinx was not about to serve as the merchant's pilot across it.

Surviving a childhood in the marketplace of Drallar had made Flinx something of a realist. So he did not reel at the merchant's proposal and say what was on his mind: 'You revolt and nauseate me, Conda Challis, and I refuse to have anything to do with you or your sick private fantasies.' Instead he said: 'I don't know where you got the idea that I could be of such help to you.'

'You cannot deny your own history.' Challis sniggered. 'I have acquired a small but interesting file on you. Most notably, your peculiar talents figured strongly in assisting a competitor of mine named Maxim Malaika. Prior to that incident and subsequent to it you have been observed demonstrating abnormal mental abilities through the medium of cheap sideshow tricks for the receipt of a few credits from passersby. I can offer you considerably more for the use of your talents. Deny that if you can.'

'Okay, so I can work a few gimmicks and fool a few tourists,' Flinx conceded, while studying the thin silvery bracelets linking his wrists and trying to find a hidden catch. 'But what you call my "talents" are erratic, undisciplined, and beyond my control much of the time. I don't know when they come or why they go.'

Challis was nodding in a way Flinx didn't like. 'Naturally. I understand. All talents – artistic, athletic, whatever kind – require training and discipline to develop them fully. I intend to help you in mastering yours. By way of example . . .' Challis took out something that looked like an ancient pocket-watch but wasn't, pressed a tiny button. Instantly the breath fled from Flinx's lungs, and he arced forward. His hands tightened into fists as he shuddered, and he felt as if someone had taken a file to the bones in his wrists. The pain passed suddenly and he was able to lean limply backward, gasping, trembling. When he found he could open his eyes again, he saw that Challis was staring into them, expectantly interested. His stare was identical to the one a chemist would lavish on a laboratory animal just injected with a possibly fatal substance.

'That . . . wasn't necessary,' Flinx managed to whisper.

'Possibly not,' a callous Challis agreed, 'but it was instructive. I've seen your eyes roving while you've talked.

21

Really, you can't get out of here, you know. Even should you somehow manage to reach the central shaft beyond Nolly and Nanger, there are others waiting.' The merchant paused, then asked abruptly, 'Now, is what I wish truly so abhorrent to you? You'll be well rewarded. I offer you a secure existence in my company. In return you may relax as you like. You'll be called on only to help operate the jewel.'

'It's the ethics of the matter that trouble me, not the salary,' Flinx insisted.

'Oh, ethics,' Challis was amused, and he didn't try to hide it. 'Surely you can overcome that. The alternative is much less subjective.' He was tapping two fingers idly on the face of the pseudo-watch.

While pretending to enjoy it all, Flinx was thinking. His wrists were still throbbing, and the ache penetrated all the way to his shoulders. He could stand that pain again, but not often. And anything more intense would surely knock him out. His vision still had an alarming tendency to lose focus.

Yet . . . he *couldn't* do what Challis wanted. Those images – his stomach churned as he remembered – to participate in such obscenities . . . No! Flinx was considering what to say, anything to forestall the pain again, when something dry and slick pressed against his cheek. It was followed by the feathery caress of something unseen but familiar at the back of his neck.

Challis obviously saw nothing in the darkness, since when he spoke again his voice was as controlled as before. His fingers continued to play lazily over the ovoid control box. 'Come, dear boy, is there really need to prolong this further? I'm sure you gain less pleasure from it than do I.' A finger stopped tapping, edged towards the button.

'*HEY!*'

The shout came from the vicinity of the door and was followed by muffled curses and dimly perceived movement. Challis's two guards were dancing crazily about, waving and swatting at something unseen.

Challis's voice turned vicious, angry for the first time. 'What's the matter with you idiots?'

Nanger replied nervously. 'There's something in here with us.'

22

'You are both out of your small minds. We are eight floors from the surface and carefully screened against mechanical intruders. Nothing could possibly – '

Nanger interrupted the merchant's assurance with a scream the likes of which few men ever encounter. Flinx was half expecting it. Even so, the sound sent a chill down his spine. What it did to Nolly, or to Challis, who was suddenly scrambling over the back of the chair and fumbling at his belt, could only be imagined.

Flinx heard a crash, followed by a collision with something heavy and out of control. It was Nanger. The half-face had both hands clamped tight over his eyes and was staggering wildly in all directions.

'The jewel . . . watch the jewel!' a panicky Challis howled. Moving on hands and knees with surprising rapidity, he reached the edge of the table and hit a switch. Instantly the light went out. In the faint illumination from the wall window Flinx could see the merchant disconnect the top of the apparatus, the globe containing the crystal itself, and cradle it protectively in his hands as he removed it.

Suddenly there was another source of light in the room, in the form of sharp intermittent green flares from a needler. Nolly had the weapon out and was sparring desperately with an adversary that swooped and dived at him.

Then something began to buzz for attention within the table, and Challis lifted a receiver and listened. Flinx listened too, but could hear nothing. Whatever was being said elicited some furious responses from the merchant, whose easygoing manner had by now vanished completely. He mumbled something into the pickup, then let it snap back into the table. The look he threw Flinx in the near blackness was a mixture of fury and curiosity. 'I bid you adieu, dear boy. I hope we have the opportunity to meet again. I thought you merely a beggar with talents too big for his head. Apparently you may be something more. I'm sorry you elected not to co-operate. Your maternal line hinted that you might,' Challis sneered. 'I never repeat mistakes. Be warned.' Still scrambling on hands and knees, he made his way to the hidden door. As it opened, Flinx caught a glimpse of a small golden figure standing there.

'Listening again, brat-child?' Challis muttered as he rose

23

to his feet. He slapped the girl, grabbing her by one arm. She started to cry and looked away from Challis as the door cycled shut.

As Flinx turned his attention back to the other door, his mind was already awhirl at an offhand comment of the merchant's. But before he could consider all the implications of the remark. Flinx was hit with a tsunami of maniacal mental energy that nearly knocked him from the couch. It was forceful beyond imagining, powerful past anything he had ever felt from a human mind before. It held screaming images of Conda Challis coming slowly apart, like a toy doll. These visions were mixed haphazardly with other pictures, and several views of Flinx himself drifted among them.

He winced under that cyclonic wail. Some of the fleeting images were far worse than anything Challis had tried to create within the jewel. The merchant's mind may have been one of utter depravity, but the brain behind this mental storm did not stop with anything that petty.

Flinx stared back at the closing door, getting his last view of black eyes set in an angelic face. In that unformed body, he knew, dwelt a tormented child. Yet even that revelation did not spark the same wild excitement in him that Challis's last casual statement had. 'Your maternal line,' the merchant had said.

Flinx knew more about the universe than he did about his real parents. If Challis knew even a rumour of Flinx's ancestry . . . the merchant was going to get his wish for another meeting.

CHAPTER TWO

The door to the tower's central shaft opened as the only other occupant of the room sought escape. Instead of an empty elevator, he found himself confronted by a figure of gargantuan proportions that lifted him squealing from the floor and removed the needler. The new arrival quickly rendered the weapon harmless by crumpling it in a fist that had the force of a mechanical press. Nolly's fingers, which happened to be wrapped around the needler, suffered a similar fate, and a single shriek of pain preceded unconsciousness.

Small Symm ducked to clear the top of the portal, dropping the limp human shape to one side. Simultaneously a long lean shape settled easily about Flinx's shoulders, and a single damp point flickered familiarly at his ear. Reaching back, Flinx scratched under the minidrag's jaw and felt the long muscular form relax. 'Thanks, Pip.'

Rising from the chair, he moved around the tablesafe and played with the controls on the other side. Before very long he succeeded in lighting the entire room.

Where Nanger had crashed and stumbled, the expensive furnishings lay broken and twisted. His body, already growing stiff with venom-inspired death, lay crumpled across one bent chair. The unmoving form of his companion was slumped to one side of the doorway. A mangled hand oozed blood.

'I was wondering,' Flinx informed Symm, 'when you'd get here.'

'It was difficult,' the bartender apologized, his voice echoing up from that bottomless pit of a chest. 'Your pet was impatient, disappearing and then reappearing when I fell behind. How did he know how to find you?'

Flinx affectionately eyed the now somnolent scaly head. 'He smelled my fear, Life-water knows I was broadcasting it loud enough.' He held out manacled wrists. 'Can you do something about these? I have to go after Challis.'

Symm glanced at the cuffs, a look of mild surprise on his face. 'I never thought revenge was part of your makeup, Flinx.'

Reaching down with a massive thumb and forefinger, Symm carefully pinched one of the narrow confining bands. A moment's pressure caused the metal to snap with an explosive *pop*. Repeating the action freed Flinx's other hand.

Looking at this right wrist as he rubbed it with his left hand, Flinx could detect no mark – nothing to indicate the intense pain that the device had inflicted.

He debated how to respond to his friend's accusation.

How could he hope to explain the importance of Challis's remark to this good-natured hulk? 'I think Challis may know something of my real parents. I can't simply forget about it.'

The unaccustomed bitterness of Symm's answer startled him. 'What are they to you? What have they done for you? They have caused you to be treated like chattel, like a piece of property. If not for the intervention of Mother Mastiff you'd be a personal slave now, perhaps to something like Challis. Your real parents – you owe them nothing, least of all the satisfaction of showing them you've survived!'

'I don't know the circumstances of my abandonment, Symm,' Flinx finally countered. 'I have to find out, I *have* to.'

The bartender, an orphan himself, shrugged massively. 'You're an idealistic misfit, Flinx.'

'And you're an even bigger one,' the boy shot back, 'which is why you're going to help me.'

Symm muttered something unintelligible, which might have been a curse. Then again, it might not. 'Where did he get out?'

Flinx indicated the hidden doorway, and Symm walked over to the spot and leaned against the metal panel experimentally. The hinging collapsed inward with suprising ease. Beyond, they discovered a short corridor, which led to a small private lift that conveyed them rapidly to the base of the luxurious tower.

'How did you get in, anyway?' Flinx asked his friend.

Symm twitched, 'I told the security people I met that I had an appointments pass, the usual procedure in an inurb like this.'

'Didn't anyone demand to see it?'

Symm didn't crack a smile. 'Would you? Only one guard did, and I think he'll be all right if he gets proper care. Careful now,' the giant warned as the lift came to a stop. Crouching to one side, he sprang out as soon as the door slid open sufficiently to let him pass. But there was no ambush awaiting them. Instead, they found themselves in a ground-car garage, which showed ample sign of having been recently vacated.

'Keep your monumental ears open,' Flinx advised quietly. 'See if you can find out where Challis has fled. I'm

26

going to work my own sources . . .'

When they left through the open doorway of the garage, no one challenged their departure, though hidden eyes observed it. But those behind the eyes were grateful to see the pair go.

'You're sure they're not still here?' Symm wondered aloud. 'Someone could have taken the car as a diversion.'

Flinx replied with the kind of unnerving assurance Symm didn't pretend to understand, but had come to accept. 'No, they're no longer in this vicinity.'

The pair parted outside the last encircling wall of the inurb. There was no formality, no shaking of hands – nothing of the sort was required between these two.

'If you learn anything get in touch with me at Mother Mastiff's shop,' Flinx instructed the giant. 'Whatever happens, I'll let you know my plans.'

As he made his way back through the market's concentric circles, he clutched his cloak tightly about him. The last drops of the morning rain were falling. In the distance an always hopeful sun showed signs of emerging from the low, water-heavy clouds.

Plenty of activity swirled about him. At this commercial hub of the Commonwealth, business operated round the clock.

Flinx knew a great many inhabitants of this world-within-a-world on sight. Some were wealthy and great, some poor and great. A few were not human and more were less human than others though all claimed membership in the same race.

Passing the stall of the sweets vendor Kiki, he kept his attention resolutely ahead. It was too early and his stomach was too empty for candy. Besides, his innards still rocked slightly from the after-effects of Challis's seemingly harmless jewellery. So, at Chairman Nils he bought a small loaf of bran bread coated with nut butter.

Nils was a fortyish food vendor with an authoritative manner. Everyone called him the Chairman. He ruled his corner of the marketplace with the air of a dictator, never suspecting that he held this power because his fellow sellers and hawkers found it amusing to humour his gentle madness. There were never any delusions in his baked goods, however. Flinx took a ferocious bite out of the triangular loaf, enjoying the occasional crunch of chopped nuts woven into the brown butter.

A glance at the sky still hinted at the possibility of the sun breaking through, a rare occurrence in usually cloud-shrouded Drallar.

His snack finished, Flinx began moving through a section filled with handsome, permanent shopfronts – a section that was considerably different from the region of make-shift shacks and stores in which he had been raised. When he'd first proposed shifting the ancient stall from the noisome depths of the marketplace Mother Mastiff had protested vociferously. 'I wouldn't know how to act,' she had argued. 'What do I know about treating with fancy customers and rich folks?'

'Believe me, Mother' – though they both knew she wasn't his real mother, she acted as one to half the homeless in Drallar – 'they're the same as your old customers, only now the idiots will come with bigger bankrolls. Besides, what else would I do with all the money Malaika pressed on me?'

Eventually he had been forced to purchase the shop and thus present her with a *fait accompli*. She railed at him for hours when he told her – until she saw the place. Though she continued muttering dire imprecations about everything he showed her – the high-class inventory, the fancy living quarters upstairs, the automatic cooking devices – her resistance collapsed with unsurprising speed.

But there were two things she still refused to do. One was to change her handmade, homemade attire – as esoteric a collage of beads, bells, and cloth as could be imagined. The other was to use the small elevator that ran between the shop proper and the living quarters above. 'The day I can't climb a single flight of stairs,' she remonstrated, 'is the day you can have me embalmed, stuffed, and put in the window at a curio sale.' To demonstrate her determination, she proceeded at once to walk the short stairway on all fours.

No one knew how old Mother Mastiff was and she wasn't telling. Nor would she consent to submit to the extensive cosmetic surgeries Flinx could now afford, or to utilize any other artificial age-reduction device. 'I've spent too long and too much effort preparin' for the role of an aged crone, and I'm not about to give up on it now,' she told him. 'Besides, the more pitiful and decrepit I look, the

28

more polite and sympathetic the suck – the customers are.'

Not surprisingly, the shop prospered. For one thing, many of the better craftsmen in Drallar had come from equally humble origins, and they enjoyed selling their better products to her.

As Flinx rounded the corner, he saw she was waiting for him at the rear entrance. 'Out all night again. I don't suppose you've been anywhere as healthy as the Pink Palace or Sinnyville. D'you want your throat cut before you make eighteen?' she admonished, wagging a warning finger.

'Not much chance of that, Mother.' He brushed past her, but – not to be put off – she followed him into the little storeroom behind the shopfront.

'And that flyin' gargoyle of yours won't save you every time, y'know. Not in a city like this, where everyone has a handshake for you with one palm and a knife for your back in the other. Keep walkin' about at the depths of the night like this, boy, and one day they'll be bringin' you back t' me pale and empty of juice. And I warn you,' she continued, her voice rising, 'it's a cheap funeral you'll be gettin', because I'm not workin' my fingers to the quick to pay for a fancy send-off for a fool!'

A sharp buzz interrupted the tirade. 'So I'll tell you for the last time, boy . . .'

'Didn't you hear the door, Mother?' He grinned. 'First customer of the morn.'

She peered through the beads in the doorway. 'Huh. Tourists, by the look of 'em. You should see the tanzanite on the woman's ring.' She hesitated, torn between the need to satisfy affection and avarice simultaneously. 'But what's a couple of customers when . . .' another hesitation, 'still, that's twelve carats at least in the one stone. Their clothes mark 'em as Terrans maybe, too.' She finally threw up her hands in confusion and disgust. 'It's my punishment. You're a visitation for the sins of my youth. Get out of my sight, boy. Upstairs and wash yourself, and mind the disinfectant. You smell of the gutter. Dry yourself well, mind . . . you're not too big or old for me to blush your bottom.' She slipped through the screen and a radical metamorphosis took place.

'Ah sir, madam,' an oily voice cooed soothingly, the voice of everyone's favourite grandmama, 'you honour my

29

small shop. I would have been out sooner but I was tending to my poor grandson who is desperately ill and in need of much expensive treatment. The doctors fear that unless the operation is performed soon, he will lose the power of sight, and – '

Her slick spiel was cut off as the elevator door slid shut behind Flinx. Unlike Mother Mastiff, he had no compunction about using modern conveniences – certainly not now, as tired as he was from the experiences of the night before. As he stepped into the upstairs quarters he did wonder how such disparate tones could issue from the same wrinkled throat.

Later, over the evening meal (prepared by him, since Mother Mastiff had been occupied with customers all day), he began to explain what had happened. For a change, she neither harangued nor chastised him, merely listened politely until he had finished.

'So you're bound to go after him then, boy,' she finally said.

'I have to, Mother.'

'Why?'

He looked away. 'I'd rather not say.'

'All right.' She mopped up the last of her gravy with a piece of bread. 'I've heard much of the man Challis – plenty of rumours about his tastes in certain matters and none of them good. There's less known about his businesses, though word is the Challis Company has prospered since he became the head.' She grunted noisily and wiped at her mouth with a corner of her multilayered skirt.

'You sure you got to do this, boy? You've only been off-planet once before, y'know.'

'I think I can handle myself, Mother.'

'Daresay, daresay,' she replied disparagingly. 'Though by all the odds you ought to have been dead a dozen times before your fifteenth birthday, and I don't suppose that grinnin' devil could have been responsible for savin' you every time.'

She favoured a small artificial tree with a poisonous stare. Pip was coiled comfortably around one of its branches. The minidrag did not look up. The relationship between him and Mother Mastiff had always been one of uneasy truce.

'Before you take off, let me make a call,' she finished.

While Flinx finished his dessert and fought to pry the last bit of thick gelatin from his back teeth, he listened to her mutter into the pickup of a small communicator at the far end of the room. The machine gave her a mobility she hadn't possessed for decades. It was one of the few conveniences the shop provided that she'd use. It also made her the terror of every city official in any way responsible for the daily operation of the marketplace.

She was back at tableside soon. 'Your friend Challis left on the freightliner *Auriga* this morning with his daughter and a covey of servants.' Her expression contorted. 'From what I was told, he left in a real hurry. You and that great imbecile Symm must have thrown quite a scare into him, but then the giant's enough by himself to frighten the polish off a mirror.'

Flinx did not return her inquiring gaze. Instead he played with one edge of the tablecloth. 'What's the *Auriga*'s destination?'

'Hivehom,' she told him. 'The Challis Company has a lot of investments on the Mediterranea Plateau. I expect that's what he'll head for once he sets down.'

'I'd better get ready.' Flinx rose and started towards his room.

A strong, crinkled hand caught one of his wrists, and a face like a rift valley stared searchingly into his. 'Don't do this, boy,' she begged, her voice low.

He shook his head. 'No choice, Mother. I can't tell you what calls, but call it does. I have to go.'

The pressure did not ease on his wrist. 'I don't know what dealings you have with this bad man, but I can't believe it's this serious.' Flinx said nothing and she finally released him. 'If it's in you to go, go then.' She looked away. 'I don't know how your mind works, boy. Never did, never. But I do know that when you get somethin' like this into it, only you can put it out. Go then, and my blessin's with you. Even,' she concluded tightly, 'if you won't tell me the why of it.'

Bending over, he kissed the grey bun curled at the back of the old woman's head. 'Blessings on you too, Mother,' he said as she squirmed violently at the gesture.

It didn't take him long to pack the few possessions he wanted to bring with him. They didn't seem to mean much to him now. As he started to leave the room, he saw that the woman was still sitting alone at the table, a suddenly tiny and frail figure. How could he tell her he had to risk the life she'd coddled in a vain search for the people who had done nothing beyond giving him birth . . . ?

When he arrived at Drallar Port later that day, he found he was only physically tired. His mind was sharp and alert. Over the years he had gradually discovered that he required less and less sleep. Some days he could get by with as little as half an hour. His mind rested when it wasn't being pushed, which was frequently.

He no longer had to worry about how he would travel, for there were sufficient funds registered on his cardmeter to sustain him for some time yet. Malaika had been generous. Not all the determining factors were financial, however. A glance at those waiting to board the first-class section of the shuttlecraft engendered an acute sense of unease in him, so he registered for standard fare.

Travelling so would be more enlightening anyway, for his first journey on a commercial spacecraft and his second time off Moth. As he followed the line into the shuttle, passing under the mildly aristocratic eye of the steward, he was shocked to discover that his about-to-be-realized childhood dream of travelling off-planet in one of the great KK-drive freightliners no longer held any thrill for him. It worried him as he strapped into his couch.

Mother Mastiff could have explained it to him if she were there. It was called growing up.

Though tolerable, the shuttle journey was rougher than his single previous experience with the little surface-to-orbit vessels. Naturally, he told himself, the pokier commercial craft would be nowhere near as luxurious as the shuttle carried by Malaika's yacht, the *Gloryhole*. This one was designed solely to get as many beings and as much cargo as possible from the ground into free-fall as economically as possible. There they could be transferred – passengers and cargo alike, with sometimes equivalent handling – into the great globular bulk of the deepspace ship.

Following that transfer Flinx found himself assigned to a small, compactly designed cabin. He barely took the time to inspect it, and he had little to unpack. During the week-long journey he would spend the majority of travel time in the ship's several lounges, meeting fellow travellers – and learning.

The shift from sublight to KK-drive superlight velocity was hardly a surprise. He had already experienced it several times on Malaika's ship.

One part of the liner he especially enjoyed. From a forward observation lounge he could look ahead and see the immense length of the ship's connecting corridor rods stretching outward like a broad narrowing highway to join the back of the colossal curving dish of the KK field projector. It blotted out the stars ahead.

Somewhere in front of that enormous dish, he knew, the drive unit was projecting the gravity well of a small sun. It pulled the ship steadily and, in turn, the drive projector which then projected the field that much further ahead – and so on. Flinx wondered still at the explanation of it and decided that all great inventions were essentially simple.

He was amusing himself in the ship's game lounge on the third day when a neatly painted thranx in the stark brown, yellow, and green of commerce took the couch opposite. Less than a metre high at the b-thorax, he was small for a male. Both sets of wing cases still gleamed on his back, indicating that the traveller was as yet unmated. Brilliant, faceted eyes regarded Flinx through multiple gemlike lenses. The wonderful natural perfume odour of his kind drifted across the game table.

The creature glanced down at the glowing board, then its valentine-shaped head cocked curiously at the young human operating it.

'You play *hibush-hunt*? Most humans find it too complicated. You usually prefer two-dimensional games.' The insect's symbospeech was precise and textbook-flat, the variety any good businessthranx would speak.

'I've heard a little about it and I've watched it played,' Flinx told his visitor modestly. 'I really don't know how to play myself.'

Mandibles clacked in a gesture of interest and understanding, since the insect's inflexible chitonous face allowed for nothing as rubbery as a smile. A slight nod of the head was more easily imitated.

Question-response having served for a courteous greeting, the thranx settled himself more firmly on the couch, trulegs doubled up beneath the abdomen, foothands locked to support the thorax and b-thorax, and truhands moving with delicate precision over the board, adjusting the game plan. 'My name is Bisondenbit,' he declared.

'I'm called Flinx.'

'One calling?' The thranx performed an insectoid shrug. 'Well, Flinx, if you'd like to learn, I have some small skill at the game. Which is to say I know the rules. I am not a very good player, so I'll probably make a good first opponent for you.' Again the mandible clicking, accompanied this time by a whistling sound – thranx laughter.

Flinx smiled back. 'I'd like to learn very much.'

'Good, good . . . this is a standoffish group and I've been preening antennae till my nerves are beginning to twitch.' The head bobbed. 'Your biggest mistake,' Bisondenbit began in businesslike fashion, 'is that you're still neglecting the ability of your pieces to move above ground and downward, as well as through existing tunnels. You've got to keep your antennae to the board and seek to penetrate your opponent's movements.'

The thranx touched a silvery figure within the three-dimensional transparent board. 'Stay attuned now. This is a *Doan* fighter and can move only laterally and vertically, though it can never appear on the surface. This divisible piece here . . .'

Flinx got to know Bisondenbit fairly well during the remainder of the trip. He kept his actual business veiled in vague circumlocutions, but Flinx gave the impression he was an antique dealer. Perhaps there would be a chance to pick up some interesting curios for Mother Mastiff's shop.

Bisondenbit did display in full a trait which had helped endear his kind to humans: the ability to listen attentively no matter how boring the story being told. He seemed to find Flinx's judiciously censored story of his own life up to this present journey fascinating.

'Look,' he told Flinx as they shared supper in one of the ship's dining lounges, 'you've never been to Hivehom before and you're determined to look up this human what's-his-name – Challis? At least I can help you get oriented. You'll no doubt find him somewhere on the Mediterranea Plateau.

34

That's where most of the human settlers live.' The insect quivered. 'Though why anyone would choose to set up housekeeping on a chilly tundra like that is beyond my understanding.'

Flinx had to smile. The mean temperature on the Mediterranea Plateau, a level area several thousand kilometres above the steaming, humid swamplands of Hivehom, was a comfortable 22° C. The thranx preferred the high thirties, with humidity as near one hundred per cent as possible.

The word colonization was never mentioned in connection with such settlements – on either world. There were several such human regions on Hivehom, of which the Mediterranea Plateau, with a population of nearly three million, was by far the largest. The thranx welcomed such exploitation of the inhospitable regions they had always shunned. Besides, there were some four million thranx living in the Amazon basin on Terra alone – which sort of evened things out.

Most of the large human-dominated concerns, Bisondenbit explained, made their headquarters on the southern edge of the Plateau, near the big shuttleport at Chitteranx. This Challis had no doubt located himself there, too.

'The human city there has a thranx name – Azerick,' Bisondenbit went on, whistling softly. 'That's High Thranx for "frozen waste", which in this case has a double meaning I won't go into, except to say that it's a good thing you humans have a sense of humour approximating our own. After we land, I'll be happy to take you up there myself, though I won't stay long. I'm not equipped for arctic travel. Furthermore, Azerick is not cheap.' He hesitated politely. 'You look pretty young for a human out travelling on his own. You have funds?'

'I can scrape by,' Flinx admitted cautiously. Probably it was his innate distrust of others, though he had to admit that in the past few days Bisondenbit had been not only helpful but downright friendly.

They boarded the shuttle together. Flinx sat near a glass-alloy port, where he would have a good view of the principal thranx world, one of the Commonwealth's dual capitals. The planet swung lazily below him as the shuttle separated from the freightliner and commenced its descent. Two large moons glowed whitely above the far horizon, one partly hidden by the planet. Wherever the cloud cover broke,

Flinx could see hints of blue from Hivehom's small oceans, rich green from its thick jungles.

Suddenly he felt the force of gravity pressing him back in his seat as the shuttle dropped tail first through the clouds ..

CHAPTER THREE

Chitteranx was impressive. Though a small port for a world as populous and developed as Hivehom, it still dwarfed the shuttleport of Drallar.

'The city is mostly underground, of course. All thranx cities are, though the surface is well utilized.' The jewelled head shook in puzzlement. 'Why you humans have always chosen to build up instead of down is something I'll never comprehend.'

Flinx's attention was more engaged by the view through the transparent access corridor than by the standard sights of the shuttle terminal. Lush jungle practically overgrew the plastic walls. It was raining outside – steaming, rather. The heat in the terminal was oppressive, despite the fact that it was a compromise between the delightful weather outside – as Bisondenbit called it – and the arctic air atop the nearby Plateau.

Rain, Flinx had grown up with on Moth, but the humidity was something new and unpleasant. Humans could tolerate a hothouse climate, but not for long without protection, and never comfortably.

Bisondenbit, however, could only grumble about the chill inside the terminal. When Flinx remonstrated, he told him, 'This is the principal human port of entry on Hivehom. If we'd landed near the equator, at *Daret* or *Ab-Neub*, you'd be wilting, Flinx.' He looked around as they emerged from the terminal proper into a cluster of roofed-over commercial buildings.

'Before I have to accompany you up to the Plateau, and struggle into a hotsuit, let me enjoy a rational climate for a

36

while. What about a drink?'

'I'd really like to start looking for Challis as soon as – '

'The plateau shuttles run every ten chronits,' Bisondenbit insisted. 'Do come. Besides, you still haven't told me: What do you keep in that box?' A truhand gestured at the large square case Flinx lugged with his left hand.

'It must be something exotic and valuable, judging from the care with which you've handled it.'

'It's exotic, I suppose,' he admitted, 'but not particularly valuable.'

They found a small eating place just inside the climate-controlled cluster of buildings. Only a few humans were present, though it was crowded with thranx. Flinx was thoroughly enchanted with the thranx resting couches, the subdued lighting which made even midday appear dim, and the ornately carved, communal drinking canisters suspended from the ceiling above each booth.

Bisondenbit selected an isolated table at the back of the room and made helpful, though unnecessary recommendations. Flinx had no trouble deciphering the menu which was printed in four languages: High Thranx, Low Thranx, symbospeech and Terranglo.

Bisondenbit ordered after Flinx opted for one of the several thousand liqueurs which the thranx were masters at concocting.

'When do you want to go back to the terminal to pick up the rest of your luggage?' the insect asked casually, after their drinks arrived. He noted with approval that Flinx disdained a glass in favour of one of the weaving-spouted tankards used by the thranx themselves.

'This is it,' Flinx told him, indicating his small shoulder bag and the single large perforated case. Bisondenbit didn't try to conceal his surprise.

'That's all you've brought all this way with you, without knowing how long it will take you to find this human Challis?'

'I've always travelled light,' was his companion's explanation. The drink was typically sweet, with a faint flavour of raisin. It went down warm and smooth. The trip, he decided, was beginning to catch up with him. He was more tired than he should be this early in the day. Obviously he wasn't quite the urbane interstellar traveller he pictured himself as.

'Besides, it shouldn't be hard to find Challis. Certainly he'll be staying at his local company headquarters.' Flinx let another swallow of the thick, honeylike fluid slide down his throat, then frowned. Despite his age, he considered himself a good judge of intoxicants, but this new brew was apparently more potent than the menu description indicated. He found his vision blurring slightly.

Bisondenbit peered at him solicitously. 'Are you all right? If you've never had Sookcha before, it can be a bit overwhelming. Packs quite a concussion?'

'Punch,' Flinx corrected thickly.

'Yes, quite a punch. Don't worry . . . the feeling will pass quick enough.'

But Flinx felt himself growing steadily groggier. 'I think . . . if I could just get outside. A little fresh air . . .' He started to get up, but discovered his legs responded with indifference while his feet moved as if he were walking on an oiled treadmill. It was impossible to get any traction.

Abandoning the effort, he found that his muscular system was entering a state of anarchy. 'That's funny,' he murmured 'I can't seem to move.'

'No need to be concerned,' Bisondenbit assured him, leaning across the table and staring at him with an intensity that was new to Flinx. 'I'll see that you're properly taken care of.'

As all visual images faded, Flinx feared his strange, new acquaintance would do just that . . .

Flinx awoke to the harmony of destruction, accompanied by curses uttered in several languages. Blinking – his eyelids felt as if they were lined with platinum – he fought unsuccessfully to move his arms and legs. Failing this, he settled for holding his eyes partially open. Dim light from an unseen source illuminated the little room in which he lay. Spartan furnishings of rough-hewn wood were backed by smooth walls of argent gunite. As his perceptions cleared he discovered that metal bands at his wrists and ankles secured him to a crude wooden platform that was neither bed nor table.

He lay quietly. For one thing, his stomach was performing gymnastics and it would be best to keep the surroundings subdued until the internal histrionics ceased. For another, the sensations and sounds surrounding him indicated it would be unwise to call attention to his new consciousness.

The sounds of destruction were being produced by the methodical dissection of his personal effects. Looking slowly to his right, he saw the shredded remains of his shoulder bag and clothing. These were being inspected by three humans and a single thranx. Recognizing the latter as his former games mentor and would-be friend, Bisondenbit, he damned his own naïveté.

Back in Drallar he would never hade been so loquacious with a total stranger. But he had been three days isolated and friendless on board ship when the thranx had approached him with his offer of games instruction. Gratitude had shunted aside instinctive caution.

'No weapons, no poison, no beamer, needler – not even a threatening note,' complained one of the men in fluent symbospeech.

'What's worse,' one of his companions chipped in, 'no money. Nothing but a lousy cardmeter.' He held up the compact computer unit which registered and transferred credit in unforgeable fashion, and tossed it disgustedly on to a nearby table. It landed among the rest of Flinx's few possessions. Flinx noted that there was one remaining object they had not yet broken into.

'That's not my fault,' Bisondenbit complained, glaring with eyes of shattered prism at the three tall humans. 'I didn't promise to deliver any fringe benefits. If you don't think I've earned my fee I'll go straight to Challis himself.'

One of the men looked resigned. Taking a double handful of small metal rectangles from one pocket, he handed them to Bisondenbit. The thranx counted them carefully.

The human who had paid him looked over at the restraining bonds, and Flinx closed his eyes just in time. 'That's a lot of money. I don't know why Challis is so afraid – this is just a kid. But he thinks it's worth the fee you demanded. Don't understand it, though.'

The man indicated the biggest of the three. 'Charlie, here, could break him in two with one hand.' Turning, he tapped the large sealed case. 'What's in this?'

'I don't know,' the thranx admitted. 'He kept it in his cabin all the time.'

The third man spoke up. His tone was vaguely contemptuous. 'You can all stop worrying about it. I've been examining that container with appropriate instrumentation while the rest of you have been occupying yourselves with a harmless wardrobe.' He gave the bag a shove. 'There's no indication it contains anything mechanical or explosive. Readings indicated that it's full of shaped organics and organic analogues – probably the rest of his clothing.' He sighed. 'Might as well check it out. We're paid to be thorough.' Taking a pair of thick metal clippers from a neat tool case, he snipped through the squat combination lock. That done, the top of the case opened easily. He peered inside, grunted. 'Clothes, all right. Looks like another couple of suits and – ' He started to removed the first set of clothing – then screamed and, stumbling backward, clawed at the left side of his face, which was suddenly bubbling like hot mud. A narrow, beltlike shape erupted from the open case.

Bisondenbit chattered something in High Thranx and vanished out the single door. The one called Charlie fell backward across Flinx's pinioned form, his beamer firing wildly at the ceiling as he dug in awful silence at his own eyes. The leader of the little group of humans was close on Bisondenbit's abdomen when something hit him at the back of his neck. Howling, he fell back into the room and started rolling across the floor.

Less than a minute had passed.

Something long and smooth slid on to Flinx's chest.

'That's enough, Pip,' he said to his pet. But the minidrag was beyond persuasion. His inspection over, he took to the air again and began darting and striking at the man on the floor. Gaping holes appeared in the supplicant's clothing and skin wherever the venom struck. Eventually the man stopped rolling.

The first man who had been struck was already dead, while the second lay moaning against a wall behind Flinx. Pieces of skin hung loosely from his cheek and neck; and a flash of white showed where Pip's extremely corrosive poison had exposed the bone.

Meanwhile the minidrag settled gently on Flinx's stomach, slid upward caressingly. The long tongue darted out again and again to touch lips and chin. 'The right hand, Pip,' Flinx instructed, 'my right hand.' In the darkness the reptile eyed him questioningly.

Flinx snapped his fingers in a special way and now the

minidrag half crawled, half fluttered over to the hand in question, rested his head in the open palm. A few scratches and then the hand closed gently but firmly. The snake offered no resistence.

Adjusting his pet with some difficulty, Flinx aligned Pip's snout with the place where the metal band was locked to the table. His fingers moved, massaging various muscles behind the jaw. A few droplets of poison oozed from the tapered tube which ran through the minidrag's lower palate.

There was a sizzling sound.

Flinx waited until the noise died away, then pulled hard. A second pull and the rotted metal gave way. Transferring Pip, with greater control now, he repeated the process on his other bindings, the snake doing his bidding through each step.

As he was freeing his left leg, Flinx noticed a movement on his right. So did Pip, and the minidrag took to the air again.

The single survivor shrieked as the dragon shape moved close. 'Get away, get away, don't let it near me!' he gibbered in total terror.

'*Pip!*' Flinx commanded. A hushed pause. The minidrag continued to hover nervously before the crouching man, its wings a hummingbird blur, soulless, cold-blooded eyes staring into those of the bleeding human whose clavicle showed pale through dissolved clothing.

Flinx finally ripped clear of the last strap. Getting slowly to his feet, he made his way carefully to the other table. The clothes he'd been wearing were an unsalvageable mess. He began to slip into the second jumpsuit, in whose folds Pip had been so comfortably coiled.

'I'm sorry for your friends, but not too sorry,' he murmured. Zipping up the suit, Flinx turned to the shocked creature on the floor. 'Tell me the whole story and don't leave out any details. The more questions I have to ask, the more impatient Pip will get.'

A stream of information poured from the man's lips. 'Your thranx friend is a small-time criminal.'

'Antique services,' Flinx muttered. 'Very funny. Go on.'

'It struck him odd that a kid like you, travelling alone, would be so interested in looking up Conda Challis. On a hunch he beamed Challis's offices here and told them about you. Someone high up got upset as hell and told him to deliver you to us, to be checked out.'

'Makes sense,' Flinx agreed. 'What was supposed to happen to me after I was – er – checked out?'

The man huddled into the corner farthest away from the fluttering minidrag, whispered, 'Use your head – what do you think?'

'Challis claimed he was the thorough type,' Flinx observed 'I could have been an innocent passenger – it wouldn't have mattered.' Repacking his few intact belongings in the hand case, Flinx started for the door that Bisondenbit had exited through only moments before.

'What about me?' the man mumbled. 'Are you going to kill me?'

Flinx turned in surprise, his eyes narrowing as he regarded the human wreck who had confidently pawed through his luggage just minutes before. 'No. What for? Tell me where I can find Conda Challis. Then I'd advise you to get to a hospital.'

'He's on the top floor of the executive pylon at the far end of the complex.'

'What complex?' Flinx asked, puzzled.

'That's right – you still don't know where you are, do you?' Flinx shook his head. 'This is the fourth sublevel of the Challis Hivehom Mining Components plant. The Challis family's very big in mining machinery.

'Go to the corridor outside the door, turn to your left, and keep on until you reach a row of lifts. They all go to the surface. From there anyone can direct you to the executive pylon – the plant grounds are hexagon-shaped and the pylon's at the northeast corner.'

'Thanks,' said Flinx. 'You've been helpful.'

'Not helpful, you poisonous little bastard,' the un-employed cripple muttered painfully as soon as Flinx had departed, 'just pragmatic.' He began to crawl slowly towards the open door.

In the corridor, once assured that no one waited in ambush, Flinx snapped his fingers again. 'Pip . . . rest now.'

The minidrag hissed agreeably and fluttered down into the open case, burying itself quietly within the folded shreds of torn clothing. Flinx snapped the latch shut. At the first opportunity he would have to replace the ruined lock, or

42

else chance some innocent bystander suffering the same fate as his three former captors.

No one challenged him as he continued on towards the lifts. The numbers alongside the doors were labelled 4-B, 3-B and so on to zero, where the count began again in normal fashion. Four levels above ground and four below, Flinx noted. Zero ought to take him to the surface, and that was the button he pressed when a car finally arrived.

The lift deposited him in an efficiently designed four-storey glass antechamber. A steady stream of humans and thranx utilized the lifts around him. 'Your pardon,' a triad of thranx trilled, as they made their way purposefully into the lift he had just vacated.

Although every eye seemed focused on him, in reality no one was paying him the least attention. No reason they should, he thought, relaxing. Only one man and a few of his minions would be hunting him.

A large desk conveniently labelled *Information* was set just inside the transparent façade of the vaulted chamber. A single thranx sat behind it. Flinx strolled over, trying to give the impression that he knew exactly what he was about.

'Excuse me,' he began, in fluent High Thranx, 'can you tell me how to get to the executive pylon from here?'

The elderly, rather officious-looking insect turned to face him. He was painted black and yellow, Flinx noted, and was utterly devoid of the enamel chiton inlay the thranx were so fond of. A pure business type.

'Northeast quadrant,' the thranx said sharply, implying that the asker should know better. 'You go out the main door there,' he continued, pointing with a truhand as a foothand supported his thorax on the table edge, 'and turn left down H portal. The pylon is a full twelve floors with carport on top.'

'Blessings of the Hive on you,' Flinx said easily. The oldster eyed him sharply.

'Say, what do you want with . . . ?'

But Flinx had already been swallowed up by the bustling crowd. The officer hunted for him a moment longer, then gave up and went back to his job.

Flinx made rapid progress across the factory grounds. A friendly worker gave him ready directions the one time he found himself lost. When he finally spied the unmistakable

43

shape of the executive pylon, he slowed, suddenly aware that from this point on he had no idea how to proceed.

Challis's reaction to his unexpected appearance was going to be something less than loving. And this time he, if not his underlings, would be prepared to deal with Pip. For all his lethal abilities, the minidrag was far from invulnerable.

Somehow, he was going to have to slip inside the tower and find out where Challis was. Even from here he could sense the powerful emanations of a smaller, darker presence. But he had no guarantee that he would find Mahnahmi and Challis together. Did the girl sense his presence as well? It was a sobering thought.

Deciding to move fast and purposefully, he strode boldly through the tower's main entrance. But this was no factory annex. An efficient-looking thranx with three inlaid chevrons on his b-thorax was there to intercept him – politely, of course.

'Swarm be with your buisness,' the insect murmured. 'You will state both it and your name, please.'

Flinx was about to answer when a door on one side burst open. A squad of heavily armed thranx gushed out, the leader pointing and shouting. 'That's the one – restrain him!'

Reacting swiftly, the officer who had confronted Flinx put a truhand on one arm. Flinx brought his leg up and kicked reluctantly. The armourlike chiton was practically invulnerable – except at the joints, where Flinx's foot struck. The joint cracked audibly and the officer let out an agonized chirp as Flinx broke for the rank of lifts directly ahead.

Jumping inside, he swung clear and hit the topmost switch, noticing that it was for the eleventh floor. A key was required to reach the twelfth.

Several beamers pierced the lift doors even as the car began its ascent. Fortunately they didn't strike any vital machinery and his ride wasn't slowed, though the three molten-edged holes bored in the door provided plenty of food for thought.

An angry pounding and banging inside the carrybag attracted his attention. Once the latch was popped a furious Pip rocketed out. After a rapid inspection of the lift's interior the minidrag settled nervously around Flinx's right

44

shoulder. It coiled tightly there, muscles tense with excitement.

There was no point in keeping the reptile concealed any longer, since they clearly knew who he was. But who/what had given him away?

Mahnahmi – it had to be! He almost felt as if he could sense a girlish, mocking laughter. Her capacity for mischief remained an unknown quantity. It was possible that her mental talents exceeded his own both in strength and lack of discipline. Of course, no one would believe that if he had the chance to tell of it. Mahnahmi had her role of goggle-eyed, innocent infant perfected.

The question, though, was whether her maliciousness was grounded in calculation or merely in a desire for undisciplined destruction. He sensed that she could change from hate to love, each equally intense, at a moment's thought. If only she would realize that he meant her no harm . . . then it came to him that she probably did.

He was a source of potential amusement to her, nothing more.

Some simple manipulations sufficed to jimmy the door mechanism. When the car passed the tenth floor he jumped clear, then turned to watch it continue past him. Frantically, he began to hunt around the room that appeared to be a combination of offices and living quarters, probably belonging to one of Challis's principal assistants. Or maybe the plant manager.

If there were no stairways he would be trapped here. He didn't think Challis's bodyguard was so stupid as to allow him to descend and escape.

At least these quarters were deserted. As he considered his situation, a violent explosion sounded above. Looking up, he saw shredded metal and plastic alloy fall smoking back down the lift shaft.

He suddenly realized that there was only one way to deal with Mahnahmi's mischief. Consciously, he fought to blank his mind, to suppress every consideration of subsequent action, every hint of preconception. The dark cloud which had hovered nearby slowly faded. He could no longer detect Mahnahmi's presence – and she should be equally blind to his whereabouts. There was a chance she, like everyone else, would momentarily think that he had died in the ambush of the lift car.

A quick patrol revealed that these quarters had only one entrance – the single, now useless lift. No other lift opened on this level. That left one way in to the floor above – the roof carport. Gradually his gaze came to rest on the curving window that looked out across the plant and to the Plateau beyond.

Flinx moved to the window, found it opened easily. The side of the pylon was marked with decorative ripples and thranx pebbling. He looked upward, considered one additional possibility.

At least they wouldn't be expecting him any more.

His mind briefly registered the magnificent panorama of the Mediterranea Plateau, dotted with factories and human settlements. In the distance the mist-filled lowlands stretched to the horizon.

The footing on the rippled metal exterior of the building was not as sure as he would have liked, but he would manage. At least he had to climb only one floor. Moving through the apartment-office, he located the bathroom, opened the window there, and started up.

Unless the floor plan upstairs was radically different, he should encounter another bathroom, perhaps larger but hopefully unoccupied, above the one he had just exited from. That would be the best place from which to make an unobtrusive entrance.

Moving hands and feet methodically, he made slow but steady progress upward, never looking back. In Drallar he had climbed greater heights on wet, less certain surfaces – and at a younger age at that. Still, he moved cautiously here.

The absence of wind was a blessing. In good time he encountered a ledge. There was a window above it. Reaching, he pulled himself up so that he was staring through the transparent pane, and observed with satisfaction that the window was open a few centimetres. Then he noticed the two figures standing at the back of the room. One was fat and sweating, a condition not due to recent exercise. The other was small, blonde, and wide-eyed.

Suddenly they saw him.

'Don't let him get me, Daddy,' she said in mock fright. Opening his mind, Flinx sensed the excitement racing

46

through hers and he felt sick.

'I don't know why you persist in tormenting me,' Challis said in confusion, his beamer now focused on Flinx's shoulder. 'I didn't hurt you badly. You've turned into something of a pest. Good-bye.' His finger started to tighten on the trigger.

Pip was off Flinx's shoulder instantly. Challis saw the snake move, shifted his aim, and fired. Remembrance of what the minidrag was capable of shook the merchant, and his shot went wild. It struck the wooden moulding above the window, missing Pip and Flinx completely. Whatever the moulding was made of, it burned with a satisfying fury. In seconds the gap between window and Challis was filled with flame and smoke.

While the smoke chased the merchant from the room and prevented him from getting a clear shot, it also left Flinx pinned outside the window. He started downward as rapidly as he dared, Pip thrumming angrily around his head and looking for something to kill. Flinx doubted he could make the ground safely before Challis got word to the guards below. Slowly he descended past one floor, a second, a third. On the fourth floor down he noticed that the reflective one-way panelling had broken and been repaired with transparent film.

Two sharp kicks enlarged the opening and he jumped through – to find himself confronting a single startled woman.

She screamed.

'Please,' he begged, making calming sounds and moving towards her. 'Don't do that. I don't mean you any harm.'

She screamed again.

Flinx made violent shushing motions with his hands. 'Be quiet . . . they'll find me.'

She continued to scream.

Flinx halted and thought furiously what to do. Someone was bound to hear the noise any second.

Pip solved the immediate problem. He lurched speculatively at the woman. She saw the long, sinuous, quick-moving reptilian form, mouth agape, rushing towards her on broad membranous wings.

She fainted.

That stopped the screaming, but Flinx was still trapped

47

in a now alerted building with next to no prospect of slipping out unseen. His gaze travelled frantically around the room, searching for a large carton to hide in or a weapon or . . . anything useful. Eventually his attention returned to the woman. She had fallen awkwardly and he moved to shift her into a more natural resting position. As he propped her up, Flinx noticed a bathroom nearby. His gaze shot back to the girl . . .

A minute later several heavily armed guards burst into the unlocked room. It seemed to be deserted. They fanned out, made a quick inspection of every possible hiding place. One guard entered the bathroom, noticed feminine legs beneath the privacy shield, and hastily withdrew, apologizing. With his comrades he left and moved on to inspect the next office.

Three offices later it occurred to him that the woman hadn't responded to his apology – not with a thank you, not with a frosty acknowledgement, not with a curse. Nothing. That struck him as being strange and he mentioned the fact to his superior.

Together they dashed back to the office in question, entered the bathroom. The legs were still in the same position. Cautiously, the officer knocked on the shield, cleared his throat appraisingly. When there was no response, he directed the other two men to stand back and cover the shield exitway, which he then opened from the outside.

The woman was just opening her eyes. She found herself sitting stark naked on the convenience, staring into the muzzles of two energy weapons held in the steady grip of a pair of resolute-looking, uniformed men.

She fainted again.

By the time the badly shaken woman had been revived once more, Flinx was well clear of the tower. No one had noticed the lithe, short-haired woman leaving the building. Flinx had made excellent use of the cosmetics found in the woman's desk – in Drallar it was useful to have knowledge of abilities others might find absurd or even disreputable. Only one clerk had noticed anything unusual. But he wasn't about to mention to his fellows that the double leather belt encircling the woman's waist had moved independently of her walk.

Finally away from both the tower and the Challis plant, Flinx discarded the woman's clothing and let Pip slip free

48

from around his belly. Disdaining normal transportation channels as too dangerous now, he made his way to the edge of the escarpment.

The two-thousand-kilometre drop was breathtaking, but he couldn't risk waiting around the Plateau for some of Challis's armed servants to challenge him in the street. Nor did he want to risk awkward questions from the authorities. So he took a deep breath, selected what looked like the least-sheer cliff and began his descent.

The basalt was nearly vertical, but crumbling and weathered, so he encountered an abundance of handholds. Even so, he doubted that Challis would imagine that anyone would consider descending the escarpment by hand and foot.

Flinx came upon some bad places, but the overgrowth of dangling vines and creepers enabled him to bypass these successfully. His arms began to ache, and once, when a foot momentarily became numb, he was lift clinging precariously by fingers and one set of toes to tiny cracks in the rock.

At the thousand-kilometre mark, the cliff started to angle slightly away from him, making climbing much easier. He increased his pace. Finally, bruised, scratched, and utterly exhausted, Flinx reached the jungle at the bottom. Pausing a moment to orient himself, he headed immediately in what he hoped was the direction of the port. He had chosen his place of descent with care, so he didn't have far to go through the dense vegetation.

But he was totally unaware that he was struggling over a region as densely populated as any of Terra's major cities. An entire thranx metropolis lay below him, hewn in traditional fashion, from the earth and rock beneath the sweltering surface. Flinx walked upon a green cloud that hovered over the city.

Totally drained and beginning to wish Challis *had* shot him, he shoved himself through one more stubborn cluster of bushes . . . then stumbled on to the surface of a neatly paved roadway. Two more days, and he had made his way back to Chitteranx Port. Those he met cautiously avoided him. He was quite aware of the sight he must present after his scramble down the cliff wall and his hike through the jungle.

A few thranx did take pity on the poor human, enough to provide him with sufficient food and water to continue on.

The sight of the port outskirts cheered him immensely. Pip took to the air at Flinx's shout of joy before settling back on his master's shoulder. Flinx glanced up at the minidrag, who looked relaxed and comfortable in the tropical heat so like that of his native world of Alaspin.

'You can afford to look content, spade-face,' Flinx addressed his companion enviously. While he had fought his way down the cliff centimetre by centimetre, Pip had fluttered and soared freely nearby, always urging him on faster and faster, when a single misstep could have meant quick death.

The clerk at the overbank counter in the port terminal was human, but that didn't prevent him from maintaining his composure at the sight of a dirty, ragged youth approaching. A wise man. he had learned early in life a basic dictum: odd appearance may indicate wealth or eccentricity, with the two not necessarily mutually exclusive.

So he treated the ragamuffin as he would have any well-dressed, clearly affluent arrival. 'May I be of service, sir?' he inquired politely, unobtrusively turning his head to one side.

Flinx explained his needs. The information he provided was fed to a computer. A short while later the machine insisted that the person standing before the counter – name Flinx, given recorded name Philip Lynx, retina pattern so-and-so, pulse variables such-and-such, heart configuration thus-and-that – was indeed a registered depositor at the King's Bank on Moth, in the city of Drallar, and that his present drawable balance as of this date was . . .

The clerk stood a little straighter, fought to face Flinx. 'Now then, sir, how did you happen to lose your registered cardmeter?'

'I had an accident,' Flinx explained cryptically, 'and it fell out of my pocket.'

'Yes.' The clerk continued to smile. 'No need to worry. As you know, only you can utilize a personal cardmeter. We will note the disappearance of your old cardmeter and within the hour you will have a new one waiting at this desk for you.'

'I can wait. However,' he indicated his clothing with an eloquent sweep of his hands, 'I'd like to buy some new clothes, and get cleaned up a little.'

'Naturally,' the clerk agreed, reaching professionally into a drawer. 'If you'll just sign this slip and permit me to register your eyeprint on it, we can advance you whatever you require.'

Flinx applied for a ridiculously modest amount, listened to the clerk's directions as to where he could hire a bath and buy clothing, and left with a grateful handshake.

The jumpsuit he eventually chose was more elaborate than the two Hivehom had already appropriated, but he felt he owed himself a little luxury after what he had been through.

The bath occupied most of the rest of the hour, and when he returned to the overbank desk he once more resembled a human being instead of a denizen of Hivehom's jungles. As promised, his new cardmeter was ready for him.

'Anything else I can do for you, sir?'

'Thanks, you've done more than enough. I . . .' He paused, looked to his left. 'Excuse me, but I see an old friend.'

He left the clerk with an open mouth and a tip of ten per cent of his total withdrawal.

The central terminal floor was high-domed and filled with the noise of travellers arriving and departing. The smallish thranx Flinx strode up behind was engaged in activity of a different sort.

'I think you'd better give that lady back her abdomen purse,' he whispered to the insectoid lightfinger. As he spoke, a lavishly inlaid and chiton-bejewelled thranx matron, her flaking exoskeleton elegantly streaked with silver, turned to stare curiously at him.

At the same time the thranx Flinx had surprised started visibly and whirled to confront his accuser. 'Sir, if you think that I have . . .' The voice turned to a clacking gargle. Flinx smiled engagingly as Pip stirred on his shoulder.

'Hello. Bisondenbit.'

The concept of compound eyes bugging outward was unreasonable from a physiological standpoint, but that was the impression Flinx received. Bisondenbit's antennae were quivering so violently Flinx thought they might shake free, and the thranx was staring in expectant terror at the lethal length of Pip.

'The abdomen purse,' Flinx repeated softly, 'and calm down before you crack your braincase.'

51

'Y-ye-yes,' Bisondenbit stuttered. Interesting! Flinx had never heard a thranx stutter before. Turning to the old female, Bisondenbit reached into an overly capacious b-thorax pouch and withdrew a small, six-sided bag of woven gold-coloured metal.

'You just dropped this, Queen Mother,' he muttered reluctantly, using the formalized honorific. 'The hooks have come all unbent . . . see?'

The matron was checking her own abdomen with a foot-hand while reaching for the purse with a truhand.

'I don't understand. I was certain it was secured . . .' She broke off, ducked her head and executed a movement with skull and antennae indicative of profound thanks. adding verbally, 'Your service is much appreciated, warsire.'

Flinx flinched when she bestowed the undeserved compliment on Bisondenbit.

That worthy's courteous pose lasted until the matron had passed out of hearing range. Then he turned nervous eyes on Flinx. 'I didn't want you killed . I didn't want anyone killed,' he stammered rapidly, 'they said nothing to me about a killing. I only was to bring you to . . .'

'Settle down,' Flinx advised him. 'And stop yammering of death. There are already too many deaths in this.'

'Oh, on that I concur.' the thranx confessed, the tension leaving him slowly. 'None of my doing.' Abruptly his attitude changed from one of fear to one of intense curiosity. 'How did you manage to escape the tower and leave the Plateau? I am told many were watching for you but none saw you leave.'

'I flew down,' Flinx said, 'after I made myself invisible.'

Bisondenbit eyed him uncertainly, started to laugh, stopped, then stared again. 'You are a most peculiar fellow, even for a human. I do not know whether to believe you or not.' He suddenly looked around the busy terminal, his nervousness returning. 'Powerful people around Challis want to know your whereabouts. There is talk of a large reward, to be paid without questions. The only clue anyone has as to your escape, however, resides in a woman who is confined to a hospital. She is hysterical still.'

'I'm sorry for that,' Flinx murmured honestly.

'It is not good for me to be seen with you – you have become a desired commodity.'

'It's always nice to be wanted,' Flinx replied, blithely ignoring Bisondenbit's fear for his own safety. 'By the way, I didn't know that the thranx counted pickpocketing among their talents.'

'From a digital standpoint we've always been adroit. Many humans have acquired equally, ah, useful abilities from us.'

'I can imagine,' Flinx snorted. 'I happen to live in a city overstocked with such abilities. But I haven't time to debate the morality of dubious cultural exchanges. Just tell me where I can find Conda Challis.'

Bisondenbit eyed the youth as if he had suddenly sprouted an extra pair of hands. 'He almost killed you. It seems he wants another chance. I can't believe you will continue to seek out such a powerful enemy. I consider myself a fair judge of human types. You do not appear revenge-motivated.'

'I'm not,' Flinx confessed uneasily, aware that Small Symm had assumed he was following Challis for the same reason. People persisted in ascribing to him motives he didn't possess.

'If not revenge, then what is it you follow him for . . . not that it makes me sad to see a being of Challis's reputation squirm a little, even if it be bad for business.'

'Just tell me where he is.'

'If you'll tell me why you seek him.'

Flinx nudged Pip and the flying snake stirred, yawned to show a sac-backed gullet. 'I don't think that's necessary,' Flinx said softly, meaningfully. A terrified Bisondenbit threw up truhands and foothands in feeble defence.

'Never mind,' sighed Flinx, tired of threatening. 'If I tell you it might even filter convincingly back to Challis. I just think he holds information on who my real parents are and what happened to them after they . . abandoned me.'

'Parents?' Bisondenbit looked quizzical. 'I was told you had threatened Challis.'

'Not true. He's paranoid because of an incident in our mutual past. He wanted me to do something and I didn't want to do it.'

'For that you've killed several people?'

'I haven't killed anyone,' Flinx protested unhappily. 'Pip has, and then only to defend me.'

'Well, the dead are the dead,' Bisondenbit observed

53

profoundly. He gazed in disbelief at Flinx. 'I did not believe any being, even a human, could be so obsessed with perverse desire. Does it matter more than your life to know who your parents were?'

'We don't have the tradition of a general hivemother that I could trace myself to and through,' Flinx explained. 'Yes, it matters that much to me.'

The insect shook his double-lobed head 'Then I wish you musical hunting in your mad quest. In another time, another place, I would maybe be your clanmate.' Leaning forward, he extended antennae. After a moment's hesitation, Flinx touched his own forehead to the proffered protrusions. He straightened, gave the slight thranx a warning look.

'Try,' he said to Bisondenbit, 'to keep your truhands to your own thorax.'

'I don't know why my activities should concern you, as long as you are not affected,' the thranx protested. He was almost happy, now that it appeared Flinx wasn't going to murder him. 'Are you going to report me to the authorities?'

'Only for procrastination.' Flinx said impatiently. 'You still haven't told me where Challis is.'

'Send him a tape of your request,' the thranx advised. 'Would you believe it?'

Bisondenbit's mandibles clicked. 'I understand. You are a strange individual, man-boy.'

'You're no incubator yourself, Bisondenbit. Where?'

Shoulder chiton moved to produce a ruffling sound, like cardboard being scraped across a carpet. Bisondenbit spoke with a modicum of pride.

'I'm not one of Challis's hired grubs – I'll tell you. You drove him from Moth, it seems; and now you've chased him off Hivehom. The Challis Company's home office is in Terra's capital, and I presume that's where he's fled. No doubt he'll be expecting you, if he hasn't died of fright by now. May you find him before the many-who-pursue find *you*.' He started to leave, then paused curiously.

'Good-bye, Bisondenbit,' Flinx said firmly. The thranx started to speak, but spotted the minidrag moving and thought better of it. He walked away, looking back over his shoulder occasionally and muttering to himself, unsatisfied. For his part Flinx felt no guilt in letting the pickpocket go free. It was not for one who had performed his fair share of borderline activities to judge another.

Why wouldn't Challis believe that his purpose in seeking him out was for nothing so useless and primitive as revenge? Challis could understand only his own kind of mind, Flinx decided.

Somehow, he would have to find a way around it.

From Hivehom to the Commonwealth's second capital world of Terra was a considerable journey, even at maximum drive. But eventually Flinx found himself drinking in a view of it from another shuttlecraft port as the little transfer ship dropped free of the freightliner.

This was the green legend, *Terra magnificat*, spawning-place of mankind, second capital of the Commonwealth and home of the United Church. This was the world where once a primitive primate had suddenly risen to stand on hind feet to be nearer the sky, never dreaming he would one day step beyond it.

And yet, save for the royal blue of the oceans, the globe itself was unremarkable, mostly swirling white clouds and brown splotches of land.

He hadn't known what to expect . . . golden spires piercing the cloudtops, perhaps, or formed crags of chromium backing against the seas – all that was at once absurd and sublime. Although he couldn't see it, Terra possessed both in munificent quantities, albeit in forms far more muted than his grandiose visions.

Surely, Flinx thought as the shuttle dropped into the outer atmosphere, the omnipresent emerald of Hivehom was more striking and, for the matter, the lambent yellow ring-wings of Moth were more sheerly spectacular.

But somewhere down there his great to the second or third power grandfather had lived and died . . .

CHAPTER FOUR

Descending on a west-to-east path, the shuttle passed over the big approach station at Perth before beginning its final powerglide over the endless agricult fields of central Australia. Flinx had passing views of isolated towns and food-processing plants and the shining solar power stations ringing the industrial metropolis of Alice Springs. He patted the shiny new case sitting by his feet, heard the relaxed hiss from within, and strapped himself down for landing.

The shuttle was dropping towards the largest shuttleport on Terra. The port formed the base of an enormous urban T whose cap stretched north and south to embrace the warm Pacific. Brisbane had been Terra's capital city for hundreds of years now, and it's port, with long, open approaches over the continental centre and the open Pacific, was the planet's busiest. It was also convenient to the large thranx settlements in North Australia and on New Guinea, and to the United Church headquarters at Denpasar.

There was a gentle bump, and he was down.

No one took any notice of him in the terminal, nor later as he walked through the streets of the vast city. He felt very much alone, even more so than he had on Hivehom.

The capital surprised him. There were no soaring towers here. Brisbane had none of the commercial intensity of West North America's city of Lala or of London or Jakutsk, or even of the marketplace in Drallar. The streets were almost quiet, still bearing in places a certain quaintness with architecture that reached back through to the pre-Amalgamation time.

As for the government buildings, they at least were properly immense. But they were built low to the ground and, because they were landscaped on all sides, seemed to reach outward like verdant ripples in a metal and stone pond.

Locating the headquarters of the Challis Company was a simple matter. Careful research then gave him the location of the family residence. But gaining entrance to that isolated and protected sanctum was another matter.

Bisondenbit's comments came back to him. How could he reach Challis and explain his purpose before the merchant had him killed?

Somehow he must extend the time Challis would grant him before destruction. Somehow . . . he checked his cardmeter. He was not wealthy, but he was certainly far above beggar status. If he could stretch things a bit, he would have a few weeks to find the proper company to implement his plan.

There was one such firm located in the southern manufacturing sector of the capital. A secretary shuffled him to a vice-president, who gazed with a bemused expression at the crude plans Flinx had prepared and passed him on to the company's president.

An engineer, the president had no difficulty with the mechanical aspects of the request. Her concern was with other matters.

'You'll need this many?' she inquired, pursing her lips and idly brushing away a wisp of grey hair.

'Probably, if I know the people involved. I think I do.'

She made calculations on a tiny desk computer, looked back at his list again. 'We can produce what you want, but the time involved and the degree of precision you desire will require a lot of money.'

Flinx gave her the name of a local bank and a number. A short conversation via machine finally caused a smile to crease the older woman's face. 'I'm glad that's out of the way. Money matters always make me feel a little dirty, you know? Uh . . . may I ask what you're going to use these for?'

'No,' Flinx replied amiably as Pip shifted lazily on his shoulder. 'That's why I came to you – a small firm with a big reputation.'

'You'll be available for programming?' she asked uncertainly.

'Direct transfer, if need be.'

That appeared to settle things in the president's mind. She rose, extended a hand. 'Then I think we can help you, Mr . . . ?'

57

He shook her hand, smiled. 'Just use the bank number I gave you.'

'As you wish,' she agreed, openly disappointed.

The contrast between the rich blue of the ocean and the sandy hills of the Gold Coast was soft and striking. One high ridge in particular was dotted with widely spaced, luxurious private residences, each carefully situated to drink in as much of the wide bay as possible – and to provide discreet, patrollable open space between neighbours.

One home was spectacular in its unobtrusiveness. It was set back in the cliffs like a topaz in gold. Devoid of sharp corners, it seemed to be part of the grass-dusted bluff itself. Only the sweeping, free-form glassalloy windows hinted that habitation lay behind.

Nearby, curling breakers assaulted the shore with geometric regularity, small cousins of more mature waves to the south. There, at an ancient village named Suferspardise, many-toned humans and not a few adaptive aliens rode the surf, borne landward in the slick wet teeth of suiciding waves.

Flinx was there now, but he was watching, not participating. He sat relaxed on a low hill above the beach, studying the most recent converts to an archaic sport. Nearby rested his rented groundcar.

At the moment Flinx was observing a mixed group of young adults, all of whom were at once older and younger than himself. They were students at one of the many great universities that maintained branches in the capital. This party disdained boards in favour of the briefer, more violent experiences of body surfing. He saw a number of young thranx among them, which was only natural. The deep blue of the males and the rich aquamarine of the females was almost invisible against the water, and showed clearly only when a comber broke into white foam.

Body surfing was hardly an activity native to the thranx, but like many human sports it had been adopted joyfully by them. They brought their own beauty to it. While a thranx in the water could never match the seal-like suppleness of a human, when it came to nakedly riding the waves they were far superior. Flinx saw their buoyant, hard-shelled bodies dancing at the forefront of successive waves, b-thorax

58

pushed forward to permit air to reach breathing spicules.

Occasionally a human would mount the back of a thranx friend for a double ride. It was no inconvenience to the insectoid mount, whose body was harder and nearly as buoyant as the elliptical boards themselves.

Flinx sighed, His adolescence had been filled with less innocent activities. Circumstances had made him grow up too fast.

Looking down at the sand he put out a foot to impede the progress of a perambulating hermit crab. A toe nudged it on to its side. The tiny crustacean flailed furiously at the air with minute hairy legs and hurled motes of indignant anger at its enormous assailant. Regaining its balance, it continued on its undistinguished way, moving just a little faster than normal. A pity, Flinx thought, that humans couldn't be equally self-contained.

Looking up and down the coast, where a citrine house lay concealed by curving cliffs, Flinx reflected that Challis should be arriving there soon from his offices in the capital.

A gull cried wildly above, reminding him that it was time . . .

Conda Challis had all but forgotten his young pursuer as he stepped from the groundcar. Mahnahmi ran from the house to greet him, and they both saw the solemn figure in the grey jumpsuit moving up the walk at the same time. Somehow he had penetrated outer defences.

Mahnahmi drew in her breath, and Challis turned a shade paler than his normal near-albino self. '*Francis* . . .'

Challis's personal bodyguard did not wait for further verbal command. Having observed the reaction of both his employer and employer's daughter, he immediately deduced that this person approaching was something to be killed and not talked to. Pistol out, he was firing before Challis could conclude his order.

Of course, the person coming up the walk might be harmless. But Challis had forgiven him such oversights in the past, and that reinforced the man's already supreme confidence.

Challis's policy seemed to pay off, for the wildly gesticulating figure of the red-haird youth disintegrated in the awesome blast from the illegally overcharged beamer.

59

'And that,' the shaken merchant muttered with grim satisfaction, 'is finally that, I never expected him to get this close. Thank you, Francis.'

The guard holstered his weapon, nodded once, and headed in to check the house.

Mahnahmi had her arms around Challis's waist. Normally, the merchant disdained coddling the child, but at the moment he was shaken almost to the point of normalcy, so he didn't shove her away.

'I'm glad you killed him,' she sniffed. Challis looked down at her oddly.

'You are? But why? Why should he have frightened you?'

'Well . . .' there was hesitation in the angelic voice, 'he was frightening you, and so that frightened me, Daddy.'

'Um,' Challis grunted. At times the child's comments could be startlingly mature. But then, he reminded himself, smilingly, she was being raised surrounded by adults. In another three or four years, if not sooner she would be ready for another kind of education.

Mahnahmi shuddered and hid her face, hid it so that Challis could not see that the shudder was of revulsion and not fear. Francis returned and took no notice of her. She had experienced the thoughts Challis was now thinking all her life, knew exactly what they were like. They were always sticky and greasy, like the trail a snail left behind it.

'Welcome home, sir. Dinner will be ready soon,' the servant at the interior door said. 'There is someone to see you. No weapons, I checked thoroughly. He insists you know him. He is waiting in the front portico.'

Challis snorted irritably, pushed Mahnahmi away ungently. It was unusual for anyone to come here to conduct business. The Challis offices in the tritower downtown were perfectly accessible to legitimate clients and he preferred to keep his personal residence as private as possible.

Still, it might be Cartesan with information on that purchase of bulk ore from Santos V, or possibly . . . he strolled towards the portico, Mahnahmi trailing behind him.

A figure seated with its back to him stared out the broad, curving window at the ocean below. Challis frowned as he began, 'I don't think . . .'

The figure turned. Having just barely regained his composure, Challis was caught completely unprepared. The organic circuits that controlled the muscles of his artificial left eye twitched, sending it rolling crazily in its socket and further confusing his thoughts.

'Look,' the red-haired figure began rapidly, 'you've got to listen to me. I don't mean you any harm. I only want . . .'

'Francis!' the terrified merchant shrieked at the sight of the ghost.

'Just give me a minute, one minute to explain,' Flinx pressed. 'You're only going to ruin your furniture if . . .' He started to rise.

Challis jumped backward, clear of the room, and stabbed frantically at a concealed switch. A duplicate of that switch was set just outside of every room in the house. It was his final security and now it worked with gratifying efficiency.

A network of blue beams shot from concealed lenses in the walls, crisscrossing the room like a cat's cradle of light. Two of them neatly bisected the form standing before him. He had had to wait until the figure rose or the beams would have passed over it.

Now the merchant let out a nervous little laugh as the figure collapsed, awkwardly falling against the couch and then tumbling to the floor. Behind him, Mahnahmi stared with wide eyes.

Challis fought to steady his breathing, then walked cautiously towards the unmoving figure. He kicked at it, gently at first, then good and hard. It did not give under his boot as it should have.

Leaning over he examined the two punctures the beams had made in the upper torso. There was no blood, and inside both holes, he saw something charred that wasn't flesh and bone. The smell drifting from the figure was a familiar one - but the wrong one.

'Circuitry and coagulated jellastic!' he muttered. 'No wonder there were two of him. Robots.'

'A robot?' a small voice squeaked behind him. 'No wonder I couldn't - ' She shut up abruptly. Challis frowned, half turned to face her.

'What was that, Mahnahmi?'

She put a finger in her mouth, sucked innocently on it as she gazed at the twisted figure on the floor. 'Couldn't see

61

any blood,' she finished facilely.

'Yes, but . . .' A sudden thought brought concern to his face. 'Where's Francis?'

'Sleeping,' a new voice informed him. The merchant's hands fell helplessly to his side, and Mahnahmi drew away as Flinx walked into the room, smiling softly. Unlike the previous two, this youth had a gently stirring reptile coiled about his right shoulder.

'I'm sorry. I'm afraid I had to knock him out – and your overzealous butler, too. You have a nervous staff, Challis.' His hand came up to touch the wall next to the concealed hallway switch controlling the multiple beamers. 'That's a neat trick.'

Challis debated whether he ought to drop to the floor, then looked from the switch back to Flinx and licked his lips.

'Will you stop with your paranoia?' the youth pleaded. 'If I wanted to kill you I could have hit that control already, couldn't I?' He tapped the wall next to it.

Challis dropped, relaxing even as he fell below the lethal level of the beams. But Mahnahmi was running in a crouch towards him, screaming with child-fury: 'Kill him, Daddy, kill him!'

'Get away, child,' Challis said abruptly, slapping her aside. He climbed slowly, carefully, back to his feet and stared at the silent figure in the hall. 'You're right . . . you could have killed me easily just now, and you did not. Why?'

Flinx leaned against the door jamb. 'I've been trying to tell you all along. That incident on Moth is past, finished, done with. I haven't been following you to kill you, Challis. Not all the way to Hivehom and certainly not here.'

'I can't believe . . . maybe you do mean what you say,' the merchant confessed, words coming with difficulty as he fought to readjust his thinking. 'Is it the real you, this time?'

'Yes.' The youth nodded, indicated his shoulder where Pip yawned impressively. 'I'm never without Pip. In addition to being *my* insurance, he's my friend. You should have noticed that the mechanicals appeared without reptilian companionship.'

'Kill him!' Mahnahmi screamed again.

Challis turned on her. 'Shut up, or I'll let Francis play

with you when he comes to. Why this sudden fury, Mahnah-mi. He's right . . . I could be dead a couple of times over by now, if he really desired that. I'm beginning to think he's telling the truth. Why are you so – '

'Because he . . .' she started to say, then subsided suddenly and looked quietly at the floor. 'Because he frightens me.'

'Then go where he won't frighten you. Go to your room. Go on, get out.'

The golden-haired child turned and stalked petulantly towards a door at the far end of the chamber, muttering something under her breath that Challis would not have appreciated, had he been able to hear her.

He turned curiously back to Flinx. 'If you don't want me dead, then why in Aucreden's name have you chased me halfway across the Commonwelath?' He quickly became a solicitous host. 'Come in, have a drink then. You'll stay for the evening meal?'

Flinx shook his head, grinning in a way Challis didn't like. 'I don't want your friendship, Challis. Only some information.'

'If it's about the Janus jewels or anything related to them. I can't tell you anything.'

'It has nothing to do with that, or with your attempt to force me to participate in your private depravities. When you were . . . leaving your house in Drallar, you said something about the characteristics of my maternal line.'

Challis looked puzzled. 'If you say I did, then I guess I did. What of it?'

'I know nothing whatsoever of my true parents. All my seller could give my adoptive mother was my name. Nothing more.' He leaned forward eagerly. 'I think you know more.'

'Well, I . . . I hadn't given it any thought.'

'You said you had a file on me . . . that you had amassed information on my background.'

'That's true. To insure that you really possessed the kind of talent I was hunting for, it was necessary to research your personal history as completely as possible.'

'Where did you find the information?'

'I see no reason to keep it from you, except that I don't know.' Flinx's hand moved a little nearer the fatal switch. 'It's true, it's true!' Challis howled, panicky again. 'Do you think I keep track of every source of minor information my people unearth?' He drew himself up with exaggerated pride. 'I happen to be the head of one of – '

'Yes, yes,' Flinx admitted impatiently. 'Don't regale me with a list of your titles. Can you locate the information source? Let's see if your retrieval system is as efficient as you claim it is.'

'If I do,' the merchant said sharply, 'will that be the last I see of you?'

'I'll have no further interest in you, Challis.'

The merchant came to a decision. 'Wait here.' Turning, he made his way to the far end of the room. There he rolled back the top of what looked to be an antique wooden desk. It's interior turned out to be filled with no-nonsense components combined in the form of an elaborate console. Challis' fingers moved rapidly on the control keys. This produced several minutes of involved blinking and noises from hidden depths within the desk.

Eventually he was rewarded with a small printout which he inserted into a playback.

'Here it is. Come look for yourself.'

'Thanks, but I'll stay here. You read it to me.'

Challis shook his head at this unreasonable lack of trust, then turned his attention to the magnified readout. 'Male child,' he began mechanically, 'registered age seven months with Church-sponsored orphanage in Allahabad, Terra, India Province. This information is followed by some staff speculation matching identity points . . . cornea prints, fingerprints, retina prints, skull shape, and so on, with purely physical superficialities such as hair and eye colour, finger rings and the like.

'These vital statistics are matched to an orphan aged five years who was sold under the name Philip Lynx at such-and-such a date in the free body market in Drallar, Moth. My people apparently felt there were sufficient similarities to link the two.'

'Is the name . . does it tell . . . ?' Flinx had to know whether the name Lynx was lineal, or given only because he was the offspring of a Lynx – that is, a sophisticated, independent woman who was mistress by her choice rather than by the man's. free to come and go as she wished.

Challis was unable to tell him. 'It does not. If you want

64

additional information you'll probably have to hunt it out of the original Church records – assuming you'll be allowed access to them. You could begin in Allahabad, of course, but without a look at the original records it would be hard to tell where to start. Besides, Deopasar itself is much closer.'

'Then I'll go there.'

'You'll never gain access to those records. Do you think, dear boy, anyone who wishes is permitted the use of the original Church files?'

'Just tell me where it is.'

Challis grinned. 'On an island called Bali, about five thousand kilometres northwest of here in the Indonesian archipelago.'

'Thank you, Challis. You won't see me again.' He turned, left the hall.

As soon as the youth was out of sight Challis's attention was drawn to several tiny screens set into a console. One showed his visitor about to leave via the front door. Challis touched a switch. The red-haired figure grabbed the door mechanism – and both he and the door dissolved in a blinding flash. The concussion shook the merchant where he stood.

'I don't make it easy for unwanted guests to get in,' he told the console grimly. 'But once in, I see to it they don't get out.'

Challis had not become what he was by leaving anything to chance. Perhaps the boy's absurd tale was true – and then, perhaps it was only a device to lure Challis into some unimaginable, fiendish trap. That the lad was cunning he had amply demonstrated. In any case, it cost nothing to make sure.

Only his life.

Shutting down the console, he walked leisurely towards the front of the house. He was surprised to see Mahnahmi standing in the hallway. Behind her, smoke still drifted from the blackened metal frame of the doorway, which now bordered a roughly rectangular crater. The depression extended the length of the hall and well out into the ferrocrete walk leading to the entrance.

The girl was holding something. It was a piece of arm. Variously coloured fluids dripped from it and tiny threads of material hung loosely from both torn ends.

Challis was struck with a mixture of fear and admiration as he stared at the section of limb Mahnahmi was examining so intently. For the first time he began to wonder just what sort of creature he had selected for an enemy. That it was more than an unusually clever seventeen-year-old boy he had suspected ever since that incredible escape on Hivehom. Now he was certain of it.

The arm, of course, was mechanical. The Flinx he thought to be real had been but a more convincing automaton, as Mahnahmi could have told him. Now Challis had gone and spoiled her game. But the left-over pieces were interesting. She studied the armature in seemingly casual fashion, compared it to a nearby fragment of mechanical flying snake.

It just wasn't fair! Since Challis had told the machine what it wanted to know, against her advice, she would never see the real Flinx again. And he had been so much fun.

She would have to find someone else's mind to play with . . .

Flinx watched the hermit crab, its terrestrial explorations concluded, disappear in an obliging wavelet. At the same time he flicked off the recorder at his belt. The tape had recorded nothing since the third simulacrum of himself had been destroyed by the merchant.

Rising, Flinx brushed the sand from the bottom of his jumpsuit and thought sorrowful thoughts about the unfounded paranoia of Conda Challis. Everything he could learn from the fat trader he had finally learned, and the information was carefully stored in the little belt recorder, which functioned over surprising distances. The simulacrums had been an expensive gamble that had worked.

Flinx returned to the rented groundcar. A special console had been rigged on one seat with five telltales at its centre. Three were dark, while two still winked a steady green. Challis might have been interested to know that had he destroyed his third visitor before answering its questions, there were two additional elaborate Flinxes in waiting.

For a delicious moment Flinx savoured the thought of sending both of them into the merchant's bedroom tonight.

But . . . no. That would place him in the position of rendering a judgement of sorts on another.

Instead he gave the two remaining simulacrums the return-to-base signal. The two remaining lights began to blink steadily, indicating they were operating properly and were in motion. They were on their way back to the fabrication plant from which Flinx had ordered them. There, their intricate innards would be salvaged, along with a concomitant part of Flinx's badly depleted bank account.

Starting up the powerful little car, he set it for a formal flight pattern leading to the atmospheric shuttleport. That strictly planetary terminal lay far to the south of the capital, nearer the suburban industrial city of Sydney.

Challis had hinted it would be difficult for a stranger to gain admittance to the United Church headquarters. Well, he would know soon enough. There was an obscure genealogy there that he wanted very much to trace.

CHAPTER FIVE

Suborbital flights to and from every major city and province on Terra were regularly scheduled at the huge port. The clerk Flinx encountered was straight of body but mentally geniculate from a quarter century of answering the same inane questions. Not only could he expect no promotion, but he suspected that his youngest daughter was dating two old men and a young woman simultaneously. As Flinx drew near, the man was reflecting that in his day, children had behaved differently.

'I just tried to buy a ticket to a city called Denpasar,' Flinx explained, 'and the light on the dispenser flashed *No Such Destination*. Why?'

'Where are you from, young sir?' the clerk inquired politely.

Flinx was startled. He hadn't been called 'sir' but a few times in his whole life. He started to reply 'Drallar, Moth,' but suddenly recalled an early dictum of Mother Mastiff's.

'Always answer a question as concise as you can, boy,' she had instructed him. 'It makes folks think of you as intelligent and non-borin', while givin' 'em as little information about yourself as possible.'

So he said simply, 'Off-planet.'

'Far off-planet, I'll venture,' the clerk added. 'Didn't you know, young sir, that Bali is a closed island? Only three classes of people are allowed to travel there.' He ticked them off on his fingers as he spoke. 'Balinese and their relatives, Church personnel, and government officials with special clearance.'

He studied Flinx carefully. 'You could pass for Balinese, excepting that carrot top of yours, so you're obviously not a native. You don't claim to be an official of the Church and – ' he couldn't repress a little smile ' – I don't think you're a special government representative. Why did you want to go there, anyway?'

Flinx shrugged elaborately. 'I'd heard it was the seat of the United Church. I thought it would be an interesting place to visit while I'm touring Terra, that's all.'

Ah, a standard query. Any incipeint suspicions the old man might have had died aborning. 'That's understandable. If you're interested in the same kind of countryside as Bali, though, you can get as close as . . .' he paused to check a thick tape playing on the screen before him, '. . . the eastern tip of the island of Java. I've been there myself. You can see the island from Banjuwangi and Surabaja's a fine old city, very picturesque. You might even take a day-flyer over to Komodo, where the dinosaur-rebreeding station is. But Bali itself,' the man shook his head regretfully, 'might as well try landing on the Imperial Home world than get into Denpasar. Oh, if you could slip onto a shuttle going in you might get into the city. But you'd never get *off* the island without having to answer some hard questions.'

'I see,' Flinx replied, smiling gratefully. 'I didn't know. You've been very helpful.'

'That's all right, sir. Enjoy the rest of your stay on Terra.'

Flinx left in a pensive mood. So there was a chance he could get on to the island, somehow. But did he want to have to answer those hard questions on his departure? He did not.

That left him with the problem of gaining admittance to a place no one was allowed into. No, he reminded himself, whispering to the case and its leathery contents, that wasn't entirely true. Three classes of people were permitted on to the island.

He didn't think it would be easy to forge government identification, and he was too young to claim to be anything worthwhile. There did exist the possibility of palming himself off as an acolyte of the Church. But what about . . . ? Hadn't the old man said that save for his red hair he could pass for Balinese?

Passing a three-story-high interior panel of polished metal, Flinx caught sight of his reflection. A little hair dye, a crash course in the local dialect, a small boat – surely it couldn't be that easy!

But there was the chance this plan was so simple that he might be overlooked by those on the watch for more sophisticated infiltrators. And Flinx had often seen how possession of a certain amount of brass – nonmetallic variety – could be more useful in fooling bureaucracy than all the formal identification in the Arm.

Turning, he retraced his path to the ticket dispensers. A punched demand and the subsequent insertion of his card-meter produced a one-way shuttle ticket for Surabaja . . .

The ancient market town had preserved much of its seventeenth-century flavour. Flinx felt right at home, learning something he had long suspected: one crowded marketplace is much like any other, no matter where one travels.

Everyone spoke Terranglo and symbospeech in addition to the old local dialect known as Bahsa Indonesia. Flinx easily secured black dye, and with his hair colour changed he quickly became one of the locals. A stay of several weeks was sufficient to provide him, a natural linguist, with an efficient smattering of the language.

Procuring a small boat was simple enough. If the ploy failed he could always fall back on the story that he was a simple fisherman whose automatic pilot had failed, causing him to be blown off course. Besides, for any off-world spy the really hard part would be passing customs at Terra port-of-entry, and Flinx had already accomplished that.

So it was that after several days of calm, automatic sailing he found himself in sight of the towering peaks of Mounts Agung and Batur, the two volcanoes that dominated the island.

Under cover of a moonless night, he made his approach at the northernmost tip of the magnificent empty beach called Kuta, on the western side of the island. No patrol appeared to challenge him as he drew his small boat up on the sand. No automated beamers popped from concealed pits to incinerate him where he stood.

So far he had been completely successful. That didn't lessen his sense of unease, however. It was one thing to stand on an empty beach, quite another to penetrate the recesses of the Church itself.

Making his way inland with his single bit of baggage – the perforated case holding a few clothes, and Pip – it wasn't long before he encountered a small, unpaved road through the jungle that fringed the beach. After a walk of several hours he was able to hail a groundcar cultivator. The farmer driving it provided him with a ride into Bena and from there it was easy to hire an automatic bekak into Denpasar proper.

Everything went as well as he dared hope. The farmer had assumed he was a stranger visiting relatives in the city, and Flinx saw no reason to argue with a story so conveniently provided. Nor had the young farmer shown any desire to switch from Terranglo to Bahasa Indonesia, so Flinx's hastily acquired vocabulary was not put to the test.

The innkeeper made Flinx welcome, though she insisted on seeing the animal in the bag. Flinx showed her, hoping that the woman wasn't the garrulous sort. If word got around to representatives of the Church, someone might grow curious about the presence here of such an exotic and dangerous off-world species as the minidrag.

But Flinx refused to worry. After all, he was ensconced in a comfortable room in the city he had been told he would have trouble reaching. Tomorrow he would set about the business of penetrating the Church system.

The first thing he had to find out was where on the island the genealogical records were stored, then what procedures one was required to go through to gain access to them. He might yet have to resort to forgery. More likely he would end up stealing a Church uniform and brazening his way into the facility.

Flinx the priest – he went to sleep smiling at the thought, and at Mother Mastiff's reaction to him in Church garb . . .

The next morning, he began his private assault on the inner sanctums of the most powerful single organization in the Commonwealth.

The first step was to select a car with a talkative driver. Flinx chose the oldest one he could find, operating on the theory that older men engaged in such professions were more inclined to gabble excessively and otherwise mind their own business. Flinx's driver was a white-maned patriarch with a large drooping moustache. He was slight and wiry, as were most of the locals. The women had a uniform doll-like beauty and appeared to age in jumps, from fourteen to eighty with no in-between.

A few of them had already regarded Flinx somewhat less than casually, something he was becoming used to as he grew older. There was no time for that now, however.

'What did you have in mind for today's journey, sir?'

'I'm just a visitor, here to see my cousins in Singaradja. Before I'm swamped with uncles and aunts, I'd like to see the island unencumbered by family talk. The old temples . . . and the new.'

The oldster didn't bat an eye, merely nodded and started his engine. The tour was as thorough as the old man was loquacious. He showed Flinx the grand beaches at Kuta where the huge breakers of the Sunda Bali rolled in, unaware that Flinx had negotiated those same waves the night before. He took him to the great oceanographic research station at Sanur, and to the sprawling grounds of the Church University on Denpasar's outskirts.

He showed him various branches of Church research facilities, all built in the old Balinese style replete with ferrocrete sculptures lining every lintel and wall. He drove him over the ancient rice paddies that terraced the toy mountains – the most beautiful on all Terra, the old man insisted, even if the farmers in their wide hats now rode small mechanical cultivators instead of water buffalo.

Half a day passed before Flinx was moved to comment, 'It's not at all like what I expected the headquarters of the United Church to be.'

'Well, what did you expect?' asked the old man. 'A reproduction on a grander scale of the Commonwealth Enclave in Brisbane? Black and bronze-mirrored domes and kilo-high spires done in mosaic?'

Flinx leaned back in the worn old seat next to the driver and looked sheepish. 'I have never been to the capital, of course, but I have seen pictures. I guess I expected something similar, yes.' The old man smiled warmly.

'I am no expert on the mind of the Church, son, but it seems to my farmer's soul to be a collection of uncomplicated gentle folk. The University is the largest Church building on the island, the astrophysics laboratory, at four stories, its tallest.' He became silent for a while as they cruised above a river gorge.

'Why do you suppose,' he asked finally, 'the United Church decided centuries ago to locate its headquarters on this island?'

'I don't know,' Flinx replied honestly. 'I hadn't thought about it. To be nearer the capital, I suppose.'

The old driver shook his head. 'The Church was here long before Brisbane was made Terra's capital city. For someone who travels about with a Garuda spirit for a companion, you seem rather ignorant, son.'

'Garuda spirit?' Flinx saw the driver looking back at the somnolent reptilian head that had peeked out from inside his jumpsuit. He thought frantically, then relaxed.

'But the Garuda is a bird, not a snake.'

'It is the spirit I see in your pet, not the shape,' the driver explained.

'That's good then,' Flinx acknowledged, remembering that the monstrous Garuda bird was a good creature, despite its fearsome appearance. 'What is the reason for the Church's presence here, if not to be near the capital?'

'I believe it is because the values of the Church and of the Balinese people are so very similar. Both stress creativity and gentleness. All of our own arrogance and animosity is subsumed in our ancient mythology.'

Flinx regarded the old man with new respect and new curiosity. At the moment he sounded like something more than merely an old groundcar driver – but that was Flinx's overly suspicious mind looking to create trouble again.

'Our most aggressive movement is a shrug,' the old man

continued, staring lovingly at the surrounding landscape. 'It is the result of living in one of the galaxy's most beautiful places.'

A light rain had begun to fall. The old man closed the car's open top and switched on the air-conditioning. Flinx, who prided himself on his adaptability in strange environments and who until now had been forced to play the role of near-native, let out a mental sigh of relief at the first cooling caress of the air-conditioner.

The humidity in one of the galaxy's most beautiful places could be stifling. No wonder the thranx members of the Church had agreed to build its headquarters here, those many centuries ago.

They paused in Ubud, and Flinx made a show of looking at the famous wood carvings in the shops the old man had recommended. This was not an exclusively Balinese custom. Mother Mastiff had her arrangements with guides in Drallar too.

The tour continued, and the need to show interest became more and more of a burden. Flinx yawned through the elephant cave, blinked at the sacred springs, and saw temples built on temples.

An appropriate location for the home of the Church, Flinx thought, as the clouds cleared and a double rainbow appeared behind the smoking cone of 15,000-kilometre-high Mount Agung. The aquamarine robes and jumpsuits of passing Church personnel blended as naturally with the still flourishing jungle vegetation as the fruit trees which stood stolid watch over roadways and fields and rice terraces.

'It's all very beautiful,' Flinx finally told the old driver, 'though I'd still like to see the Church headquarters.'

'Church headquarters?' the old man looked uncertain, pulled at his moustache. 'But the entire island is the headquarters of the United Church.'

'Yes, I know,' Flinx said, trying not to seem impatient. 'I mean the headquarters of the headquarters.'

'Well,' the old man looked up and left off pulling his moustache, 'the nearest thing to that would be the Administration Depot, but why anyone would want to see that I don't know.' Surprisingly, he smiled, showing white teeth beneath his wrinkled upper lip.

'Still expecting towers of precious metal and amethyst

arches, eh son?' Flinx looked embarrassed. 'I'll tell you, though the Depot is nothing to waste one's time with, it's in a setting the Buddha himself would envy.'

The driver made up his mind. 'Come then, I'll take you there, if you've set your mind on it.'

They continued north out of Ubud, passing steeper and steeper terraces as they mounted an old roadway. It showed no evidence of the heavy traffic Flinx would expect to be en route to and from the headquarters of the headquarters. Maybe the old man was right. Maybe the facility he sought didn't exist.

Maybe he was wasting his time.

He leaned out the window, saw that his initial estimate of the road condition still held. The grass covering the path was several centimetres tall. Thick and healthy, it showed none of the characteristic bends the steady passage of groundcars over it would have produced.

Eventually the car sighed to a stop. The oldster motioned for Flinx to get out and he did so, whereupon the driver guided him to the edge of a steep precipice.

Flinx peered cautiously over the side. At the bottom of a valley several thousand kilometres below lay a broad, shallow lake. Irrigated fields and scattered farmers' homes dotted the greenery.

At the far end of the lake, near the base of smouldering Mount Agung, sprawled a tight group of modest boxlike two-storey structures enamelled a bright aquamarine. They were strictly utilitarian in appearance if not downright ugly. There wasn't an arch or tower among them.

A few antennae sprouted flowers of abstract metal mesh at one end of the complex, and there was a small clearing nearby that was barely large enough to accommodate a small atmospheric shuttle.

Was that all?

Flinx stared at it disbelievingly. 'Are you sure that's it?'

'That is the Administration Depot, yes. I have never been there myself, but I am told it is mostly used for storing old records.'

'But the Church Chancellory . . . ?' Flinx started to protest.

'Ah, you mean the place where the Counsellors meet? It's the low clamshell-like building that I showed you in Denpasar itself, the one next to the solar research station. Remember it?' Flinx searched his memory, found that he did. It had been only slightly more impressive in appearance than the disappointing cluster of small buildings below.

'The Council of the Church meets there once a year, and that is where their decisions are made. I can take you back there, if you wish?'

Flinx shook his head, unable to hide his disappointment. But . . . if this was a warehouse for old records, it might contain what he'd come to see. If not – well, he could set about solving the problem of leaving this island without incurring unwanted questions. Perhaps in India province, in Allahabad . . .

'You said you've never been inside,' he turned to the old man. 'Does the Church forbid visitors there?'

His driver looked amused. 'Not that I ever heard of. There is no reason to go there. But if you wish . . .'

Flinx started back towards the car. 'Let's go. You can leave me there.'

'Are you certain, son?' the old man asked with concern, eyeing the sun in its low-hanging position in the damp sky. 'It will grow dark soon. You may have trouble finding a ride back to the city.'

'But I thought . . .' Flinx began.

The old man shook his head slowly, spoke with patience. 'You still do not listen. Did I not say it was merely a place of storage? There is no traffic down there, in the valley. It is a place of slow-growing things, dull and far from any town. Were I a Churchman, I would far rather be stationed in Benoa or Denpasar. It is lonely here. But,' he shrugged at last, 'it is your money. At least it will be a warm night.'

They climbed back into the car and he started down a winding narrow path Flinx hadn't seen before. 'If you do not get a ride back you might try sleeping on the ground. Mind the centipedes, though; they have a nasty bite. I am sure some farmer will give you a ride back to the city in the morning – if you rise early enough to catch him.'

'Thanks,' Flinx said, his gaze fixed on the valley below. With its shining lake snug against the base of the great volcano, it was attractive indeed, though his attention was still drawn to the prosaic architecture of the Depot. It became even less impressive as they drew nearer. The aquamarine enamel seemed stark against the rich natural browns and greens of the vegetation ringing the mountain. As they reached the valley floor Flinx saw that the structures were devoid of windows. Befitting, he thought grimly, a facility devoted to things and not people.

The car pulled up before what must have been the main entrance, since it was the only entrance. No massive sculptures depicting the brotherhood of the humanx, no playing fountains flanked the simple double-glass door. A few undistinguished-looking groundcars were parked in the small open hangar to one side.

Flinx opened the door, climbed out. Pip stirred within the loose folds of the jumpsuit and Flinx hushed his restless pet as he handed the old driver his cardmeter.

The driver slipped it into a large slot in his dash, waited until the compact instrument ceased humming. The transfer of funds completed, he handed the cardmeter back to Flinx.

'Good luck to you, son. I hope your visit proves worth all your trouble to come here.' He waved from the car as it started back towards the mountain road.

'Trouble' is an inadequate word, old man, Flinx thought as he called a farewell to him. '*Selamat seang!*'

Flinx stood alone before the Depot for a moment, listening to the soft trickle of water dropping from terrace to terrace. The soft *phutt-putt* of a mechanical cultivator guided by the hand of a farmer drifted across the fields to him. According to the old guide, the people were in the process of harvesting their fifth rice crop of the year and had begun sowing the sixth.

By now, Flinx was sick of agriculture, temples – and the island itself. He would inspect what this unprepossessing structure had to offer, try the city records in Allahabad, and be on his way home to Moth in a few days, with or without information.

He berated himself for not taking the shuttleport clerk's indirect suggestion and contriving to come here via the diplomatic atmospheric shuttle from South Brisbane. Instead he had wasted weeks on learning the local language and piloting the small boat.

He expected an armed fortress with walls half a kilometre thick and bristling with beamers and SCCAM projectors. Instead he found himself stalking an island of rice farmers

76

and students. Even the Chancellory was out of session.

Flinx mounted the few steps and pushed through the double doors, noting with disgust that they opened manually and without challenge. A short hallway opened into a small circular high-domed chamber. His gaze was drawn upwards – where it froze. The dome was filled with a tridee projection of the entire inhabited galaxy. Each Commonwealth world was plainly marked by colour and minute block letters in symbospeech.

Flinx studied it, picking out Terra and Hivehom first because of their brighter colours, then moving on to Evorai, Amropolous, Calm Nursery – thranx worlds all. Then on to the human planets of Repler, Moth, Catchalot, and Centaurus III and V. Half-lights indicated the outposts of humanx exploration, fringe worlds like Burley with its vast store of metals, Rhyinpine of the troglodytes and endless caverns, and the frigid globe of far distant Tran-ky-ky.

His eyes lowered to the curving floor of the chamber, and at last he found his mosaic, though the motif in the floor was simple. It consisted of four circles, two representing Terra's hemispheres and the other two Hivehom's. They formed a box with a single smaller sphere at their centre, tangent to all four circular maps. The central sphere contained a vertical hourglass of blue, representing Terra, crossed by a horizontal hourglass of green, standing for Hivehom. Where they met the colours merged to form aquamarine – the signet colour of the United Church.

Three halls broke the walls around him, one vanishing into the distance ahead, the others to left and right. Each wall between was filled with engravings of impressive figures from the history of the Church – thranx and human both – in modest pose. Most impressive was a scene picturing the signing of the Amalgamation that formally united thranx and mankind. The Fourth Last Resort, David Malkezinski, touched forehead to antennae with the tri-eint Arlenduva, while the insect's truhand was locked in the human's right palm.

To the right of this relief were engraved some of the basic maxims of the Church: Man is animal; thranx is insect – both are of the species Brother . . . Advise not civilization; physical force reciprocates mentally . . . if God wished man and thranx to devote themselves to Him, He would not have made the worlds so complicated . . . Self-righteousness is the key to destruction – the list went on and on.

Opposite that wall was an engraved list of recent philosophical pronouncements, which Flinx read with interest. He had just finished the one about hedonism violating the Prime Edict and was on to the admonition to distrust anything that smacks of absolute right when his attention was broken by a voice.

'Can I help you, sir?'

'*What?*'

Flinx turned, startled, to see a young woman in aquamarine robes staring quizzically back at him. She was seated near the corridor at the far left, behind a sparsely covered desk. He hadn't even noticed her until she spoke.

'I said, may I help you.' She walked over to stand next to him, stared into his eyes. That alone was unusual. Most new acquaintances found their first gaze going somewhat lower, to the scaly shape wrapped around Flinx's shoulder or, in this instance, peeping out of his suit front.

But this slim girl ignored the flying snake. That smacked of poor vision or great self-confidence, Flinx thought. Her indifference to the snake was the first impressive thing he had encountered on this island.

'Sorry,' he lied easily, 'I was just about to come over and talk to you. Did I keep you waiting?'

'Oh no . . . I just thought you might be getting tired. You've been studying the maps and inscriptions for over an hour now.'

His gaze went instantly to the glass doors, and he saw that she was telling the truth. A tropical night black as a gambler's conscience had settled outside.

He was uneasy and upset. It felt as if he had been eyeing the engravings in the little domed alcove for only a few minutes. His gaze travelled again over the three-dimensional map overhead, to the inlaid pictorials and the subtly inscribed sayings. Did those carefully raised colours and words and reliefs conceal some kind of mnemonic device, something to capture an observer into absorbing them despite himself?

His speculation was abruptly cut off by the girl's soft voice: 'Please come over to the desk. I can help you better from there.'

Still dazed, Flinx followed her without protest. A few papers and several small screens rested on the desktop, and he saw switches set in ranks of panels at the far side.

'I've been studying,' she explained apologetically, 'or I would have come over sooner. Besides, you seemed to be enjoying yourself. Nonetheless, I thought I'd better find out if you needed anything since I go off shift soon and my replacement would start ignoring you all over again.'

If that was a lie, Flinx thought, it was a smooth one. 'What are you studying?'

'Spiritual assignation and philosophical equations as they relate to high-order demographic fluxation.'

'I beg your pardon?'

'Diplomatic corps. Now,' she continued brightly, 'what can I help you with?'

Flinx found himself staring at the unlocked glass doors, the tridee map overhead, the words and pictures engraved on the encircling walls. In his thoughts he matched them with the simple exterior of this structure, compared that to his vaunted imaginary pictures of what it ought to look like.

Everything he'd encountered on this island, from the unpretentiousness of this Depot to the language of his driver, was a mixture of the simple and the sophisticated. A dangerously uncertain mixture. For a moment he seriously considered forgetting the whole thing, including his purpose in travelling across half the Commonwealth, and turning to walk out those unguarded doors. He had spent much of his frenetic young life trying to avoid attention, but whatever he told this girl now promised to deliver him to questioners.

Instead of leaving, he said, 'I was raised by a foster parent who had no idea who my parents were. I still don't know. I don't know for certain who I am or where I come from, and it may not matter much to anyone else, but it matters to me.'

'It would matter to me, also,' the girl replied seriously. 'But what makes you think we can help you find out?'

'An acquaintance indicated he had found some information on my parentage, some hints that physically I could match up with a child born here on Terra, in the city of Allahabad. I do know my real name as it read on the . . on the slaver's records, but I don't know if it's a family name or one given me well after my birth.

'It's Philip Lynx.' He pronounced it carefully, distinctly, but it still wasn't his name. It belonged to an alien; it was a stranger's name. He was just Flinx.

'I was told that this was a storage facility for Church records, although,' he indicated the little chamber with its three connecting halls, 'these buildings hardly look big enough to hold even a portion of those records.'

'We're very space-efficient,' she told him, as if that should explain it. 'The records for Allahabad are kept here, as are the records of every being registered with the Church,' Her eyes shifted, but not to look at Pip.

Flinx turned, thinking she was staring at something behind him. When he saw nothing and turned back, he saw she was smiling at him.

'It's your hair,' she said easily. 'The dye is beginning to come off.' His hand went instinctively to his scalp, felt of the dampness there. When he brought it down, it was stained black.

'You've been out in the city too long. Whoever sold you that dye cheated you. Why dye it, anyway – the red is attractive enough.'

'A friend thought otherwise.' He couldn't tell from her thoughts if she believed him; but she chose not to press the matter, touching instead a switch on her desk.

'Allahabad, you said?' He nodded. She bent over the desk, addressed a speaker. 'Check for records on a Philip Lynx,' she told it, 'Allahabad-born.' She looked up at him. 'Spelling?'

Flinx spread his hands. 'L-y-n-x, P-h-i-l-i-p was the way it was listed on the slaver's sheet, but that could be a misspelling.'

'Or a corruption,' she added, turning to the speaker again. 'Check also variational spellings. Also all inquiries into said records for the past . . . five years,' Then she clicked off.

'Why that last?' he inquired. Her expression was grim.

'Your acquaintance should not have had access to your records. Those are between you and the Church. Yet it seems someone managed to gain permission to see them. You're going to be asked some hard questions later, if you are this Philip Lynx.'

'And if I'm not?'

'You'll be asked questions anyway – only you won't be

80

looking at anyone's files.' She smiled pleasantly. 'It's not your wrongdoing, it seems . . . though someone is going to lose his robes. The lower grades are always vulnerable to bribery, especially when the request is for seemingly harmless information.'

'No need to worry about that,' Flinx told her. 'About the only thing I'm sure of in this galaxy is that I'm me.' He grinned. 'Whoever that is.'

She did not return the smile. 'That's what we're going to find out.'

Once Flinx's identity was established, through various checks, the girl became friendly once more. 'It's late,' she observed when the identification precedures had concluded. 'Why don't you wait and begin your retrieval in the morning There's a dormitory for visitors and you can share cafeteria food with the staff, if you have the money. If not, you can claim charity, though the Church frowns on direct handouts.'

'I can pay,' Flinx insisted.

'All right.' She pointed to the far corridor. 'Follow the yellow strip on the floor. It'll take you to the visitors' bureau. They'll handle things from there.'

Flinx started towards the hallway, looked back. 'What about the retrieval? How do I begin?'

'Come back to this desk tomorrow. I'm on duty ten to six all week. After that you'd have to hunt to find me again. I have to transfer to another manual task, but for the rest of this week, I can help you. My name's Mona Tantivy.' She paused, watched Flinx's retreating form, then called to him as he entered the corridor. 'What if the name Philip Lynx doesn't match up with the child born in Allahabad?'

'Then,' Flinx shouted back to her, 'you can call me anything you want . . .'

CHAPTER SIX

The cubicle they assigned him was small and simply furnished. He spent an hour washing off the dust of days, and a pleasant surprise awaited him when he exited the shower – his jumpsuit had been taken away and cleaned. It was a good thing he had taken Pip into the bath with him.

Feeling uncomfortably clean, he was directed to the nearest food service facility and soon found himself mingling with a crush of aquamarine robes and suits.

The facility itself was a surprise, decorated with local shrubs and fountains, its lushness in stark contrast to the spartan exterior of the building. It was divided into three sections by semipermeable panelling.

One section was adjusted to the midtemperate zone climate most favoured by humans, while the area farthest from the door was almost misted over from the heat and humidity favoured by the thranx. The eating area in between was by far the largest. Here the two environments blended imperfectly, to form a climate a touch warm and damp for humans, slightly dry and cool to the thranx, yet suitable to both. All three areas were crowded.

He was thankful for the presence of several humans and thranx who wore something other than the Church colour; it made him feel considerably less conspicuous.

The smells of recently prepared food were everywhere. While a few of the aromas were exotic, they couldn't compete with the incredible variety of odours always present in the marketplace in Drallar. Even so, he found himself salivating. He had had nothing to eat since his brief breakfast in the city early that morning.

A short time after placing his order with the autochef he was rewarded with a flavourful steak of uncertain origin and an assortment of breads and vegetables. But when he inquired again about the rest of his order, a small screen lit up: *No intoxicants of any sort, however mild, are permitted in Depot commissaries.*

Flinx swallowed his disppointment – a poor substitute for the beer he had ordered – and settled for iced shaka.

Pip was curled about his shoulder once again. The flying snake had aroused a few comments but not fear. The creatures in the facility – they ranged in age from less than his own to elders well over a hundred – were peculiarly indifferent to the possibility of the minidrag suddenly spewing corrosive death.

Flinx took a seat by himself. His ears were no larger than normal, and his talent no sharper than usual, but his hearing was well trained. To survive in Drallar, one had to utilize all one's senses to the utmost. Listening to the conversation around him in the food service facility, they served to satiate his curiosity.

To his left a pair of elderly thranx were arguing over the validity of performing genetic manipulation with unhatched eggs. It had something to do with the scorm process as opposed to the oppordian method, and there was much talk of the morality of inducing mutation by prenatal suggestion in unformed pupae.

Hunting for something less incomprehensible, he overheard an old woman with two cream-coloured stripes on her suit sleeve lecturing a group of acolytes: two human, two thranx. A hydrogen atom was emblazoned above the stripes.

'So you see, if you check the research which has been performed on Pluto, Gorisa, and Tipendemos over the last eight years, you'll find that any additional modifications to the SCCAM weapons system must take into account the stress limitations of the osmiridium casing itself.'

A bite of bread and yet another wisp of conversation, this from a middle-aged man behind him with a lush white beard: 'Production levels on Kansastan and Inter-Kansastan in the Bryan Sector suggest that with proper preatmospheric seeding, food grain production can be increased as much as twenty per cent over the next three planting years.'

Flinx frowned as he considered this intense babble, but it wasn't the absence of theology in the discussions that troubled him. He really couldn't judge, but even to his untrained ears it seemed that a lot of very sensitive matters

83

were being freely discussed in the presence of non-Church personnel. Whether that proved the Church was inefficient or only typically humanx he could not decide. Though security wasn't his problem, it troubled him nonetheless as he finished his meal.

He was still troubled the following morning, as he made his way back to the desk in the entrance chamber. Mona Tantivy was on duty, and she smiled when she saw him approach. Traffic was moving briskly through the chamber now as Church personnel bustled from one corridor to another and through the doubleglass entranceway.

'Ready?' she asked.

'I'd like to get this over with as soon as possible,' he said, in a sharper tone than he intended. Flinx, aware he was trembling slightly, resolutely calmed himself.

The woman pursed her lips reprovingly. 'Don't act as if you're going to be inoculated or something.'

'In a sense that's just how I feel,' he replied grimly.

And it was. Flinx had grown up with a deficient image of self. If he found no remedy here, he would likely carry that cross with him forever.

The woman nodded slowly, pressed a switch. A few minutes later a fortyish human with a build like a wrestler came out of the near corridor. His smile was identical to Tantivy's, and he projected the same desire to aid and be helpful. Flinx wondered if this attitude was natural or if that, too, was part of the Church course of instruction: Advanced Personality Manipulation through Traditional Facial Gesticulation – or something similar.

Angrily Flinx thrust his instinctive sarcasm aside. All that mattered was seeing what he had come for.

'My name's Namoto,' the blocky oriental said, introducing himself with smile and handshake. 'I'm pleased to meet you, Mr Lynx.'

Flinx put up a restraining hand. 'Let's not call me that until we prove it. Just Flinx, please.'

The smile didn't fade. 'All right, whoever you be. Come with me and we'll see if we can find out who you are.'

After what seemed like twenty minutes of walking through hallways and featureless corridors, Flinx was thoroughly disoriented. 'It's hard to believe that the

Church records of every human being in the Commonwealth . . .'

'. . . and of every thranx,' Namoto finished for him, 'are
all stored in this small building, but it is true. Information
storage is a thousand-year-old science, Flinx. The art of
document reduction has been developed to a high degree.
Most of the records in this building would be invisible under
a standard microscope. Our scanners and imprinters work
with much finer resolutions.' He paused before a door that
looked no different from a hundred already passed.

'We're here.'

The single word engraved in the translucent door said
simply. *Genealogy*. Behind this door were the early histories
of billions of humanx lives – though not all of them. There
were still those who did not wish to be documented by anything other than their own epitaph, and a few of them
achieved this.

On the other hand, Flinx had been undocumented his
whole life, and he was tired of it.

'There could be a large number of Philip Lynxes still
alive,' Namoto suggested as he keyed the door, 'although
because of certain colloquial sociological connotations, it
is a less common name than many.'

'I know what it means,' Flinx snapped. Pip shifted
uneasily on his master's shoulder at the sudden flare of
mental violence.

The room was enormous. Mostly it consisted of seemingly
endless aisles alternating with rows of enclosed metal that
stretched from floor to ceiling. No row appeared different
from its neighbour.

Flinx was led to a row of ten booths. Two were occupied
by researchers, the rest were empty. Namoto sat down before
the single large screen in the walled booth and gestured for
Flinx to sit next to him. Then he pressed both thumbs to a
pair of hollows set in the screen's side.

A light winked on beneath them and the screen lit up.
Namoto leaned forward, said, 'My name is ShigetaNamoto.'
He relaxed. There was a pause; the machine hummed, and a
green light winked on above the screen's centre.

'You are recognized, Padre Namoto,' the machine
intoned. 'Awaiting requests.'

'Report results of previous night's search on one human male named Lynx, Philip. Hold alternate spellings till directed.' He turned, whispered to Flinx, 'For a start we'll assume the name on the slaver's record was correct.'

'Possible place of origin,' he told the machine, 'Allahabad, India Province, Terra.' The Padre looked over at his anxious companion. 'How old are you . . . or do you know?'

'Mother Mastiff tells me I should be about seventeen, though she can't be sure. Sometimes I feel like I'm seven hundred.'

'And sometimes I feel like I'm seven,' the massive Churchman countered pleasantly, returning his attention to the machine.

'Age approximation noted,' the device stated. 'Results of search appear.'

Namoto studied the list. 'I was right . . . it's not a common name. There are records of only three Philip Lynxes having been born and registered at Allahabad within the last half century. Only one of them fits your age bracket.' He addressed the machine once more.

'Further information desired.'

There was a brief hum, then the screen lit brightly with the legend: TRANSFERRING ALLAHABAD TERMINAL. Then a moment later: TRANSFER COMPLETED . . . CODE LENGTH.

Namoto gazed at the numbers following. 'Doesn't seem to be much information at all. I hope it's worth . . .' He paused, suddenly concerned. 'Are you all right, Flinx? You're shivering.'

'I'm fine . . . it's a lot cooler in here than outside, that's all. Hurry up.'

Namoto nodded. 'Decide transfer.'

Flinx's hands tightened convulsively on his thighs as each word was printed out . . .

LYNX, PHILIP . . . TRUE NAME . . . BORN 533 A.A., 2933 OLD CALENDAR IN THE SUBURB OF SARNATH, GREATER URBAN ALLAHABAD, INDIA PROVINCE, TERRA.

There was a pause during which nothing further appeared on the screen. Flinx turned to Namoto, almost shouting. 'Is that all?'

'Gentle, Flinx . . . see, more comes.' And the printout continued again.

NOTES ADDITIONAL: RECORDS OF ASSISTING SEMI-PHY-

SICIAN AND MONITORING MEDITECH INDICATE PRESENCE OF
UNUSUALLY HIGH BIRTH AURA IN R-WAVE MATERNITY
CHAMBER READINGS . . . NO UNUSUAL OR ADVERSE REACTION
FROM MOTHER . . . R-WAVE READOUTS INDICATE POTENTIAL
OF POSSIBLE ABNORMAL TALENTS, CLASS ONE . . .

DELIVERY NORMAL . . . NO R-WAVE REACTION ASCRIB-
ABLE TO TRAUMA . . . MONITORS POSTOPERATIVE CHECK
NORMAL . . . INFANT OTHERWISE NORMAL AND HEALTHY . . .

MOTHER AGED 22 . . . NAME: ANASAGE . . . GRAND-
PARENTS UNKNOWN . . .

Namoto did not look at Flinx as the readout concluded:
FATHER UNKNOWN, NOT PRESENT AT BIRTHING . . .

Flinx fought to relax. Now that this ordeal was over he
wondered at his tension. What information there was told
him little – and as for the last, well, he had been called a
bastard before and far worse than that. But all this new
information still did not tell him if Lynx was a lineal name,
or one applied solely to him at birth. Without that – or
additional information – he might as well not have bothered.

'Any information,' he asked in a soft monotone, 'on the
postdelivery status of the . . .' the word came surprisingly
easy now, 'mother?'

Namoto requested it of the machine. The reply was short,
eloquent.

MOTHER DECEASED . . . OFF-PLANET, 537 A.A. . . . ADDI-
TIONAL DETAIL AVAILABLE . . .

'Explain the . . .' Flinx began, but Namoto hushed him.
'Just a minute, Philip.'

Pip stirred nervously as his master bristled in reaction.
'Don't call me that. It's Flinx, just *Flinx*.'

'Grant me the minute anyhow.' Namoto used a small
keyboard to instruct the machine manually. There was a low
whine from sealed depths. A tiny wheel of millimetre-wide
tape, so narrow as to be almost invisible, was ejected from
an almost invisible slot. At the same time the screen lit for
the last time.

PRINTOUT OF DELIVERED INFORMATION ACCOMPLISHED
. . . SECONDARY INFORMATION WITHDRAWN TEN STANDARD
MONTHS TWO WEEKS FOUR DAYS PRIOR THIS DATE . . .

Namoto's gaze narrowed. 'Someone's been tampering
with your file, all right.' To the machine, 'Identify with-
drawing authority.'

'Neat,' was all Namoto said. 'Your acquaintance wanted
to make certain no one else had access to whatever information he stole.'

A red-tinged image grew in his mind – Challis! The
merchant had fooled him even at the point of imagined
death. He had confessed to the Flinx simulacrum where he
had obtained his information on Flinx, without finding it
necessary to add that the critical information was no longer
there.

What he had left in the Church archives was just enough
to satisfy any casual inspector and to prevent any cancellation alarms from being activated.

And Flinx doubted that Challis was awaiting his return
back in the capital. So he would have to start his hunt all
over again – with no hint of where the merchant had fled to
this time. A quiet voice nearby was speaking to him.

Namoto had keyed the machine release and was offering
him the tape. 'Here's a copy of what the thief left in the
archive.' Flinx took it, his movements slow and stunned.
'I'm sorry about the rest, whatever it consists of. I suspect if
you want to know the contents you're going to have to find
your acquaintance again and ask him some direct questions.
And when you do, I'd appreciate it if you'd contact the
nearest Church authorities.' The padre was not smiling.
'Theft of Church records is a rather serious offence.

'This tape – and the one that was stolen – is a many-
times-enlarged duplicate of the archive original. Any micro-
scopic scanner will play it back.' He rose. 'If you want to see
it again use the machine in the booth two alcoves over. I'll
be at the monitor's desk if you want me for anything.'

Flinx nodded slowly as the padre turned, walked away.
Challis! Thief, would-be murderer, casual destroyer of
other's lives – next time he might let Pip kill him. The
Commonwealth would be a little cleaner for the absence of
. . . Something burned his shoulder and nearly yanked him
from the chair.

Pip had all but exploded from his shoulder perch, fast
enough to mark the skin beneath Flinx's jumpsuit. Fumbling
the cassette into a pocket, he scrambled to his feet and raced
down the aisle after his panicked pet.

'Pip . . . wait , . . there's nothing wrong . . . !'

The minidrag had already reached the entrance. Both Namoto and the monitor on duty had moved away from the desk. They were watching the snake warily while backing slowly away. The minidrag beat at the translucent plexite for a moment as Flinx rushed from the booth aisle. He was calling to the reptile verbally and mentally, praying that the snake would relax before someone, gentle and understanding or not, took a shot at him.

The minidrag backed off, fluttering and twisting in the air, and spat once. A loud hissing sound, and a large irregular hole appeared in the door. Flinx made a desperate grab for the receding tail, but too late – the elusive reptile had already squeezed through the aperture.

'Open the door,' he yelled. 'I've got to go after him!'

The attendant stood paralysed until Namoto murmured tensely, 'Open the door, Yena.'

Yena moved rapidly then. 'Yes, sir – should I sound an alarm?'

Namoto looked to Flinx, who was ready to rip the door from its glide. 'Pip wouldn't hurt anyone unless he sensed a threat to me.'

'Then what's the matter with him?' the padre asked as the door slid back. Flinx plunged through, the padre close behind.

'I don't know . . . there he goes! Pip . . . !'

The curling tail was just vanishing around a bend in the corridor. Flinx plunged after.

In the twists and turns of the labyrinthine building, Flinx occasionally lost sight of his pet, But ashen-faced human personnel and thranx with uncontrollably shivering antennae marked the minidrag's path as clearly as a trail of crimson lacquer. Despite his bulk, Padre Namoto remained close behind Flinx.

It felt as if they had run around kilometres of corners before they finally caught up with the minidrag. Pip was beating leathery wings against another doorway, much larger than any Flinx had seen so far.

Only this time there was more than a single studious monitor in attendance. Two men wearing aquamarine uniforms were crouched behind a flanking tubular barrier. Each had a small beamer trained on the fluttering minidrag.

Flinx could see a small knot of Church personnel huddled expectantly at the far end of the corridor.

'Don't shoot!' he howled frantically. 'He won't hurt anyone!' Slowing, he moved closer to his pet. But Pip refused every summons, remaining resolutely out of grabbing range as he continued to beat at the doors.

'Whatever's berserked him is on the other side.' He called to the two armed men. 'Let him through.'

'That's a restricted area, boy,' one of them said, trying to divide his attention between the flying snake and this new arrival.

'Let us through,' a slightly winded Namoto ordered, moving out where he could be seen clearly. The guard's voice turned respectful.

'Sorry, Padre, we didn't know you were in charge of this.'

'I'm not, the snake is. But open the doors anyway. My authority.'

Flinx had barely a minute to wonder exactly how important his helpful guide was before the surprisingly thick double doors started to separate. Pip squeezed through the minimal opening and an impatient Flinx had to wait another moment before the gap was wide enough to admit him.

Then he was on the other side, which proved to be a corridor no different from any of the many he had already traversed.

Except . . .

Except for the bank of six lifts before him. Two padre-elects were waiting in front of the lift at far left. One was a very old, tall, and oddly deformed human. He stood next to a young female thranx.

Pip was hovering in midair as Flinx and Namoto slipped into the corridor. Then he suddenly dived at the couple, completely ignoring the other Church personnel who were beginning to notice the presence of the venomous reptile in their midst.

'Call him off, Flinx,' Namoto ordered. There was no hint of obsequiousness in his voice now. He had his beamer out and aimed.

Flinx suddenly sensed what had pulled so strongly at his pet. As Pip dived, the bent old man ducked and dodged with shocking agility, fairly throwing his young companion against the lift door. She twisted herself as she was shoved. It was sufficient to prevent a nasty break, but too weak to keep her from slamming hard into the unyielding metal. Shiny blue-green legs collapsed and she folded up against the door.

The old cleric's extraordinary suppleness caused Namoto and the others to delay intervening. Producing a beamer of his own from within the folds of his robes, the man – who had yet to utter a word, even a simple cry for help – took a wild shot at Pip. The minidrag spat, and inhuman reflexes enabled his target to just avoid the corrosive venom. It scorched the finish on the wall behind him.

'*Pip, that's enough!*' Something in his master's voice apparently satisfied the minidrag. Hesitating briefly, the reptile pivoted in midair and raced back to Flinx. But the flying snake still felt uncomfortable enough to disdain his normal shoulder perch, opting instead to remain hovering warily near Flinx's right ear.

For several silent seconds a mass of people were momentarily unified by the paralysis of uncertainty. Then Namoto broke the spell. 'What branch are you working with, sir?' he inquired of the object of Pip's assault. 'I don't believe I recognize . . .'

The padre became silent as the beamer recently directed against the snake shifted to cover him. Trying to look in every direction at once, the man moved a shifting, glacial glare over the small crowd which had gathered. No one challenged him, electing instead to wait and watch.

'Keep back, all of you,' he finally warned. His accent was one Flinx did not recognize, the words almost more whistled than articulated.

As the man began backing towards the portal Flinx and Namoto had just passed through, Flinx cautiously edged around to where he could aid the injured young thranx. She was just regaining consciousness when he came near her. Getting both hands around her thorax, he lifted steadily. 'He . . . threatened to kill me,' she was murmuring groggily, still none too steady on trulegs and foothands. He could feel her b-thorax pulsing with uneven breathing.

Abruptly in control of herself again, the thranx looked accusingly across at her attacker. 'He said if I didn't take him down to command level he'd kill me!'

'You can't get out of this building, sir,' Namoto informed the man whom the girl had just accused. 'I'm going to have to ask you to put down that beamer and come with me.' The beamer waved at him and the padre ceased his approach after a single step.

'To be rational is to live,' the man whistle-talked.

Without releasing his grip on the beamer, the man reached into the folds of his robes – exceptionally voluminous they were, Flinx noted. A moment's search produced a small brown cube sporting wires and several awkwardly installed knobs.

'This is a hundred-gram casing of kelite – enough to kill everyone in this corridor.' His explanation was enough to send the younger of the watching acolytes scurrying in retreat.

Namoto didn't budge. 'No volume of explosives could get you out of this complex,' he informed the nervous man, his voice steady now. 'Furthermore, although that cube looks like a kelite casing, I find that most unlikely, since no volume of explosives can get *into* this complex without being detected. Furthermore, I don't think you're an authorized member of the Church. If that's true, then you can't be in possession of an activated beamer.'

The padre took another step forward.

'Keep away, or you'll find out whether it's activated or not!' the man shouted shrilly.

Every eye in the corridor was locked on the two principals in the threatening standoff – every intelligent eye.

Flinx thought he saw something move close to the ceiling, suddenly glanced to his right. Pip was no longer there.

There was no way of telling whether the same thought occurred simultaneously to the old man, or whether he simply detected motion overhead. Whatever the cause, he was ducking and firing before Flinx could shout to his pet.

Namoto had been right and wrong. The tiny weapon looked like a beamer but wasn't. Instead it fired a tiny projectile that just passed under the minidrag's writhing body. The projectile hit the far wall and bounced to the floor. Whatever it was was nonexplosive, all right; but Flinx doubted its harmlessness.

This time, Pip was too close to dodge. Powerful muscles in jaws and neck forced the poison out through the hypodermal tube in the minidrag's mouth. The poison missed the eyes, but despite his uncanny agility, the old man couldn't avoid the attack completely. The venom grazed head and neck. A sizzling sound came from dissolving flesh, and the man emitted an unexpected piercing hiss, sounding like an ancient steam engine blowing its safety valve.

It was not a sound the human throat could manufacture. Namoto and Flinx rushed the falling figure. But even as he was collapsing he was fumbling with the cube of 'kelite'.

The confidence of a dying man was reason enough for Namoto to fall to the floor and yell a warning to everyone else. Suddenly there was a muffled explosion – but one far smaller than kelite would have produced, and it did not come from the brownish cube. A few screams from the crowd, and the threat was past.

As Flinx climbed back to his feet, he realized that Namoto's observations were once again confused. First, the beamer had turned out to be a weapon, but not a beamer. And now it seemed this intruder had succeeded in smuggling a minimal amount of explosive into the complex, but not enough to hurt anyone else. If it was indeed kelite, it was a minute amount; but nonetheless, it made an impressive mess of the man's middle. His internals were scattered all over this end of the corridor.

Flinx was still panting when Pip settled around his shoulder once again. Moving forward, he joined Namoto in examining the wreckage of what minutes before had been a living creature.

With death imminent, the creature's mind had cleared, his thoughts strengthened multifold. Flinx suddenly found his head assailed with a swirl of unexpected images and word-pictures, but it was the familiarity of one which shocked him so badly that he stumbled.

Flinx could sense the ghostly rippling picture of a fat man he desired strongly to see again, the man he had given up hope of ever relocating: Conda Challis. This vision was mixed with a world-picture and the picture-world had the name Ulru-Ujurr. Many other images competed for his attention, but the unexpected sight of Challis in the dying intruder's mind overwhelmed them beyond identification.

Pip had sensed his master's fury at that very individual long minutes ago, back in the archives. Then this wretched person suddenly – undoubtedly – pictured the very same merchant, in terms unfavourable to Flinx. So Pip had reacted in proportion to Flinx's emotional state. Whether the minidrag would still have attacked the stranger had he not drawn a weapon was something Flinx would never know.

Namoto was studying the corpse. The explosion had been contained but intense. Little was left to connect the head and upper torso with the legs. Most of the body between had been destroyed.

Reaching down, the padre felt what appeared to be a piece of loose skin. He tugged . . . and the skin came away, revealing a second epidermis beneath. It was shiny, pebbled, and scaly – as inhuman as that final cry had been.

As inhuman as the thoughts Flinx had entered.

A low murmur of astonishment began to rise in the crowd, continuing as Namoto, kneeling, pulled and tore away the intricate molding which formed the false facial structure. When the entire skull had been exposed, Namoto rose, his gaze moving to the sample of forged flesh he held in one hand. 'A nye,' he observed matter-of-factly. He dropped the shard of skin, wiped his hands on his lower robe.

'An adult AAnn,' someone in the crowd muttered.

'In *here*!'

'But why? What did he hope to accomplish with so small an explosive?'

Someone called for attention from the back of the crowd, held up a tiny shape. 'Crystal syringe-dart,' she explained. 'That's how he got past the detectors – no beamer, no explosive-shell weapon.'

'Surely,' someone approached Namoto, 'he didn't come all this way with all this elaborate preparation, just to kill someone with a little dart gun?'

'I don't think so, either,' the padre commented, gazing down at the body. 'That explosive – that was a suicide charge, designed to kill him in the event of discovery. But perhaps it was also there to destroy something else.'

'What kind of something else?' the same person wondered.

'I don't know. But we're going to analyse this corpse before we dispose of it,' Kneeling again, Namoto pawed slowly through the cauterized meat. 'He was well armed as

94

far as it went – his insides are full of pulverized crystal. Must have been carrying several dozen of those syringe-darts.'

Flinx jerked at the observation, started to say something – then turned his budding comment into a yawn. He couldn't prove a thing, and it was an insane supposition anyway. Besides, if by some miracle he were half right, he would certainly be subjected to a year of questioning by Church investigators. He might never find Conda Challis then. Worse, by that time the indifferent merchant might have destroyed the missing record he had stolen, that remaining piece in the puzzle of Flinx's life.

So he could not afford to venture a childish opinion on what those fragments might be of.

A full crew of uniformed personnel entered the corridor. Some began dispersing the still buzzing crowd while others commenced an intensive examination of the corpse.

One small, very dark human glanced casually at the organic debris, then walked briskly over to confront the padre.

'Hello, Namoto.'

'Sir,' the padre acknowledged, with so much respect in his voice that Flinx was drawn from his own personal thoughts to consideration of the new arrival. 'He was well disguised.'

'An AAnn,' the short package of mental energy noted. 'They're feeling awfully bold when they try to slip one of their own in *here*. I wonder what his purpose was?'

Flinx had an idea, but it formed part of the information he had chosen not to disclose. Let these brilliant Churchmen figure it out for themselves. After he recovered the lost piece of himself from Challis, then he would tell them what he had guessed. Not before.

While the new man talked with Namoto, Flinx turned his attention back to the swarm of specialists studying the corpse. This was not the first time he had encountered the reptilian AAnn, though it was the first time in the flesh.

An uneasy truce existed between the Humanx Commonwealth and the extensive stellar empire of the AAnn. But that didn't keep the reptilians from probing for weak sport within the humanx-thranx alliance at every opportunity.

'Who penetrated its disguise?'

'I did, sir,' Flinx informed him, 'or rather, my pet did, Pip.' He fondled the smooth triangular head and the minidrag's eyes closed with pleasure.

'How,' Namoto asked pointedly, 'did the snake know?' He turned to his superior, added for his benefit, 'We were in genealogy at the time, sir, halfway around the complex.'

Flinx's reply walked a fine line between truth and prevarication. What he left out was more important, however, than what he said.

'The minidrag can sense danger, sir,' he explained smoothly. 'Pip's an emphatic telepath and we've been together long enough to develop a special rapport. He obviously felt the AAnn posed a threat, however distant, to me and he reacted accordingly.'

'Obviously,' murmured the smaller man noncommittally. He turned to face the young thranx. 'How are you involved in this, Padre-elect?'

She stopped preening her antennae, snapped to a pose of semiattention. 'I was on monitor duty at the lift station, sir. I thought it was a human. He approached me and said he had to go down to command level.'

Down to – Flinx's mind started envisioning what wasn't visible.

'I wondered why he didn't simply use his own lift pass. No one without a pass should be allowed this far. He had one, and showed it to me. He insisted that either it didn't work or else that the lift receptor was out of order.'

She looked downward. 'I suppose I ought to have sensed something then, but I did not.'

Namoto spoke comfortingly. 'How could you know? As you say, he got this far. His forgery wasn't good enough to fool the lift security 'puter, though.'

'Anyway,' she continued, 'I tried my own pass on Lift One, and it responded perfectly. Then I tried his and it didn't even key the *Acknowledge* light. So he asked me to call a lift for him. I told him it would be better to have his pass checked for malfunction, first. He said he didn't have time, but I was obstinate. That's when he pulled the weapon and told me to call him a lift or he'd kill me.'

Flinx noted that she was still unsteady despite the support of four limbs.

'Then these two gentlemen arrived, just as I was about to call the lift.' She indicated Flinx and Namoto.

'You couldn't sound an alarm?' the smaller man wondered gruffly.

She made an elabotate thranx gesture of helplessness with her truhands.

'When he pulled the weapon I was away from the silent alarm at the desk, sir, I couldn't think of a reason to get back to it . . . and, I was frightened, sir. I'm sorry. It was so unexpected . . .' She shivered again. 'I had no reason to suspect it was an AAnn.'

'He looked human to everybody else,' Flinx said comfortingly. The valentine-shaped head looked gratefully across at him. Though that face was incapable of a smile, she clicked her mandibles at him in thanks.

'Every experience that doesn't end in death is valuable,' the short man pontificated. That appeared to end her involvement as far as he was concerned. His attention was directed again to the people working with the body.

'Get this cleaned up and report to me as soon as preliminary analysis is completed,' he snapped. His motions, Flinx noted, were quick, sharp, as if he moved as well as thought faster than the average being. One of those movements fixed Flinx under a penetrating stare. 'That's an interesting pet you have, son. An emphatic telepath, you say?'

'From a world called Alaspin, sir,' Flinx supplied helpfully.

The man nodded. 'I know of them, but I never expected to see one. Certainly not a tame one. He senses danger to you, *hmmm*?'

Flinx smiled slightly. 'He makes a very good bodyguard.'

'I dare say.' He extended a hand too big for his body. 'I'm Counsellor Second Joshua Jiwe.'

Flinx now understood the deference which had been shown this man. He shook his hand slowly. 'I never expected to meet anyone so high in the Church hierarchy, sir.' Though he didn't add that in Bran Tse-Mallory and Truzenzuzex, who had been with him in the hunt for the Tar-Aiym Krang, he had met two who had at one time ranked even higher.

'I'm in charge of Depot security.' Again that head whipped around, instead of turning normally, to face

Namoto. 'What do you know about this young man?'

'He's come a long way in search of his natural parents. I've been doing my best to help him locate traces of them.'

'I see.' Jiwe spun on Flinx again. 'No doubt you're anxious to leave?'

'I've done everything here I can,' Flinx admitted. Jiwe could be the man to ask the awkward questions Flinx always feared.

The Counsellor Second reminded him of a *Canish*, a small, superactive little carnivore that haunted the chill forests of Moth. It was a quick, sharp-eyed killer whose movements were as hard to pin down as a muffled curse in a crowd. and a threat to creatures many times its size.

Like this Jiwe, Flinx suspected. The man was too interested in Pip and in the minidrag's relationship to Flinx. It was difficult to concentrate on Jiwe, however, when Flinx's mind was still astorm with the knowledge that Conda Challis had appeared in the thoughts of the dying AAnn. What had a human merchant to do with the lizards?

'Are you all right, Flinx?' Namoto was eyeing him concernedly. 'You looked dazed.'

'I was. I was drifting home in my mind . . . where my body ought to be headed.'

'And where is that?' Jiwe inquired interestedly.

Damn the man! 'A central trading world, name of Moth, city of Drallar.'

The Counsellor looked thoughtful. 'I know the world. Interesting, a lightly populated planet with a long history of settlement. Very independent-minded people. The local government's a benevolent monarchy, I believe.'

Flinx nodded.

'An indifferent monarchy would be more accurate, I think,' ventured Namoto.

The Counsellor smiled. 'It all amounts to the same thing as far as the locals are concerned.' He even grinned like a *Canish*, Flinx mused.

'And you say you can occasionally sense his thoughts and he yours, son?'

'Feelings, not thoughts, sir,' Flinx corrected hastily.

The Counsellor seemed to consider for a moment before asking, 'I wonder if you'd have a minute or two to spare? We won't delay your departure very long. If you'll just accompany us downstairs . . .'

'Sir . . .' Namoto started to interrupt, but the Counsellor waved his objection away.

'It doesn't matter. This is a perceptive young man and he's heard more than enough to know by now that there are levels to the Depot below what is visible on the surface. I think he's sufficiently mature to know when to keep his mouth shut and what not to talk loosely about.' He stared piercingly at Flinx. 'Aren't you, son?'

Flinx nodded vigorously, and the Counsellor rewarded him with another quasi-carnivorous smile. 'Good . . . I like a free spirit. Now then, we have a small problem we've been unable to solve. You might be able to approach it differently than anyone else. All I ask is that you make an effort for us. Afterwards, regardless of the results, we'll put you on an atmospheric shuttle free to anywhere on Terra. What do you say?'

Since he couldn't very well refuse the offer without making the Counsellor twice as suspicious of his peculiar abilities as he already was, Flinx smiled cheerfully and replied with a marvellous imitation of innocent enthusiasm.

'I'll be happy to do anything I can, of course!'

'I thought you might say that. I hoped so. Padre Namoto, you might as well join us – this could be instructive. Someone else can temporarily cover your normal duties.' He gestured at the reptilian corpse. 'Security will be working with this mess for quite a while yet.'

Then he turned to face the young thranx. 'Padre-elect Sylzenzuzex, you were about to call a lift. Do so now.'

'Yes, sir,' She appeared to have recovered completely from the shock of her near-abduction. Returning the Counsellor's request with a poised salute of truhand and left antennae, she moved to the nearest lift door and inserted a complex three-pronged card into a slot on its right.

Following an intricate push-and-twist of the card, the slot immediately lit with a soft green glow. A matching tell-tale winked on above the doorway, *beeped* three times. Sliding silently aside, the door revealed an elevator car of surprising size.

Flinx entered after the padre-elect. Something . . . something about her was nudging a familiar memory. The thought faded as his attention was caught by the rank of numbers set just inside the door.

In descending order the panel read: 2-1-0-1-2-3 – and so on down to twelve. Twelve storeys below ground level and only three above. Mentally, he smiled remembering. Now he was certain that his groundcar driver had been something more than a talkative oldster. But he hadn't lied to Flinx – he had simply described the Depot only as it was, without bothering to mention what couldn't be seen.

The thranx inserted the card into a slot below the panel of numbers. Flinx saw there were no switches, buttons, or other controls. Someone without a card might force the doorway into a lift, but without that intricate triangle-shape it could not be activated.

She cocked her head towards Jiwe. 'Sir?'

'Seventh level,' the Counsellor directed her, 'quadrant thirty-three.'

'That's the hospital, isn't it, sir? I don't get out that way very often.'

'That's right, Padre-elect.'

Inserting the card into the slot, she made another complex turn with it. The number seven lit on the panel, and a long series of tiny numbers appeared within the material of the card itself. Holding it firmly in place, she slipped one digit over the number 33. As soon as the light was covered, the door slid shut.

Flinx felt the lift move downward, accelerate, and shift in directions he could not follow. Several minutes later it stopped. Combining changes of direction with an approximation of their steady, smooth speed, he decided rapidly that they were no longer beneath the visible structure of the Depot.

When the door finally slid aside Flinx stepped out into a crowd of humans and thranx that was startling in its density. Here white was the predominant colour of clothing, though every uniform, robe, or jumpsuit was touched at some spot or another with the identifying aquamarine.

Jiwe and Namoto led while Flinx lagged behind, keeping pace with the young thranx. His nagging supposition concerning her had blossomed impossibly.

She spoke first, however, reaching up to put a delicate truhand on his free shoulder. 'I did not have a chance to thank you and your pet for saving my life. My delay shames me. Accept those thanks now.'

He inhaled deeply of her natural fragrance. 'All the thanks belong to Pip, not me,' he mumbled, embarrassed. 'Listen, what did the Counsellor call you?'

'Padre-elect. The rank is approximately – '

'Not that,' he corrected curiously. 'Your name.'

'Oh . . Sylzenzuzex.'

'That would break down as Syl, of the Hive Zen, family Zu, the Clan Zex?'

'That's right,' she acknowledged, unsurprised. Any human could break down a thranx name. 'What's yours?'

'Flinx . . . yes, one calling. But I've another reason for making certain of yours, one that goes beyond exchanging identification.' They rounded a bend in the pastel-walled corridor.

'You see, I think I know your uncle . . .'

CHAPTER SEVEN

Thranx are stiff-jointed but extremely sure of foot. Nevertheless, Flinx's pronouncement caused his insectoid companion to stumble. Multiple-lensed eyes regarded him with astonishment.

'My . . . *what*?'

Flinx hesitated as they turned still another corner. How far did this underground world extend laterally, he wondered. Perhaps for the length and breadth of the whole island?

'I might not have the pronunciation correct,' he said awkwardly. 'But aren't you related to an old philosoph named Truzenzuzex?'

'Say that one more time,' she coaxed him. He did so. 'You're sure of that stress on the family syllable?' A positive nod. 'I'm not sure "uncle" would be a proper Terranglo analog, but yes, we are closely related. I haven't seen Tru in several years, not since my adolescence began.'

'You know him well?'

'Not really. He was one of those childish gods – you understand, an adult whom other adults idolized? How do you happen to know him?'

'We were companions on a journey not long ago,' Flinx explained.

'He was an Eint, you know,' she went on thoughtfully. 'Very famous, very controversial in his beliefs. Too controversial, many in the Clan thought. Then when I heard he had left the Church . . .'

The sentence died quickly. 'It is not discussed in the Clan. I've heard practically nothing of him since he vanished many years ago to engage in private research with a human stingship partner of his youth.'

'Bran Tse-Mallory,' Flinx supplied, reminiscing.

The girl nearly stumbled again. 'I've never known a human so full of the nectar of the unexpected. You are a strange being, Flinx-man.'

When the question of his strangeness came up it was always a good time to change the subject.

He gestured upward. 'So the Records Depot aboveground isn't much more than camouflage for the *real* Church centre.'

'I . . .' She looked ahead and Flinx noted that the Counsellor hadn't missed a word of their conversation, judging from the speed with which he replied.

'Go ahead and tell him, padre-elect. If we don't he'll probably divine it anyway. How about it, son – are you clairvoyant?'

'If I was, I wouldn't be asking, would I?' Flinx shot back nervously, trying to conceal his increasing unease at the Counsellor's pointed comments. He had to get out of here. If he was still present when word of his extraordinary escape on Hivehom trickled down to Jiwe's level, they might never let him go. He would become something he had always fought to avoid – a curiosity, to be studied and examined like a pinned butterfly under glass.

But he couldn't turn and run. He would have to wait this out.

Now that she'd been granted permission, Sylzenzuzex explained enthusiastically, 'The aboveground Depot is fully utilized, but the majority of the installation extends under much of Bali, in many directions. There are only two ways in and out. Through the records centre, above and behind us now, and through the undersea shuttleport facing Lombok.' Her eyes glistened.

'It's a wonderful place. So much to study. So much to learn here, Flinx!'

Flinx's reaction so far had been something less than boundless enthusiasm. He suspected Sylzenzuzex came from a rather coddled family. His own blithe trust of honoured people and institutions had died somewhere between the ages of eight and nine.

He noticed how the overhead fluorescents filled her enormous eyes with ever-changing rainbows. 'The active volcanic throat of Mount Agung is channelled and controlled. It supplies all the power the Church complex requires. The entire island is completely self-contained and self-sustaining. It . . .'

She broke off as Namoto and Jiwe stopped in front of a door flanked by two Church guards wearing aquamarine uniforms. Their apparent relaxation, Flinx sensed, was deceptive, as was the casual way they seemed to hold their beamers.

Proper identification was exchanged, and they were admitted to a much smaller corridor. Two additional screenings by six more armed men and thranx finally gained them entrance to a modest chamber. In the centre of this room was a narrow bed. It sat like a spider in its web at the centre of a gleaming mass of highly sophisticated medical machinery.

As they moved towards the bed Flinx saw it contained a single immobile man. His eyes were open, staring at nothing. Indirect, carefully aligned lighting insured that his vacant eyes would not be damaged and a tiny device regularly moistened his frozen-open orbs. Awake but unaware, conscious but not cognizant, the man floated nude save for wires and tubes on a bed of clear medical gelatin.

Flinx tried to follow the maze of lines and cables and circuitry that stopped just short of metallic mummification, decided that more than anything else the immobile man resembled an overutilized power terminal.

Jiwe glanced once at the sleeper. 'This is Mordecai

Povalo.' He turned to Flinx. 'Ever hear of him?'

Flinx hadn't.

The Counsellor leaned over the motionless figure. 'He's been hovering between life and death for weeks now. On certain days he'll show some slight improvement. Other days will require the efforts of a dozen physicians to keep him living. Whether he had any will to live left no one can tell.

'The technicians insist his mind is still active, still functioning. His body tolerates the machines that keep it running. Although his eyes are open we can't tell if they're registering images. Just because his visual centres continue to operate doesn't mean he's seeing anything.'

Flinx found himself drawn to the frozen figure. 'Will he ever come out of his coma?'

'According to the doctors it's not properly a coma. They don't have a term for it yet. Whatever it is . . . no. They expect him to stay like this until his mind quits or his body finally rejects the life-sustaining equipment.'

'Then why,' Flinx wanted to know, 'keep him alive?'

On Evoria there dwelt a thranx Di-eint called Tintonurac, who was universally famed for his brilliance – though at present, he wore the look of a happy idiot.

Of course, his insectoid face could not produce a human expression, but in the years since the Amalgamation humans had learned to read thranx expressions with the same facility their quasi-symbiotic insect associates had learned to interpret mankind's.

No human orathranx noticed his expression at the moment, an expression alien to the face of the most acclaimed member of his Hive.

Head of his clan, he was a credit to his aunts and uncles, to his hive-mother and to his real parents. Tintonurac's particular wizardry lay in the ability to translate the concepts and schemes of others into reality – for he was a Master Fabricator, or precision engineer. Not only did his mechanical creations improve upon their originator's initial drawings, they were as attractive to look upon as they were supremely functional. Debate raged among his admirers as to whether their idol should more properly be considered a sculptor than an engineer.

Among his many products were a device which neatly dispatched a virulent human disease, an energy multiplex system for the hydroelectric plants so prevalent on thranx worlds, and an improved fire-control system for the sometimes wild yet irresistible SCCAM weapons system that was the mainstay of the combined human-thranx peaceforcer fleet. There were still others, some more esoteric than believable, which only his magic could transform into working devices.

But none of his inventions was the cause of his giddily pleased expression in this eighth month of the tail end of the Season of High Pollen on Evoria. The source of his pleasure was a glistening object that he kept concealed in a drawer of his workbench. He was staring at it now, revelling in its message and its glory as he sat at work in the laboratory, his six assistants attending to business around him. All were respected scientists and engineers in their own right. Of the group, four were thranx and two human. It was a measure of the admiration accorded Tintonurac that such people would volunteer to serve as his assistants, when they could easily have had laboratories and staffs of their own.

The Di-eint's mandibles moved in thranx laughter as he chuckled at a new thought. How curious a thing to occur to him! What might it be like to combine the two liquid metals in the flasks in his truhand's left with the catalyst solvent locked in its container across the room?

Acting as if half asleep, Tintonurac walked to the cabinet and removed the solvent. Turning back to his lounge-seat, he discovered that the pleasure grew deeper and more profound as he pursued this course of action.

Dridenvopa was working with the human Cassidy, but not so intensely that he failed to notice the Di-eint's actions. Distracted, he left his work to stare as Tintonurac poured the syrupy contents of one flask into a second. Bejewelled compound eyes glittered uncertainly when the contents of the overfull flask gushed the new mixture on to the bench, then to the floor. The Di-eint was as clean in his physical manipulations as in his mental, and this was not like him. Nor was the mask of pure, unthinking delight on his face.

Dridenvopa started to comment, then held himself back. Surely the Di-eint knew what he was doing. That reassuring thought sent him back to his own task, until he and Cassidy

105

both noticed the brightly labelled container the Di-eint was transferring from a foothand to a truhand.

'Isn't that . . . ?' the human Cassidy began in puzzled symbospeech, the all-purpose galactic patois, as the Di-eint unlocked the container. Instead of finishing the question he let out a strange human yowl and tried to cross metres of inter-vening benches and equipment before the inevitable occurred. But he was unable to get there in time to prevent a small portion of the harmless liquid in the container from entering the flask of the harmless mixed liquid metal. Together, these harmless substances formed a rapidly expanding ball so hot and intense as to make white phosphorus seem arctic cold.

Despite the increasing incandescence, Tintonurac con-centrated on the pleased beauty within the object . . .

The always efficient fire-fighting arm of the local thranx municipality arrived with its usual speed. All that remained for them to lavish their attention on was a scorched region between two buildings. The incredible heat had incinerated the metal walls of the laboratory. Its organic inhabitants had perished.

The investigators decided that someone had made an unusual yet possible mistake. Even the most brilliant scientist could make a fatal slip, even a thranx could lethally err, when hypnotized by a magnificence that the investigators might have understood, had it not been cremated along with the rest of the laboratory's contents – as had been intended.

Jiwe reflected on Flinx's question. 'Because he's sympto-matic of something which has been happening with dis-tressing frequency lately throughout the Commonwealth. Most people refuse to see any pattern to it, any connection between incidents. A very few, myself among them, aren't so certain these events are unrelated.

'Over the past several years, important people with unique talents have exhibited an unnerving tendency to blow themselves to bits, along with a sometimes equally unique apparatus. Taken individually, these incidents affect only the immolated. Taken collectively, they constitute something potentially dangerous to a great many others.'

The silence in the chamber was punctuated only by the efficient hum of life-sustaining equipment, the eerie wheeze of a mechanical zombie.

'Out of dozens, Povalo here is the only one who wasn't quite thorough enough in doing away with himself. Though for all the difference, he might as well be dead. He's certainly no good to himself any more.'

'You say some of you believe these suicides are all linked,' Flinx ventured. 'Have you discovered anything to connect them?'

'Nothing positive,' Jiwe admitted, 'which is why there are so few of us. All of them did have *one* thing in common, though. Not one appeared to have any reason for wanting to kill himself. I happen to think that's mighty significant. But the Council doesn't agree.'

Flinx showed little interest. Now was the time to quash personal curiosity and get about the business of getting out. 'What do you want of me?'

Jiwe moved to a nearby chair, threw himself into it. 'Povalo was a wealthy, intelligent, wholly self-possessed engineer doing important research. Now he's a vegetable. I want to know why a man like that – why many humans and thranx like that – seem to find it suddenly necessary to murder themselves. Yes, self-murder . . . I can't call it suicide when I truly believe it's something else.'

'What am I supposed to do?' Flinx asked warily.

'You detected that AAnn infiltrator when no one else suspected his presence.'

'That was just an accident,' Flinx explained. He scratched Pip's jaw. 'It happens only when Pip gets excited, when he perceives a possible threat to me.' He indicated Povalo. 'Your subject is hardly a threat.'

'I'm not expecting a thing,' Jiwe calmed him, 'I'm just asking you to try. I'll try tarot readers and tea leaves after you've failed.'

Flinx sighed elaborately. 'If you insist . . .'

'Ask,' the Counsellor reminded him gently, 'not insist.'

Semantics, Flinx thought sardonically; but he dutifully turned to face the bed and concentrated on its limp occupant. He struggled to reach past those sightless eyes, more afraid of what he might discover than what he might not.

Pip tightened reflexively on his shoulder, sensing his master's effort. Flinx hoped without much confidence that Jiwe hadn't noticed the minidrag's reaction. What he had failed to consider was that his very unease as he concentrated on Povalo was enough to stimulate Pip. There *was* a threat present, even if only in his own mind.

No faint haze obscured his vision. There was no lilting music in his ears to distract him. The bed, its cocoon of circuitry, the shining equipment, and the translucent gelatin suspension – all were clear as ever to his eyes. And yet . . . there was something in his mind that he saw without those eyes, something that hadn't been there a moment ago. It was part of the creature on the bed.

A young man in the fullness of youth – an idealized distortion of Mordecai Povalo – was courting a woman of supernal beauty. Together they floated in thick cumulus clouds engorged with moist love. Side by side they dived ecstatically to the glassy green depths of a shallow ocean. From time to time the figures changed slightly, in build, in colouring, but the subject was ever the same.

In the magnificence of youth, Povalo-plus courted a woman of supple grace, swirling and spinning in love-turns about her as they floated among pink clouds . . .

Without warning the woman disappeared – swam off, flew off, ran away, depending on the terrain of the moment. Distraught beyond hope, the man walked to a workbench, depressed a switch on a tiny instrument board which would make everything well again.

Flinx blinked once, looked away from the bed. Jiwe was watching him intently. 'I'm sorry,' he said softly.

'I couldn't detect a thing.'

The Counsellor held his stare a moment longer, then slumped back into the chair. He appeared to age ten years.

'I got what I expected. I thank you for trying, Flinx.'

'May I leave, now?'

'Hm? Oh, yes, of course. Padre-elect,' he directed Sylzenzuzex, 'you'd better go with our young friend and show him his way out.' Then he looked again at Flinx. 'I'll authorize a blank voucher for travel anywhere on Terra. You can pick it up on your way out.'

'If it's all right with you, sir,' Flinx declared, 'I'd like to make one more trip to Records, I think I might find some related information on my parents. And I'd like to replay the copy of the information I already have.'

Jiwe looked blankly at Namoto, who reminded him: 'The boy's parents, remember?'

'Yes. Naturally any help we can give you we will gladly provide. Padre-elect, you can assist our friend Flinx in finding any information he requires. One last thing, son,' Jiwe finished, managing to smile slightly again, 'if you run into any more visitors who smell like an old jacket instead of a human or thranx, please speak up before your pet assassinates them?'

'I'll do that, sir,' Flinx agreed, smiling back. His relief as they left the room was considerable.

'Where do you want to go?' Sylzenzuzex inquired as they re-entered the main hospital corridor. 'Back to Genealogy?'

'No . . . I think I've gotten all I can from there. Let's try your Galographics Department. I think I may have located the world my parents moved to.' This was a lie.

'No problem,' Sylzenzuzex assured him, her mandibles clacking politely.

As they continued down the corridor, Flinx mulled over what he had seen in Povalo's mind. The idealized vision of himself, the woman, the clouds, seas, and rolling hills – all gentle, simple images of an uncomplicated paradise.

Except for the console. Everything had been all golden and red and green. He had not seen reality, of course, but merely a simulation of it which the comatose engineer had thought was reality.

Those simple colours. The shifting body outlines. Flinx had seen them before.

Just prior to his death, the engineer Mordecai Povalo had owned and played with a Janus jewel.

Povalo's jewel naturally led Flinx to think of Conda Challis and his own little crystal playhouse. Conda Challis had been in the mind of the infiltrating AAnn, along with the unknown world Ulru-Ujurr.

A bizarre series of coincidences which undoubtedly led nowhere. Never mind the AAnn and to perdition with poor Mordecai Povalo! Flinx had no room in his mind for anything now save Challis and the information he had removed from the Church archive.

That was why he was going to Galographics. His parents . . . they could quite easily have died right here on Terra. To find out for certain he had to find Challis; and the merchant might well have fled to an unfamiliar globe like this Ulru-Ujurr – if indeed such a world existed and was not merely some aspect of the AAnn's mind that Flinx had mis-interpreted.

It felt as if they had walked for hours before they reached the bank of lifts again. Once more Sylzenzuzex employed the complex card key, once more they travelled an angular pathway.

The level they eventually stepped on to was deserted, a far cry from the bustle of the hospital section. She led him past doors with long compound names engraved in them until they entered the one they sought.

Physically, Galographics looked like a duplicate of the Genealogy Archives, with one exception. This room was smaller and it contained more booths. Furthermore, the monitoring attendant here was much younger than the one he had encountered before.

'I'd like some help hunting up an obscure world.'

The attendant drew herself up proudly. 'Information retrieval eliminates obscurity. It is the natural building block of the Church, on which all other studies must be based. For without access to knowledge, how can one learn about learning?'

'Please,' Flinx said, 'no more than two maxims per speech.' Behind him, Sylzenzuzex's mandibles clicked in barely stifled amusement.

The attendant's professional smile froze. 'You can use the catalogue spools, three aisles down.' She pointed.

Flinx and Sylzenzuzex walked towards the indicated row. 'The world I want to check on is called Ulru-Ujurr.'

'Ujurr,' she echoed in symbospeech, the odd word sounding more natural when spoken in her consonant-oriented voice. Flinx watched her closely, but she gave no sign that she had ever heard the name before.

He couldn't immediately decide whether that was good or bad.

'Is that symbospeech spelling?' she asked after he made a show of blocking it out. 'The tape doesn't say for sure. There may be variables. Let's try phonetic first, though.' The attendant appeared to hesitate slightly, wondering if perhaps a Church tape would be so unspecific. But there were variable spellings of far better known worlds, she reminded herself.

They walked down an aisle lined by the vast, nearly

featureless walls of the information storage banks. In those metal ramparts, Flinx knew, were stored trillions of bits of information on every known world within and without the Commonwealth.

These records probably had an annex buried somewhere beneath them in the true labyrinth of the Depot complex, an annex closed to casual inspection. For that reason, if Flinx's globular quarry happened to be of some secretive, restricted nature, it might not appear in the spools here.

He was somewhat surprised when they found what appeared to be the proper compartment. Sylzenzuzex pressed a switch nearby and the metal wall responded with oral confirmation.

'It could be a different Ulru-Ujurr,' she warned him, as she studied the labels and minute inscriptions identifying the spool case. 'But there don't appear to be any cross-references to another world with a similar name.'

'Let's try it,' Flinx instructed impatiently.

She inserted a card key into the appropriate slot. It was a far simpler device than the one used to operate the multi-level lifts. They were rewarded with a tiny spool of thread-thin tape. She squinted at it – though that was merely an impression Flinx interpreted by her movements, rather than by a physical gesture, since she had no eyelids to narrow.

'It's so hard to tell, but it seems as if there's very little on this tape,' she finally told him. 'Sometimes, though, you can find a spool that looks like it contains two hundred words and in actuality it holds two million. They could make this system more efficient.'

Flinx marvelled at anyone who could call such a system inefficient. But, he reminded himself, even the lowliest members of the Church hierarchy were constantly exhorted to find ways to improve the organization. Spiritual methodology, they called it.

Only a few of the booths were occupied. They found one at the end of a row, isolated from the other users.

Flinx took the chair provided for humans, while Sylzenzuzex folded herself into the narrow bench designed for thranx and inserted the fragment of sealed plastic into the playback receptor. Then she activated the viewscreen, using the same procedure Namoto had employed earlier. The screen lit up immediately.

Displayed was the expected statistical profile: Ulru-Ujurr was approximately twenty per cent larger than Terra or Hivehom, though its composition produced a gravity only minimally stronger. Its atmosphere was breathable and uncomplicated and it contained plenty of water. There were extensive ice caps at both poles. Further indicative of the planet's cool climate was the extent of apparent glaciation. It was a mountainous world, its temperate zone boasting intemperate weather, and primarily ice north of that.

'It's not a true iceworld,' Flinx commented, 'but it's cooler than many which are suited to humanx habitation.' He examined the extensive list closely, then frowned. 'A little cold weather shouldn't discourage all humanx settlement on an otherwise favourable world, but I don't see any indication of even a scientific monitoring post. Every inhabitable world has at least that. Moth supports a good-sized population, and there are humanx settlements of size on far less hospitable planets. I don't understand, Sylzenzuzex.'

His companion was all but quivering with imagined cold, ' "Cool," he calls it, "Habitable." For you humans, perhaps, Flinx. For a thranx it's a frozen hell.'

'I admit it's far from your conception of the ideal.' He turned back to the readout. 'Apparently there's both animal and vegetable native life, but no descriptions or details. I can see how the terrain would restrict such studies, but not eliminate them totally the way they seem to have been.' He was growing more and more puzzled.

'There aren't any significant deposits of heavy metals or radioactives.'

In short, although people *could* live on Ulru-Ujurr – there just wasn't anything to entice them there. The planet lay on the fringe of the Commonwealth, barely within its spatial borders, and it was comparatively distant from the nearest settled world. Not an attractive place to settle.

But dammit, there ought to be some sort of outpost!

That was the end of the tape except for one barely legible addendum: THOSE DESIROUS OF OBTAINING ADDITIONAL STATISTICAL DETAIL CONSULT APPENDIX 4325 SECTION BMQ . . .

'I presume you're as tired of reading statistics as I am,' Sylzenzuzex said as she set the tiny tape to rewind. 'As far as your parents are concerned, this world certainly looks like a dead end. What do you wish to see now?'

Trying to keep his tone casual, he said, 'Let's go ahead and finish with this one first.'

'But that means digging through the sub-indexes,' she protested, 'Surely you . . .'

'Let's make sure of this,' he interrupted patiently.

She made a thranx sound indicating moderate resignation coupled with overtones of amusement, but she didn't argue further.

After nearly an hour of cross-checking they hunted down Appendix 4325, Section BMQ; obtained the necessary sub-index, and prodded the somehow reluctant machine to produce the requested tape sub-sub-heading. Someone, Flinx thought, had gone to a lot of trouble to conceal this particular bit of information without being obvious about it.

This time his suspicions were confirmed. Slipped into the viewer and activated, the screen displayed glaring red letters which read: ULRU-UJURR . . . HABITABLE WORLD . . . THIS PLANET AND SYSTEM ARE UNDER EDICT . . .

The date of the first and only survey of the planet was listed, together with the date on which it was placed under Church Edict by the Grand Council.

That was the end of it, as far as Sylzenzuzex was concerned. 'You've reached the Hive wall. I can't imagine what led you to think your parents could be on this world. You must have made a mistake, Flinx. That world is Under Edict. That means that nothing and no one is permitted to travel within shuttle distance of its surface. There will be at least one automated peaceforcer in orbit around it, programmed to intercept and challenge anything that tries to reach the planet. Anyone ignoring the Edict . . . well,' she paused significantly, 'you can't outrun or out manoeuvre a peaceforcer.' Her eyes glistened. 'Why are you looking at me like that?'

'Because I'm going there. To Ulru-Ujurr,' he added, at her expression of disbelief.

'I retract my first evaluation,' she said sharply. 'You are more than strange, Flinx – or perhaps your mind is becoming unhinged by the traumatic events of today.'

'My mind's hinges are fastened down and working

smoothly, thanks. You want to hear something really absurd?'

She eyed him warily. 'I'm not sure.'

'I think all these suicides of important people that Jiwe is so worried about have something to do with the Janus jewel.'

'The Janus – I've heard of them, but how . . . ?'

He rushed on recklessly. 'I saw powder that might have come from a disintegrated jewel on the body of the infiltrator.'

'I thought that was from destroyed crystal syringe-darts.'

'It could also have been from a whole jewel.'

'So what?'

'So . . . I don't know what; but I just have a feeling everything ties together somehow: the jewels, the suicides, this world – and the AAnn.'

She looked at him sombrely. 'If you feel so strongly about this, then for the Hive's sake why did you not tell the Counsellor?'

'Because . . . because . . .' his thoughts slowed, ran into that ever-present warning wall, 'I can't, that's all. Besides, who'd listen to a crazy theory like that when it comes from . . .' then he smiled suddenly, 'an unhinged youngster like myself.'

'I don't think you're that young,' she countered, pointedly ignoring the comment about him being unhinged. 'Then why tell anyone . . . why tell me?'

'I . . . wanted another opinion, to see if my theory sounded as crazy out loud as it does in my head.'

Her mandibles clicked nervously. 'All right, I think it sounds crazy. Now can we forget all this and go on to the next world your research turned up?'

'My research didn't turn up any other worlds. It didn't turn up Ulru-Ujurr, either.'

She looked exasperated. 'Then where did you find the name?'

'In the . . .' He barely caught himself. He had almost confessed that he'd plucked it out of the mind of the dying AAnn. 'I can't tell you that, either.'

'How am I supposed to help you, Flinx, if you refuse to let me?'

'By coming along with me.'

She stood there dumbstruck.

'I need someone who can override a peaceforcer command. You're a padre-elect in Security or you wouldn't have been monitoring a station as sensitive as the surface lift corridor. You could do it.' He stared anxiously at her.

'You had better go talk to Counsellor Jiwe,' she told him, speaking very slowly. 'Even assuming I could do such a thing, I would never consider challenging a Church Edict.'

'Listen,' Flinx said quickly, 'a higher-ranking Church member wouldn't consider it, and would be followed, if only for protective reasons. Not even a Commonwealth military craft would. But you're not so high up in the hierarchy that it would cause alarm if you suddenly deviated from your planned activities. I'm also betting that you've something of your uncle in you, and he's the most brilliant individual I ever met.'

Sylzenzuzex was looking around with the expression of one who suddenly awakens to find herself in a locked room with a starving meat-eater.

'I am not hearing any of this,' she muttered frantically. 'I am not. It . . . it's blasphemous, and . . . idiotic.' Never taking her eyes off him, she started to slide from the bench. 'How did I get involved with you, anyway?'

'Please don't scream,' Flinx admonished her gently. 'As to your question, if you'll think a minute . . . I saved your life . . .'

CHAPTER EIGHT

She paused, all four running limbs cocked beneath her in preparation for a quick sprint towards the monitor's desk. Flinx's words rolled about in her head.

'Yes,' she finally admitted, 'you saved my life. I'd forgotten, for a moment.'

'Then by the Hive, the Mother-Queen and the miracle of metamorphosis,' he intoned solemnly, 'I now call that debt due.'

She tried to sound amused, but he could see she was shaken. 'That's a funny oath. Is it designed to tease children?'

For emphasis he repeated it again . . . this time in High Thranx. It was difficult and he stumbled over the clicks and hard glottal stops.

'So you know it,' she murmured, slumping visibly, then glancing at the monitor sitting quietly at the distant desk. Flinx knew that a single shout could bring a multitude of armed personnel – and angry questions. He was gambling everything that she wouldn't, that the ancient and powerful life-debt sworn on that high oath would restrain her.

It did. She looked at him pleadingly. 'I'm barely adult, Flinx. I still have all my wingcases and I shed my adolescent chiton only a year ago. I've never been wed. I don't want to die, Flinx, for your unexplained obsession. I love my studies and the Church and my potential future. Don't shame me before my family and my Clan. Don't . . . make me do this.'

'I'd like to help you . . . truly I would. You've apparently had more than your share of unhappiness and indifference. But please try to understand – '

'I haven't got time to understand,' he snapped shutting her up before she weakened his resolve. He *had* to get to Ulru-Ujurr, if there was even a chance Challis had fled there. 'If I'd taken time to understand, I'd be dead half a dozen times already. I call on that oath for you to pay your debt to me.'

'I agree then,' she replied in a dull voice. 'I must. You drown me in your dream.' And she added something indicative of hopelessness mixed with contempt.

For a brief moment, for a second, he was ready to tell her to disappear, to leave the room, to run away. The moment passed. He needed her.

If he went directly to someone like Jiwe and told him he had to go to Ulru-Ujurr the Counsellor would smile and shrug his shoulders. If he told him about his theory concerning the Janus jewels. Hiwe would demand details, reasons, source of suspicions. That would mean owning up to his talents, something he simply couldn't do.

The Church, for all its goodwill and good works, was still a massive bureaucracy. It would put its own concerns above his. 'Sure,' they would tell him, 'we'll help you find your real parents. But first . . .'

That 'first' could last forever, he knew, or at least until a bored Challis had destroyed the last link between Flinx and his heritage. Nor was he convinced they would help him even if he did reveal himself fully – he wasn't certain the Church's adaptability extended to breaking its own Edict.

He was going to Ulru-Ujurr, no matter what, though he couldn't tell anyone the real reason why. Not even the silently waiting Sylzenzuzex, who stared at the floor with the look of the living dead. Surely, though, she would be fully reinstated when it became known she had accompanied him under duress.

Surely . . .

After Sylzenzuzex had applied for and, as a matter of course, received her accumulated leave of several Terran weeks, they took an atmospheric shuttle back to Brisbane Shuttleport. To the questioning machine she had explained that it was time for her to visit her parents on Hivehom. Throughout it all, Flinx never wavered in his determination to take her with him. This couldn't be helped. She was frigidly polite in response to his questions. By mutual agreement they did not engage in casual small talk.

They were held up in Brisbane for over a week while Flinx concluded the complex arrangements required for renting a small, autopiloted KK-drive ship. Private vessels capable of interstellar travel were not commonly available.

Malaika had been very generous, but the three-day rental fee exhausted the remainder of Flinx's credit account. That didn't trouble him, since he was already guilty of kidnapping. It would hardly matter when the ship broker sent collectors to stalk him after three days had elapsed without his return. He would worry about repaying the astronomical debt he was about to incur another time. If he returned, he reminded himself. The Church had not slapped an Edict on Ulru-Ujurr out of bored perversity. There was a reason . . . and there was always Challis.

Sylzenzuzex knew less about astrogation than he did. If

the broker had lied to him about the little ship's self-sufficiency, they would never get to Ulru-Ujurr – or anywhere else.

As a matter of fact, she explained, her chosen field was archeology. Security was only her student specialty. Hivehom's early primitive insectoid societies had always fascinated her. She had dreamed of studying them for the rest of her life, once she graduated and returned home as a full padre – something that would never happen now, she reminded him bitterly.

He ignored her. He had to, or his resolve would crack. Once more he wondered at why an apparently innocuous, inhabitable planet like Ulru-Ujurr should have been placed Under Edict. The information they had studied in Galographics, the long lists of cold statistics that had led him in short order to abduction and fraud and debt, neglected to elaborate on that small matter.

At least one worry was quickly allayed when the powerful little vessel made the supralight jump that took them out of immediate pursuit range. According to simplified readouts, the ship was proceeding at maximum cruising speed on course for the co-ordinates Flinx had provided it.

Flinx wasn't really concerned that he was worse than broke once again. In a way he was almost relieved. He had spent his entire life in an impecunious state. The abrupt resumption of that familiar condition was like exchanging an expensive dress suit for a favourite pair of old, worn work pants.

The time they spent travelling wasn't wasted. Flinx constantly consulted and questioned the ship's computer, improving his rudimentary knowledge of navigation and ship operation while staying a respectful distance from the autopilot override. He was not ashamed of his ignorance. All KK-drive ships were essentially computer-run. Stellar distances and velocities were far too overwhelming for simple organic minds to manipulate. The humanx crew present on the large KK freightliners was there merely to serve the needs of passengers and cargo, and as a precaution. They constituted the flexible fail-safe, ready to take over in the event the ship's machine mind malfunctioned.

It was fortunate that he was so interested in the ship, because Sylzenzuzex proved to be anything but a lively

118

companion. She preferred instead to remain in her cabin, emerging only to pick up her meals from the autochef. Gradually, however, even the patience of one accustomed to underground living began to wear thin, and she spent more and more time on the falsely luxurious bridge of the ship. Still, when she deigned to say anything at all, her conversation was confined to monosyllabic comments of utter despondency.

Such willing submission to reality grated against Flinx's nature even more than her silence. 'I don't understand you, Sylzenzuzex. You're like a person attending her own wake. I told you I'll confirm that I kidnapped you against your will. Surely everyone will have to admit you're blameless for anything that happens?'

'You just don't understand,' she muttered sibilantly. 'I could not lie like that. Not to my superiors in the Church, or to my family or hive-mother. Certainly not to my parents. I went with you willingly.' Her exquisite head, shining like the sea in the overhead lighting, dipped disconsolately.

'You're not making sense,' Flinx argued vehemently. 'You had no choice! I called on you to fulfil a hereditary debt. How can anyone blame you for that? As for our forbidden destination – that was wholly my choice. You had nothing to say about my decision and you have voiced plenty of objections to it.' As he talked, his pre-prepared meal lay cooling in its container nearby. Meanwhile Pip's jet eyes stared pensively up at his troubled master.

Sylzenzuzex stared at him. 'There are still some things humans do not understand about us,' and she turned away as if those were to be her last words on the subject.

Always the convenient phrase, Flinx thought furiously. Whether human or thranx, it mattered not – always the ready willingness to seek refuge in absolutes. Why were supposedly intelligent beings so terrified of reason? He stared out the foreport, frustrated beyond measure. The universe did not run on emotional principles. He had never been able to understand how people could.

'Have it your way,' Flinx grumbled. 'We'll stick to more immediate concerns. Tell me about this peaceforcer station that's supposed to prevent us from landing on this world.'

There was a whistling sound as a large dollop of air was forced out through breathing spicules – a thranx sigh.

'Peaceforcers, more likely. There should be anywhere from one to four of them in synchronous orbit around the planet. I'm not certain because so few worlds are Under Edict that the subject is rarely brought up for discussion. So, of course there is no information whatsoever on the worlds themselves. Being Under Edict, as they say, is a situation discussed more as a possibility than a fact.

'I would imagine,' she concluded, walking over to a console and gazing idly at the instrumentation, 'that we will be signalled or intercepted in some fashion and ordered to leave.'

'What if we ignore any such warning?'

She made a thranx shrug. 'Then we're likely to have our wingcases blown off.'

Flinx's tone turned sarcastic. 'I thought the Church was an interspecies purveyor of gentleness and understanding.'

'That's right,' she shot back, 'and it provides a lot of comfort and assurance to everyone to know that the Church's decrees are enforced.' Her voice rose. 'Do you think that the Church puts a whole world Under Edict because of some Counsellor's whim?'

'I don't know,' he replied, unperturbed. 'Probably we'll get the chance to find out . . .'

Without warning a flying fortress appeared out of nowhere. One minute they were alone in free-space, cycling in towards the fourth planet of an undistinguished sun, and the next a craft with six points projecting from its principal axes had matched their speed and was cruising alongside. This ship was many times the size of their small vessel.

'Automated peaceforce station twenty-four,' a mechanical voice said pleasantly over the speakers. The tridee screen could not pick up any picture.

'To undeclared vessel class sixteen-R. In the name of the Church and the Commonwealth you are hereby notified that the world you approach is Under Edict. You are directed to reverse your present course and re-engage your double-K drive. No vessel is permitted to make shuttlefall on the fourth planet, nor to remain in the vicinity of this sun.

'You have thirty standard minutes from the conclusion of this notification to reprogramme your navigational computer. Do not, repeat, do not attempt to approach within scanner range of the fourth world. Do not attempt to move closer than five planetary diameters. Failure to comply with the aforementioned regulations will be dealt with appropriately.'

'A polite way of saying it'll blow us to small pieces,' Sylzenzuzex commented dryly. 'Now can we go back?'

Flinx didn't reply. He was busy studying the mass of metal drifting next to them. That it was supremely fast, far faster than this small craft, had already been demonstrated. Without question, several weapons of various destructive capabilities were trained on the bridge even as he wondered what to do next. They could no more make a desperate dash for the planet's surface than he could outrun a devilope on the plains bordering the Gelerian Swamp, back home.

'This is why I've brought you,' he told the waiting thranx. 'It sure wasn't for the pleasure of your company.' Flinx moved aside, revealing activated instrumentation. 'Here's the tridee. Give it your name, Church identity number, Security code – whatever it takes to gain clearance to land.'

She didn't budge, her legs seemingly rooted in the metal floor. 'But it won't listen to me.'

'Try.'

'I . . . I won't do it.'

'You're under life-oath, you've sworn on your Hive,' he reminded her between clenched teeth, hating himself more with every word.

Again the symmetrical head drooped; again the hollow, defeated voice. 'Very well.' She shuffled over to the console.

'I'm telling you for the last time,' she told him, 'that if you make me do this, it's as if you've banished me from the Church yourself, Flinx.'

'I happen to have more confidence in your own organization than you apparently do. Besides, if after a full explanation of the circumstances they actually do kick you out, then I don't think the organization's worthy of you.'

'How sure you are,' she said calmly, concluding with a sound so harsh it made Flinx flinch.

'Go ahead,' he ordered.

She tested the broadcast, then rattled off a series of superfast words and numbers. Flinx could barely identify them, much less make any sense of the steady stream of hybrid

121

babble. It occurred to him that she might just as well have given the fortress the command to destroy them. That unpleasant thought passed when nothing happened. After all, survival was as strong a thranx drive as it was a human one.

Instead, the announcement brought the hoped-for-result. 'Emergency temporary cancellation received and understood;' came the stiff voice. 'Processing.'

Two minutes stretched long as two years while Flinx waited for the final reply.

Then: 'Other stations notified. You may proceed.'

There was no time to waste on giving thanks. Flinx rushed to the navigation input and verbally instructed the ship to take up a low orbit around the temperate equatorial zone, above the largest continent. The detector devices on the ship were then to begin a search for any sign of surface communications facilities – anything that would indicate the presence of humanx settlement.

Anywhere someone like Challis could exist.

'What if there isn't anything like that,' Sylzenzuzex asked, her face paling as the ship pulled away from the orbiting fortress. 'There's a whole world down there, bigger than Hivehom, bigger than Terra.'

'There'll be some place developed,' he assured her. His confident tone belied the uncertainty in his mind.

There was. Only they didn't locate it – it found them.

'What ship . . . what ship . . . ?' the speakers crackled as soon as they entered parking orbit. The query came in perfect symbospeech, though whether from thranx or human throat he couldn't tell.

Flinx moved to the pickup. 'Who's calling?' he asked, a mite inanely.

'What ship?' the voice demanded.

This could go on for hours. He responded with the first thing that sounded halfway plausible. 'This is the private research vessel *Chamooth* on Church-related business, out from Terra.'

There, that wasn't a complete lie. His abduction of Sylzenzuzex certainly constituted Church-related business, and he had been led here by information in Church files.

A long pause followed while unseen beings at the other end of the transmission digested this. Finally: 'Shuttleport co-ordinates for you are as follows.'

Flinx scrambled to record the information. His ruse had gotten them that much. After they landed . . . well, he would proceed from there. The numbers translated into a position on a fairly small plateau in the mountains of the southern continent. According to the information, the landing strip bordered an enormous lake at the 14,000-kilometre level.

Sweating, muttering at his own awkwardness, Flinx succeeded in positioning the ship over the indicated landing spot with a minimum of corrections to the autopilot. From there it was a rocky, bouncing descent by means of auto-programmed shuttlecraft to the surface.

Sylzenzuzex was talking constantly now, mostly to her-self. 'I just don't understand,' she kept murmuring over and over, 'there shouldn't be anything down there. Not on an edicted world. Not even a Church outpost. This just doesn't make any sense.'

'Why shouldn't it make sense?' Flinx asked her, fighting to keep his seat as the tiny shuttle battled powerful cross-winds. 'Why shouldn't the Church have business on a world it wants to keep everyone else off of?'

'But only an extreme threat to the good of humanx kind is reason enough for placing a world Under Edict,' she protested, her tone one of disbelief. 'I've never heard of an exception.'

'Naturally not,' Flinx agreed, with the surety of one who had experienced many perversities of human and thranx nature. 'Because no information is available on worlds which are Under Edict. How very convenient.'

The shuttle was banking now, dipping down between vast forested mountain slopes. A denser atmosphere here raised the treeline well above what existed on Moth or Terra. Tarns and alpine lakes were everywhere. At the higher elevations, baby glaciers carved tentative paths downward – even here, near the planet's equator.

'Commencing landing approach,' the shuttle computer informed them. Flinx stared ahead, saw that the plateau the ground-based voice had mentioned was far smaller than he had hoped. This was not a true plateau, but instead a broad glacial plain ice-quarried from the mountains. One side of the plateau-plain was filled with a narrow lake that glistened like an elongated sapphire.

As the shuttle straightened out they rushed past a sheer waterfall at least a thousand metres high, falling to the canyon below in a single unbroken plunge like white steel. This, he decided, was a magnificent world.

If only the shuttle would set them down on it in one piece.

His acceleration couch trembled as the ship fired braking jets. Ahead he could now make out the landing strip that ran parallel to the deep lake. At the far end, a tiny cluster of buildings poked above the alluvial gravel and low scrub.

At least the installation here – whoever was manning it – was advanced enough to include automatic landing lock-ons. Built into the fabric of the landing strip itself, they hooked into the corresponding linkups in the belly of the shuttle. The completion of this manoeuvre was signalled by a violent lurch. Then the landing computer, somewhere below them, took over and brought the shuttle in for a smooth, safe setdown.

Sylzenzuzex stared out the side port on the left even as she was undoing her straps. 'This is insane,' she muttered, gazing at the considerable complex of structures nearby, 'there can't be a base here. There shouldn't be anything.'

'Some anythings,' he commented, gesturing towards the pair of large groundcars which were now moving on to the field towards them, 'are coming to pay their greetings. Remember now,' he reminded her as he calmed a nervous Pip and headed for the access corridor leading to the hatch, 'you're here because I forced you to come '

'But not physically,' she countered. 'I told you before, I can't lie.'

'The Horse Head,' he murmured, looking skyward. 'Be evasive then. Ah, do what you think best. I'm no more going to convert you to reason than you're going to convince me to enter your Church.'

Flinx activated the automatic lock, and it began to cycle open. If the atmosphere outside had been unbreathable, despite the information in the Galographics records, the lock would not have opened. As the door plug drew aside, a rippled ramp extended itself, sensors at its far end halting it as soon as it touched solid ground.

Pip was stirring violently, but Flinx kept a firm hand on his pet. Apparently the minidrag perceived some threat again, which would be natural if, say, this was indeed a Church installation. In any case they couldn't take on an entire party which was presumably armed. It took several minutes before he succeeded in convincing his pet to relax, regardless of what happened next.

Flinx took a deep breath as he started down the ramp. Sylzenzuzex trooped morosely behind, lost in morose thought. Despite the altitude, the air here was thick and rich in óxygen. It more than counteracted the slightly stronger gravity.

Snow-crowned crags rose around the valley on three sides. Except for the glacial plain they now stood on, the valley and mountain slopes were furred with a thick coat of great trees. Green was still the predominant colour but there was a substantial amount of yellow-hued vegetation. Their branches rose stiffly skyward, no doubt to be fully spread by the winter snowfall.

The temperature was perfect – about 20°C. At least, it was as far as Flinx was concerned. Sylzenzuzex was already cold, and the dry air did nothing to help the flexibility of her exoskeletal joints.

'Don't worry,' he said, trying to cheer her as the ground-cars drew near, 'there must be quarters provided for thranx personnel. You can warm up soon.'

And explain your story to the local authority in private if you wish, he added silently.

His thoughts were broken as the first big car pulled to a halt before them. As he waited Flinx kept a tight grip on Pip, holding the tense minidrag at the wing joints to prevent any sudden flight. Yet despite the minutes he had already spent calming his pet, Pip still struggled. When he finally settled down, he coiled painfully tight around Flinx's shoulder.

People began to emerge from the groundcar. They did not wear aquamarine robes of the Church, nor the crimson of the Commonwealth. They did not look like Commonwealth-registered operatives, either, and they were carrying ready beamers.

Seven armed men and women spread out in a half-circle which covered the two arrivals. They moved with an efficiency Flinx did not like. As the second car arrived and began to disgorge its passengers, several members of the first group broke off to run up the ramp and disappear into the shuttle.

'Now listen . . .' Flinx began easily. One of the men in the group waved his beamer threateningly.

'I don't know who you are, but for now, shut up.'

Flinx complied readily, as Sylzenzuzex – frozen now with more than the cold – stood behind him and studied their captors.

Several minutes passed before the pair who had entered the shuttle re-emerged and shouted down to their companions: 'There's no one else aboard, and no weapons.'

'Good. Resume your positions.'

Flinx turned to the squat, middle-aged woman who had spoken. She was standing directly opposite him. She had the face of one who had seen too many things too soon and whose youth had been a time of blasted hopes and unfulfilled dreams. A vivid scar ran back from a corner of one eye in a jagged curve to her ear, then down the side of her neck to disappear beneath her high collar. Its livid whiteness was shocking against her dusky skin. She flaunted the scar like a favourite necklace. He noticed that her simple garb of work pants, boots, and high-necked overblouse had seen plenty of use.

Taking out a pocket communicator, she spoke into it: 'Javits says there's no one else on board and no weapons.' A mumble too soft and distant for Flinx to understand issued from the compact unit's speaker.

'No, instruments don't show any automatic senders aboard, either. Has the ship in orbit responded again?' Another pause, then. 'It looks like there's only the two of them.'

She flipped off the unit, stuck it back in her utility belt and regarded Flinx and Sylzenzuzex. 'Does anyone know you've come here?'

'You don't expect me to make it easy for you do you?' Flinx responded, to divert attention from Sylzenzuzex as well as to answer the query.

'Funny boy.' The woman took a deliberate step forward raised the beamer back over her left shoulder. Pip stirred and she suddenly became aware that the minidrag was not a decoration.

'I wouldn't do that,' Flinx told her softly. She eyed the snake.'

'Toxic?'

'Very.'

She didn't smile back. 'We can kill it and the both of you, you know.'

'Sure,' agreed Flinx pleasantly. 'But if you swing that beamer at me, then both Pip and I are going to go for your throat. If he doesn't kill you I probably will, no matter how fast this ring of happy faces moves. On the off chance we don't, then I'll be dead and your superior will be damned displeased at not having the chance to question me. Either way, you lose.'

Fortunately the woman wasn't the type to act without thinking. She stepped back, still keeping her beamer trained on him. 'Very funny boy,' she commented tightly. 'Maybe the Madam will let me have you after she's finished asking her questions. Act as smart as you like. You've got a short future.' She gestured sharply with the beamer. 'Both of you – into the first car.'

They walked between the beamers. Flinx tensed in readiness as he entered the large compartment, saw to his disappointment that two armed and equally tense people were awaiting him inside. No chance of jumping for the controls, then. He climbed in resignedly.

Sylzenzuzex followed him, having to squat uncomfortably on the bare floor because the car was equipped only with human seating, which would not accommodate her frame. Several of the armed guards followed. To Flinx's relief, the squat woman was not among them.

A low hum rose to a whine as the groundcar lifted. Staying a metre above ground, it moved towards the nearby buildings, the second car following close behind. As they came nearer, Flinx could see that the complex was built at the edge of the forest. In the distance he could just make out several additional structures hugging the mountainside, high up among the trees.

The cars pulled up before a steeply gabled five-storey building. They were escorted inside.

'The buildings here are all slants and angles,' Flinx commented to Sylzenzuzex as they made the short walk from car to entranceway. 'The trees already show that the snowfall here must be tremendous in winter. And this is the local equivalent of the tropics.'

'Tropics,' she snorted, her mandibles clacking angrily. 'I'm freezing already.' Her voice dropped. 'It probably doesn't make any difference, since we're likely to be killed soon. Or hasn't it dawned on you that we've stumbled on to a very large illegal installation of some kind?'

'The thought occurred to me,' he replied easily.

Taking a lift to the top floor, they came out into a corridor along which a few preoccupied men and women moved on various errands. They were not so absorbed that they failed to look startled at the appearance of Flinx and Sylzenzuzex.

The group made one turn to the left, continued almost to the end of a branch corridor, then stopped. Addressing the door pickup, the squat woman requested and received permission to enter. She disappeared inside, leaving the heavily guarded twosome to wait and think, before the door slid aside once again.

'Send 'em in.'

Someone gave Flinx a hard shove that sent him stumbling forward. Sylzenzuzex was introduced into the room with equal roughness.

They stood in a luxurious chamber. Pink-tinted panels revealed a rosy vista of lake and mountains, landing field and – Flinx noted with longing – their parked shuttlecraft. It seemed very far away now.

A small waterfall danced at one end of the room, surrounded by carpets that were more fur than fabric. Thick perfume scented the air, clutched cloyingly at his senses. Behind them the door slid silently shut.

There was another person in the room.

She was seated in a lounge chair near the transparent panels, and was clad in a light gown. Her long blonde hair was done up in a triple whirl, the three braids coiled one above each ear and the last at the back of her head. At the moment she was drinking something steaming from a taganou mug.

Scarface addressed her with deference. 'They're here, Madam Rudenuaman.'

'Thank you, Linda.' The woman turned to face them. Flinx sensed Sylzenzuzex's surprise.

'She's barely older than you or I,' she whispered.

128

Flinx said nothing, merely waited impassively and gazed back into olivine eyes. No, olivine wasn't right - gangrenous would be more appropriate. There was an icy murderousness behind those eyes which he sensed more strongly than the drifting perfume.

'Before I have you killed,' the young woman began in a pleasant liquid voice, 'I require answers to a few questions. Please keep in mind that you have no hope. The only thing you have any control over whatsoever is the manner of your death. It can be quick and efficient, depending on your willingness to answer my questions, or slow and tedious if you prove reluctant. Though not boring, I assure you . . .'

CHAPTER NINE

Flinx continued to study her as she took another sip of her steaming drink. She was almost beautiful, he couldn't help but notice - though any trace of softness was absent from her face.

Reaching to one side, she picked up an intricately carved cane. With this she was able to rise and limp over to examine them more closely. She favoured her left leg.

'I am Teleen auz Rudenuaman. You are . . . ?'

'My name's Flinx,' he responded readily, seeing no profit in angering this crippled bomb of a woman.

'Sylzenzuzex,' his companion added.

The woman nodded, turned and walked back to resume her seat, instructing them both to sit also. Flinx took a chair, noticing out of the corner of an eye that the scarred woman called Linda was watching his - and Pip's - every move from her position by the door. Sylzenzuzex folded herself on the fur floor nearby.

'Next question,' the woman Rudenuaman said. 'How did you get past the Church peaceforcer?'

'We . . .' he started to say, but stopped as he felt a delicate yet firm grip on his arm. Looking past the truhand, he saw

129

Sylzenzuzex eyeing him imploringly.

'I'm sorry, Syl, but I've got an aversion to torture. We're not going anywhere and for the moment, at least, I'd like to . . .' The truhand pulled away. He did not miss the look of utter contempt she threw him.

'Sensible as well as sassy,' Rudenuaman commented approvingly. 'I've been listening to you ever since you landed.' The brief flicker of a grin vanished and she repeated impatiently. 'The fortresses, how did you get past?'

Flinx indicated Sylzenzuzex. 'My friend,' he explained, ignoring the hollow mandibular laugh that flowed from her, 'is a padre-elect currently working in Church security. She talked the peaceforcer into letting us pass.'

Rudenuaman looked thoughtful. 'The circumvention was accomplished verbally, then?' Flinx nodded. 'We'll have to see if we can do something about that.'

'About a peaceforcer fortress?' Sylzenzuzex blurted. 'How can you modify – in fact, how did *you* succeed in passing them? What are you doing here, with this illegal installation? This is an edicted world. No one but the Church or those in the highest echelons of the Commonwealth government have the codes necessary to pass a peaceforcer station; certainly no private concern has that ability.'

The woman smiled. 'This private concern does.'

'Which concern is that?' Flinx asked. She turned her unfunny grin on him.

'For a condemned man you ask a lot of questions. However, I don't have the chance to brag very often. It's Nuaman Enterprises. Ever hear of it?'

'I have,' Flinx told her, thinking that this search for his parentage was making him a lot of rotten business contacts. 'It was founded by . . .'

'By my aunt's relatives,' she finished for him, 'and then further developed by my Aunt Rashalleila, may a foulness become her soul.' The smile widened. 'But I am in charge now. I felt a change of personnel at the uppermost executive position was in order.

'Unfortunately, the first time I tried replacing her I chose for my cohort a man of muscle and no brains. No, that's not accurate. Muscle and no loyalty. It cost me,' and she frowned in reminiscence, 'a bad time. But I managed to escape from the medical hell my aunt had me committed to. My second attempt was better planned – and successful.

'It is now Rudenuaman Enterprises, you see. Me.'

'No private concern has the wherewithal to circumvent a Church peaceforcer,' Sylzenzuzex insisted.

'Despite your security clearance, stiff one, you seem to cherish all kinds of foolish notions. Not only have we, with some help, I admit, circumvented them; but they remain in operation to warn off or destroy any visitors we do not clear.

'You can see why your sudden appearance caused me considerable initial worry. But I'm not worried any more – not since you proved so co-operative in following our landing instructions. Of course, you had no reason to expect a greeting from anyone other than a bunch of surprised Churchmen.'

'You have no right . . .' Sylzenzuzex began.

'Oh, please,' a disgusted Rudenuaman muttered. 'Linda . . .'

Scarface left her place at the door. Flinx held on tightly to Pip; this was no time or place to force a final confrontation. Not yet.

The squat woman kicked suddenly and Flinx heard the crack of chiton. Sylzenzuzex let out a high, shrill whistle as one foothand collapsed at the main joint. Reddish-green blood began to leak steadily as she fell on her side, clutching with truhands and her other foothand at the injured member.

Linda turned and resumed her position at the door as if nothing had happened.

'You know she has an open circulatory system,' Flinx muttered carefully. 'She'll bleed to death.'

'She would,' Rudenuaman corrected him, 'if Linda had cracked the leg itself instead of just breaking the joint. A thranx joint will coagulate. Her leg will heal, which is more than you can say for what mine did after my aunt's medical experimenters finished with it.' She tapped her own left leg with the cane. It rang hollowly. 'Other parts of me also had to be replaced, but they left the most important thing,' she indicated her head, 'intact. That was my aunt's last mistake.'

'I've only one more question for you.' She leaned forward, and for the first time since the interrogation began seemed genuinely interested. 'What on Terra possessed you to come here, to a world Under Edict, in the first place? And only two of you, unarmed.'

'It's funny,' Flinx told her, 'but . . . I also have a question that needs to be answered.'

Seeing that he was serious, she sat back in her chair. 'You're a peculiar individual. Almost as peculiar as you are stupid. What question?'

He was suddenly overwhelmed by a multitude of conflicting possibilities. One fact was clear – whether or not she could tell him what he wished to know, he and Sylzenzuzex would die. As the silence lengthened, even Sylzenzuzex became curious enough to forget the pain in her foothand momentarily.

'I can't tell you that,' he finally answered.

Rudenuaman looked at him askance. 'Now that's strange. You've told me everything else. Why hesitate at this?'

'I could tell you, but you'd never believe me.'

'I'm pretty credulous at times,' she countered. 'Try me, and if I find it intriguing, maybe I won't kill you after all.' The thought seemed to amuse her. 'Yes, tell me and I'll let you both live. We can always use unskilled labour here. And I am not surrounded by clever types. I may keep you around for novelty, for when I'm visiting here.'

'All right,' he decided, electing to accept her offer as the best they could hope for. 'I came hoping to find the truth of my birthright.'

Her amused expression vanished. 'You're right . . . I don't believe you. Unless you can do better than that . . .'

She was interrupted by a chime and looked irritably to the door. 'Linda . . .' There was a wait while the squat woman slid the door back and silently conversed with someone outside. Simultaneously something almost forgotten suddenly howled in Flinx's mind.

That was matched by a scream which everyone could hear.

'Challis,' an angry Rudenuaman yelled, 'can't you keep that brat quiet? Why you continue to drag her around with you is something I never . . .' She broke off, looking from the merchant who was standing in the half-open doorway goggling at Flinx, to the red-haired youth, and then back at the merchant again.

'Gu . . . wha . . . *you!*' Conda Challis finally managed to blurt, like a man clearing his throat of a choking bone.

'You know this man?' Rudenuaman asked Challis. A terrible fury was building in her, as it slowly became clear how Flinx had found this world. She was only partially correct, but it was the part she could believe. 'You *know* each other? Explain yourself, Challis!'

The merchant was completely out of control. 'He knows about the jewels,' he babbled. 'I wanted him to help me play with a jewel and he . . .'

Unwittingly, the merchant had revealed something Flinx half suspected. 'So, the Janus jewels come from here. That's very interesting, and it explains a great deal.' He looked down at Sylzenzuzex.

'Most obviously, Syl, it explains why anyone would go to the incredible expense and chance the enormous penalty involved in ignoring a Church edict.'

A miniature, silvery voice exploded. 'You colossal, obese idiot!' it half screamed, half bawled.

The already battered Challis looked down, shocked to see the ever-compliant Mahnahmi making horrible faces up at him. Flinx watched with interest. The merchant had finally done something dangerous enough to cause her to break her carefully maintained shell of innocence.

Rudenuaman looked on with equal curiosity, though her real attention and anger were still reserved for Challis. She was eyeing him almost pityingly.

'You are becoming a liability, Conda. I don't know why this man has come here, but I don't think it involves the jewels. Nor does it matter anymore that you've just given away the best-kept secret in the entire Commonwealth, because it will never leave this world – certainly not with either of these two.' She indicated Flinx and Sylzenzuzex.

'But he's been following me, haunting me!' Challis protested frantically. 'It has to have something to do with the jewels.'

Rudenuaman turned to Flinx. 'You've been following Challis? But why?'

The merchant yammered on, unaware he was providing confirmation of Flinx's earlier reply. 'Oh, some blithering insanity about his ancestry!' He didn't add, much to Flinx's dismay, whether he possessed any further information on

133

that particular obsession.

'Maybe I do believe you,' Rudenuaman said cautiously to Flinx. 'If it's an excuse, it's certainly a consistent one.'

Better get her off the subject of himself, Flinx decided. 'Where are the jewels mined? Up at that big complex on the mountainside?'

'You are amusing,' she said noncommittally. 'Yes, I may keep you alive for a while. It would be a change to have some mental stimulation.' She turned sternly to face the merchant. 'As for you, Conda, you have finally allowed your private perversions to interfere with business once too often. I had hoped . . .' She shrugged. 'The fewer who know about the jewels and where they originate, the better. But considering what is at stake here I think I have to risk finding another outside distributor.'

'Teleen, no,' Challis muttered, shaking his head violently. From an immensely wealthy, powerful merchant he had suddenly been reduced to a frightened, fat old man.

'And we'll have to do something about the whining brat-child, too,' she added, turning a venomous stare on the silently watching Mahnahmi. 'Linda . . . take them over to Riles. He can do what he wants with Challis, as long as it's reasonably quick. After all,' she added magnanimously, 'he was an associate of ours for a while. As for the little whiner, save her for after-dinner entertainment. We ought to be able to make her last a few days.'

'*No!*'

Flinx felt himself lifted in the grip of a mental shriek of outrage. A tremendous force ripped through the room, tearing rugs and furniture and people from their moorings and hurling them away from the doorway. Several of the thick pink polyplexalloy panels were blown out.

Flinx fought for control of his body, managed to come to a halt against a couch firmly anchored in the floor. Pip fluttered uneasily above his head, hissing angrily but unable to do more than hold his air in the face of the gale.

Hair flying, Flinx shielded his face with one hand and squinted into the hurricane.

Sylzenzuzex had been rolled skittering into a far corner. The guard, Linda, was lying unconscious nearby. She had been standing closest to the immense blast. Teleen auz Rudenuaman lay buried in a mass of thick fur rugs and broken fixtures, while the considerable bulk of Conda Challis hugged the fixed fur near the doorway and hung on for dear life as the wind pulled and tore at him.

'You fat imbecile!' the source of that pocket typhoon was screaming at him, stamping childishly at the floor. 'You pig's ass, you jelloid moron . . . you've gone and spoiled *everything*! Why couldn't you keep your dumb mouth shut? For years I've kept you from tripping over your own tongue, for years I've made the right decisions for you when you gleefully thought it was your doing! Now you've thrown it all away, all away!' She was crying, girlish tears running down her cheeks.

'Child of my own,' Challis gasped into the wind, 'get us out of this and – '

'*Child of my own!*' she spat down at him. 'I don't know the words yet to describe what you've thought of doing to me, or what you have done – not that it would matter to you. I can't save you any more, Daddy Challis.' She glared around the room.

'You can all go to your respective hells! I'm not afraid of any of you. But I need time to grow into myself. I don't know what I am, yet.'

She glared contemptuously back at Challis. 'You've ruined my chance to grow up rich and powerful. The Devil take you.'

Turning, she disappeared, running down the corridor. 'Some day,' a mental shout stabbed fadingly at Flinx, 'I'll even be strong enough to come back for *you*.'

The wind died slowly, in increments. Flinx was able to roll over in the falling breeze and feel of his bruises. He saw that Sylzenzuzex had succeeded in protecting her broken foothand. Her hard exoskeleton had saved her from any additional injury, so that while the first wounded, she actually was the least battered of anyone in the room. Except for Pip, of course, who settled unhurt but disturbed on Flinx's shoulder. Only the force of the wind had prevented him from killing Mahnahmi.

Teleen auz Rudenuaman was more shaken than she cared to admit. 'Linda . . . Linda!' The guard was just regaining consciousness. 'Alert the base, everyone. That child is to be killed instantly. She's an Adept.'

'Yes . . . Madam,' the woman replied thickly. Her right

135

cheek was bleeding and discoloured, and she was wincing painfully as she touched her left elbow.

Rudenuaman tried to sound confident. 'I don't care what kind of magic tricks she can pull. She's only a child and she can't go anywhere.'

As if in reply, minutes later a dull rumble reached them through the broken window panels. Rudenuaman limped hurriedly to the transparent wall. Flinx was also there, in time to see something that he, alone of those in the room, wasn't surprised at.

Their shuttlecraft – and all remaining hope of escape – was shrinking rapidly into the sky at the end of the landing strip, a vanishing dot between the mountaintops.

'She . . . she can pilot a shuttle,' a dazed Challis was mumbling to himself.

'Quiet, Conda. Anyone can direct a craft attuned to accept verbal commands. Still, alone, at her age . . .'

'She's been using me. Her, using *me*,' Challis continued, oblivious to everything around him. His eyes were glazed. 'All these years I thought she was such a charming, pretty little . . . and she's been using me!' The laughter began to fall.

'Will you *shut up*!' Rudenuaman finally had to scream. But the merchant ignored her, continued to roll around on the floor roaring hysterically at the wonderful, marvellous joke that had been played on him. He was still chuckling, albeit more unevenly, when two guards arrived to escort him out.

Flinx envied him. Now he would never feel the beamer when they executed him. Shake a man's world badly enough and the man comes apart, not the world. First the sudden sight of Flinx, here, and then Mahnahmi. No, not even all the King's horses and all the King's men could put Conda Challis together again.

Rudenuaman watched until the door closed and then collapsed, exhausted, on a battered couch – one of the few left undestroyed by Mahnahmi's uncontrolled infantile violence. She debated with herself, then finally said, 'It has to be done. Call Riles.'

'Yes, Madam,' Linda acknowledged.

Momentarily forgotten, Flinx and Sylzenzuzex rested and treated each other's wounds as best they could. Before long a tall, muscular man entered the room.

'I've been briefed,' he said sharply. 'How could this happen, Rudenuaman?'

Pip bridled and Flinx put a tight restraining grip on his pet. His own senses were quivering. Something he had sensed the moment they'd left the shuttle was intensified in this newcomer's presence.

'It could not be prevented,' Rudenuaman told him, her tone surprisingly meek. 'The child is apparently a psionic of unknown potentialities. She had fooled even her own father.'

'Not a difficult task, from what I am told of how Challis behaved. He will be more useful to us dead,' the tall figure said, swinging around to face Flinx and Sylzenzuzex. 'These are the two captives who penetrated the defences?'

'Yes.'

'See that they do not also escape, if you can,' the figure snapped. 'Though if the child escapes to tell of what she knows of this place, it will not matter what is done with these two. This entire deception is beginning to weary me . . . ' Then he reached up, grabbed his chin, and pulled his face off.

A gargled clicking came from Sylzenzuzex as the irritated not-man turned to leave the room. Flinx was shaken, too. He knew now what had been troubling him and his pet, since they had landed on this world. It wasn't just that the man turned out to be an AAnn – for that was a possibility he had suspected ever since he'd fished the image of Conda Challis and Ulru-Ujurr out of the reptilian infiltrator's mind back on Terra.

It was because he knew this particular AAnn.

But the Baron Riidi WW had never set eyes on Flinx, who had never strayed within range of the tridee pickup when the Baron had pursued him and the other on board Maxim Malaika's ship, so many months ago. Flinx, however, had seen all too much of that frigid, utterly self-possessed face, had heard too many threats pronounced by that smooth voice.

Riidi WW turned at the door, and for a moment Flinx feared the AAnn aristocrat had recognized him after all. But he'd paused only to speak to Rudenuaman again.

'You had best hope that the child does not escape, Teleen.'

Though no longer conveying the impression of total

137

omnipotence, the merchantwoman was far from being cowed. 'Don't threaten me, Baron. I have resources of my own. I could make it difficult for you if I were suddenly missed.'

'My dear Rudenuaman,' he objected, 'I was not threatening you. I would not . . . you have been too valuable to us – both you and your aunt before you. I would not have any other human holding the Commonwealth end of this relationship. But if the child gets away, then by-the-sand-that-shelters-life this entire operation will have to be closed down. If a follow-up party from the Church were to discover this base and find that it is being partially funded and operated by the imperial race, that could serve as a pretext for war. While not afraid, the Empire would prefer not to engage in hostilities just now. We would be forced to destroy the mine and obliterate all trace of this installation.'

'But it would take years to replace this,' she pointed out.

'Several, at least,' the Baron concurred. 'And that is but an optimistic estimate. Suppose the Church should elect to patrol this system with crewed fortresses instead of gullible automatons? We could never come back.'

'I was right,' Sylzenzuzex declared with satisfaction. 'No private concern *does* have sufficient resources to bypass a Church peaceforcer station. Only another spatial government like the Empire could manage it.'

The Baron gave her an AAnn salute that suggested she had just won a Pyrrhic victory. 'That is quite so, young lady. Neither would the Empire be concerned, as a private corporation might be, that your Church has placed this world Under Edict. What does concern us is that it lies within Commonwealth territory. Our danger in discovery lies in the diplomatic consequences, not in some imaginary devil someone in your hierarchy places here.'

'You haven't found anything on this world to justify its quarantine?' Flinx asked, curiosity drowning his caution.

'Nothing, my young friend,' the tall AAnn replied 'It is wet and cold, but otherwise most hospitable.'

Flinx eyed the Baron closely, trying to penetrate that calculating mind, without success. His erratic talent refused to co-operate. 'You're chancing an interstellar war just to make some credit?'

'What's wrong with money? The Empire thrives on it, as

138

does your Commonwealth. Who knows,' the Baron said, smiling. 'it may be that my hand in this is concealed from my own government. What the *arkazy* does not see in the sand will not bite him, *vya-nar*?

'Now you must excuse me, for we have a runaway infant who requires scolding.' He vanished through the doorway.

Flinx had dozens of questions he could have thrown at the AAnn aristocrat. However, while the Baron had not given any sign of recognition when replying to the single question, the danger remained that in an extended conversation Flinx might let some unthinking familiarity slip. If the AAnn ever suspected that Flinx had been among those who had cheated him and the Empire of the Krang, those several months ago, he would vivisect the youth with infinite slowness. Better not take a chance.

They stayed there waiting while Teleen recomposed herself from both the ordeal of Mahnahmi's escape and from the trauma of confronting the angry Baron. Flinx watched from a broken window as a distant, concealed elevator lifted two big military shuttles from the ground beneath the landing strip. A single groundcar, no doubt containing Riidi WW, pulled up alongside one of the shuttles and several figures hurried from it to the waiting ships.

Once the groundcar had moved out of the way, the two shuttles thundered into the heavens, where they would likely rendezvous with at least one waiting AAnn naval vessel. Mahnahmi had had a good start, but Flinx knew his rented craft could never outrun even a small military ship. However, the girl's mind was like a runaway reactor: there was no telling what she was capable of under sufficient stress. The Baron, he decided, had better watch out for himself.

Turning from the window. Flinx conversed in low tones with Sylzenzuzex. Both tried to come up with reasons for the AAnn's presence here. She no more believed the Baron's casual disclaimer that he was on this world for mere profit than he did. The AAnn had been the Commonwealth's prime enemies since its inception. They never ceased searching, guardedly yet relentlessly, for a new way to hasten its destruction and hurry what they believed was their destiny to rule the cosmos and its 'lesser' races.

There had to be a deeper reason involving those unique

Janus jewels, though neither of them could think of a viable theory.

On Tharce IV lived a woman called Amasar, who was widely celebrated for her wisdom. At the moment, however, she adopted an air of drunken ecstasy as she revelled in the beauty of the object she held.

Adored by her constituents and respected by opponents, she had been the permanent representative from the Northern Hemisphere of Tharce IV to the Commonwealth Council for two decades. Her mind never rested in its search for solutions to problems or answers to questions, and she worked hours that embarrassed colleagues and assistants half her age. Currently she held the post of Counsellor Second in charge of Diplomatic Theory on the Council itself. As such she was in a position to influence strongly the direction of Commonwealth foreign policy.

She should have been studying the transcript of the up-coming agenda, but her mind was occupied instead with the magnificence dwelling in the object in her hand. Besides, on the majority of questions that would come to a vote in the Council her mind was already made up. As a respected counsellor, her advice would be a powerful influence.

Yes on this issue, nay on that one, leaning so and so on this proposal, not to withdraw on this matter, not to yield on that particular point – it was a long list.

Her mind focused elsewhere, Amasar switched off the viewer, which had been running blankly for several moments. Leaning back in her chair, she continued to stare raptly at the shining irregularity of the object on her desk.

Tomorrow she would board ship for the annual Council meeting. The gathering place varied between the dual Commonwealth capitals of Terra and Hivehom. This year the thranx capital world was to be the site. This promised to be an absorbing, stimulating session, one she was looking forward to. Several issues of vital importance were due to come to a vote, including measures involving those sly murderers, the AAnn. The Council had some who believed in moderation and appeasement of the reptiles, but not her!

But why worry about such things now? Moving as if in a dream, she opened the centre drawer of her desk to perform a final check. Everything was there: diplomatic credentials, *reservation confirmations, documentation and information tapes. Yes, it should be an interesting session this year.*

She was still aglow with pleasure as she reached into the lowermost drawer on her right, took out the small, lightweight needler, and fried that insidiously seductive thing before blowing out her brains!

The apparent suicide was recorded by the local coroner and confirmed by Commonwealth officials as another of those inexplicable occurrences that periodically afflict even the stablest of human beings. Anything could have been the cause. Too little confidence, too little money, too little affection . . .

Or too much of an especially lethal kind of beauty.

'A remarkable infant,' Teleen auz Rudenuaman finally said, interrupting their talk, She eyed them, and commented, 'This appears to be a day for unusual infants.' When her captives remained sullenly silent, she shrugged and looked out the panels again. 'I knew there was a reason for hating that brat so strongly. I admit, though, that she had me completely fooled. I wonder how long she'd been manipulating Challis to suit her own ends?'

'According to what she said, all her conscious life.' Flinx thought it a good idea to keep the merchantwoman's attention focused elsewhere. 'Are you going to kill us now?' he asked with disarming matter-of-factness, 'or have you decided to believe me?'

'My having you killed has nothing to do with your story, Flinx,' she explained, 'though Challis seems to have confirmed it. I have plenty of time to get rid of you. I still find you a novelty,' She gazed appraisingly at him. 'You're a bundle of interesting contradictions, and hard to pin down. I'm not sure I like that. I tend to get frustrated with something I don't understand. That's dangerous, because I might end up killing you on a whim, and that would only frustrate me more, since you'd die with all the answers.

'No, I think I'll wait for the Baron to return before doing anything irreversible with you two.' She showed white teeth. 'The AAnn are very adept at clearing up contradictions.'

Sylzenzuzex climbed to her trulegs and tested her injured limb. She would be forced to limp along on three supports until it healed. She glared at the merchantwoman – compound eyes being especially good for glaring.

'To work so with the sworn enemies of humanx-kind.'

Rudenuaman was not impressed. 'So much outrage over a little money.' She looked reprovingly at the thranx. 'The AAnn have given me exclusive rights to distribute the Janus jewel within the Commonwealth. In return I permit them to take a certain percentage of the production here. I supply much of the means for the mining, and they neutralized the peaceforcers.

'I've made Nuaman, now Rudenuaman, Enterprises stronger than it has ever been, stronger than it was under my aunt. We have discovered only the one pocket of jewels, which appear to be an isolated mineralogical mutation. In five to ten years we will have taken the last jewel out of that mountain. Then we will depart from here voluntarily, with the Church none the wiser and the Commonwealth hurt not at all. By that time Rudenuaman Enterprises will be in an invincible financial position. And my aunt, may she rot in limbo, would have approved. I think – '

'*I* think you're blinding yourself,' Flinx put in, 'voluntarily. There's a great deal more in this as far as the Empire is concerned than a little petty cash.'

Rudenuaman eyed him curiously. 'What gives you the right to say something like that?'

'I was at the Church administrative headquarters before we came here. During that time an AAnn in surgical disguise – similar to but rather more elaborate than what the Baron was wearing – tried to sneak into the command centre there. After he killed himself I found crystalline dust scattered all over his middle. It could have come from a pulverized Janus jewel.'

'But the crystal syringe-darts he was carrying . . .' Sylzenzuzex started to remind him.

'. . . could have been manufactured from flawed Janus jewels themselves,' he told her. 'Did you stop to think of that? Wouldn't it make a marvellous cover?' He turned to look at her. 'I don't think that infiltrator killed himself to keep from being questioned. You can't break an AAnn. I think the explosion was to destroy what he was carrying – a Janus jewel.'

'But what for?' she wondered. 'To bribe someone?'

'I don't think so . . . but I'm not sure. Not yet.'

'As if I cared what happens to the Church,' Rudenuaman added in disgust.

Sylzenzuzex responded with great dignity. 'The Church is all that stands between civilization and barbarism.'

'Now would the Commonwealth representatives like that, my dear? They appear to consider themselves the guardians of humanx accomplishment.'

'The Commonwealth stands only because it's backed by the incorruptible standards of the United Church.'

'There is someone I'd like to meet,' the merchantwoman quipped, shifting on her couch. 'An incorruptible.'

'Me too,' admitted Flinx.

Sylzenzuzex spun on him. 'Whose side are you on, anyway, Flinx?' The fine hairs rose on the back of her b-thorax.

'I don't know,' he replied feelingly. 'I haven't studied all the sides carefully enough yet.'

'Would you like to see the mine?' Teleen asked suddenly.

'Very much,' he admitted, Sylzenzuzex looked indifferent, but he could sense her interest.

'Very well,' the merchantwoman decided, apparently on impulse. 'Linda . . .'

'Groundcar, Madam – and guards?'

'Just a driver and one other.'

The squat bodyguard looked uncertain. 'Madam, do you think that . . . ?'

Rudenuaman waved her objections aside. She was in the mood to wipe away the distressing events of the afternoon. Boasting and showing off would be excellent therapy. 'You worry too much, Linda. Where can they go? Their shuttle has been stolen, the Baron has taken our craft, and this world grows progressively more inhospitable no matter which way one travels. They're not about to run away.'

'Right,' Flinx agreed. 'Besides, my companion has an injured limb.'

'Why should that matter to you?' Sylzenzuzex sneered.

He turned on her angrily. 'Because despite everything that's happened, and I regret much of it, I do care what happens to you – whether you want to believe it or not!'

Sylzenzuzex stared at his back as he spun away from her, jamming his hands into his jumpsuit pockets. Security schematics, archeologic chronophysics – all appeared simple alongside this impenetrable young human. It would not have comforted her, perhaps, to know that her opinion of him was shared in varying degrees by the other two women in the room.

No doubt Flinx would have been easier to understand if he had understood himself . . .

CHAPTER TEN

The groundcar whined smoothly, well tuned as it was, as it climbed a sloping path covered with a low growth resembling heather. Flinx leaned back and stared through the transparent roof. Just beyond the mine buildings, the mountain became nearly vertical, soaring another 2500 metres above the lake.

At the moment neither the incredible scenery, not their present dim prospects, nor Sylzenzuzex's occasional whistling moans of pain held his attention. Instead, his mind was on that stolen tape which might contain the early part of his life. And in his mind, the tape was still inextricably linked with Conda Challis, who would run from him no longer.

Flinx had already seen the sumptuous living quarters/ office occupied by Teleen auz Rudenuaman. No doubt Challis possessed a similar if less extensive chamber somewhere in the complex behind them . . . probably in the very same building. Eventually Challis's rooms would be cleaned out, his effects disposed of so that the space could be put to new uses. But for now it was doubtless sealed and undisturbed – including that tape, so tantalizingly near.

If this unpredictable young woman could be persuaded to keep them alive a while yet, he might still have the chance to see what was on that stolen spool. Though if she knew how desperately he wanted it, she might just slowly unwind it in a dish of acid before his eyes.

It was a measure of her megalomania, or confidence, that

144

she had ordered Challis killed. Someone would have to go to considerable lengths to cover up his disa, pearance – not that his company subordinates would object. Rudenuaman's agents should have no trouble locating several survivors who would be eager to take over the reins of power unquestioningly. Besides, Challis's private activities were of such a nature as to discourage close investigation. A man engaged in such distasteful hobbies could come to any number of sudden, unexpected ends.

Flinx wondered if the merchant's mind were still functional enough for him to regret the simple manner of his passing. No doubt he had conceived an eventual demise of grandiose depravity for himself.

The groundcar came to a halt level with the lowest part of the sheer-sided, gleaming metal buildings. These were constructed on a more or less flat area that had been gouged in the flank of the mountain. Suspended at a higher elevation, a series of square metal arches punctured the rock walls like silvery hypodermics sucking blood from a whale. From within the structure, clear mountain air carried to the arrivals the steady *ca-rank*, *ca-rank* of tireless machinery.

A guard who may or may not have been as human as he looked saluted casually as they entered the structure. 'The exterior building we are now in,' Rudenuaman was explaining, 'houses all our milling and processing facilities.' She waved constantly as they made their way through the building. 'This installation has cost an incredible amount of credit . . . a tiny drop when compared to the profit which we will eventually realize.'

'I still don't see why the AAnn need you so badly,' Flinx told her, his eyes taking in everything on the principle that knowledge is freedom. 'Particularly since they're the ones responsible for negating the peaceforcer fortresses.'

'I thought I'd already made that clear,' she said. 'First, the Commonwealth is a far larger market for the gems than the Empire. They have no way to market their share except through a human agent . . . me. But more important, as the Baron explained, this world lies within Commonwealth boundaries. Though comparatively isolated, there are a number of other busy, inhabited Commonwealth planets plus numerous automatic monitoring stations between here and the nearest populated Empire world. AAnn technicians require safe conduct, which Rudenuaman company ships provide.'

Flinx, thinking suddenly of the Baron's pursuit of Mahnahmi, asked. 'Then there are no Imperial military vessels in this region?'

Rudenuaman looked surprised at Flinx's naïveté. 'Do you take the Baron for a fool? It would only take the discovery of one such ship and this quadrant of space would be swarming with Commonwealth warships. The Baron,' she informed them smugly, 'is far more subtle than the AAnn are normally given credit for.'

So subtle, Flinx thought with mixed feelings, that he might have outfoxed himself. If he were chasing Mahnahmi in a freighter instead of in a destroyer or frigate, she might elude him after all. Not that he was certain he wanted that precocious talent to escape; but at least a merry chase might prolong the Baron's absence from Ulru-Ujurr for some time.

They had to resolve the situation before that happened and the Baron returned. Novelty value or no, Flinx did not think the AAnn aristocrat would tolerate his and Sylzenzuzex's continued existence. If it came to a confrontation between Flinx and Rudenuaman, she would have him and Sylzenzuzex executed without a thought in order to keep her associate placated.

Though Rudenuaman might be swayed by flattery and amusement, Flinx had no illusions about his ability to so manipulate the Baron, 'Teleen,' he began absently, 'have you ever . . .'

She turned angrily on him, voice chill and expression dark. 'Don't ever call me that or you'll die a lot quicker than otherwise. You will address me as Madam or Madam Rudenuaman, or the next way you will amuse me is with your noise as I have the skin stripped from your back.'

'Sorry . . . Madam,' he apologized carefully. 'You still insist that the AAnn's only interest in the Janus jewels is financial?' He was aware of Sylzenzuzex watching him.

'You continue to bring that up. Yes, of course I do.'

'Tell me – have you ever seen an AAnn, the Baron for example, utilize a headset linkage to create particle-plays within one of the crystals?'

'No.' She didn't appear to be disturbed by the thought.

'This is a mining outpost. There are no hedonists or idlers here.'

'Do you have a headset link here?'

'Yes.'

'And Challis . . . I presume he did, also? Colloid plays seemed to have been one of his favourite obsessions.'

'Yes, though not the only one,' she said, her mouth wrinkling in distaste.

'What about the Baron? Surely he enjoys the gems?'

'Baron Riidi WW,' she announced with confidence, 'is all business and military-minded. I have on occasion seen him relaxing at various AAnn recreations, but never with a Janus jewel.'

'What about the other AAnn of importance and rank here?'

'No, they're all fully absorbed in their assignments. Why so curious to know if I've ever seen one of the reptiles using a gem?'

'Because,' Flinx said thoughtfully. 'I don't think they can. I don't know what the Baron does with the jewels which are consigned for supposed sale within the Empire, but I'm certain they're not provided for the amusement of wealthy AAnn. Possibly for bribery purposes within the Commonwealth – I haven't worked that out yet.

'The AAnn mind is different from that of human or thranx,' he went on. 'Not necessarily inferior – probably superior in some ways – but different. I've read a little about it, and I don't believe that their brains produce the proper impulses for operating a Janus jewel linkage. They could scramble the colloidal suspension, but never organize it into anything recognizable.'

'Really,' Rudenuaman murmured at the conclusion of his little lecture. 'What makes you an expert on such matters?'

'I have big ears,' Flinx replied. Better she continued to consider him a wild guesser than a calculating thinker.

'All right, suppose they can't operate the jewels the way we can.' She shrugged indifferently. 'The beauty of the gem is still unsurpassed.'

'That's so,' he conceded, 'but to the point of justifying this kind of risky invasion of Commonwealth territory? I'm damned if I think the AAnn love beauty that much. Somehow those jewels are being used against the Commonwealth, against humanx-kind.'

Rudenuaman didn't reply, choosing to ignore what she couldn't refute. They had walked deep into the higher levels of the building. A tall AAnn approached them, his surgical disguise perfect – except now Flinx knew what it concealed and was able to recognize the reptilian beneath.

'That's Meevo FFGW,' Rudenuaman informed them, confirming Flinx's guess. 'He is the AAnn - second in command and the Baron's assistant. He's also an excellent engineer, in charge of the overall mining operation here.' She glared confidently at Flinx. 'I've thought a little about your accusations, and you know what I've decided?' She smiled. 'I don't give a god-damn what the AAnn do to the Commonwealth with their share of the jewels, as long as it doesn't interfere with my business.'

'That's about what I thought you might say.' Sylzenzu-zex's voice carried contempt in a way only the sharply clipped tones of a thranx can. Flinx thought it idiotic to antagonize their mecurial host, but she appeared unper-turbed. If anything, she was pleased to see one of her captives so upset.

'Isn't it nice to have one's thoughts confirmed?' She faced the newcomer. 'Greetings, Meevo.'

Flinx used the opportunity to study the reptilian's make-up in detail. Were a Rudenuaman ship to be stopped by Commonwealth inspectors, he doubted that any casual observer could penetrate the carefully drafted disguise.

If one knew to look closely, though, the eyes were a dead giveaway. For Meevo FFGW, like the Baron, like all AAnn, had a double eyelid. A blink would reveal the mind behind such eyes as not human.

'These are the ones who succeeded in passing the adjusted fortresses?' the AAnn lieutenant asked, glancing from Sylzenzuzex to Flinx.

'Just the two of them, yes,' Rudenuaman told him.

Meevo appeared amiably curious. 'Then why are they still alive?'

Sylzenzuzex shivered again, this time at the utterly inhumanx indifference in that voice.

'They keep me amused for now. And when the Baron returns he may have some questions of his own for them.

148

The Baron's a more efficient interrogator than I. I tend to be impatient.'

A low reptilian chuckle came from the engineer. 'I heard about the child. Most unfortunate, irritating. There is no need to worry, though. The Baron will finish her before she can contact outsiders. His efficiency extends to other areas besides questioning.' He grinned, showing false human teeth set into an elongated false human jaw. At the back of the open mouth Flinx could just make out the gleam of real, far sharper teeth.

'You find them amusing . . . curious,' the engineer concluded, with a gesture Flinx was unable to interpret. His attitude suggested that casual amusement was as alien to him as bearing living young.

Curiosity, however, was a trait the AAnn did share with their enemies. Meevo tagged along as Rudenuaman led them through the remainder of the complex.

'The milling and separation you saw downstairs. Polishing and removal of surface impurities takes place over there.' She indicated a series of doorless chambers from which musical sounds emerged.

'Are they all AAnn here except you and your bodyguard?' Sylzenzuzex wondered sardonically.

'Oh, no. We're about half and half here. There are a surprising number of talented humanx in our loving society for whom the everyday problems of living have proven too much. They've been driven by insensitive authority to seek marginally reputable work. Existence overrides any qualms they hold about such intangibles as interspecies loyalty.'

'I'll venture none of them ever gets off this world alive.'

Rudenuaman appeared genuinely surprised, 'Ridiculous woman . . . that would be bad for business. Oh, I don't mean *we* inspire their loyalty. For most of those who work here that term no longer has meaning, or they wouldn't be here in the first place. Any of them would gladly sell their knowledge of this illegal installation the moment they were discharged.

'We employ, with their knowledge and consent, a selective mind-wipe which clears their brains of all memories of their stay here. It leaves them with the vaguely uncomfortable feeling that they've undergone a long period of unconscious-

149

ness. That and their newly fat bank accounts ensure they will not give away our presence here.'

'Mind-wipe,' a stunned Sylzenzuzex muttered, 'is forbidden for use by anyone other than Commonwealth or Church high physicians, and then only in emergency circumstances!'

Rudenuaman grinned. 'You must remember to add that to your report.'

They entered a large chamber. and the temperature dropped noticeably. 'We'll be going into the main shaft,' she explained, indicating long racks of bulky overclothing hanging nearby. Sylzenzuzex saw that a number of them were designed for thranx.

'Did you think that your precious cousins were immune to the lure of credit?' Rudenuaman taunted her. 'No species has a corner on greed, child.'

'Don't call me a child,' Sylzenzuzex countered softly.

Rudenuaman's response was not what Flinx expected – the first real laugh they had heard from her. She leaned on her cane, chuckling. Curious workers turned to glance at them as they passed.

'I'll call you dead, if you prefer,' the merchantwoman finally declared, She pointed towards the long racks of overclothing. 'Now put one of those on – it's quite cold inside the mountain.'

After donning the protective outer garments, they followed her and the AAnn engineer down a wide rectangular avenue. Metal soon gave way to bare rock. Evenly spaced single-span duralloy arches helped support the roof.

Flinx's thermal suit was partly open, permitting a small reptilian head to peep out from within, eyes unblinking as it surveyed the chill surroundings. Double rows of brightly glowing light tubes cast a steady radiance throughout the tunnel.

'This section has already been played out,' Rudenuaman explained. 'The jewels lie in a vein running horizontally into the mountain.'

They slowed.

'There are several additional subsidiary shafts, running the length of lesser veins. Some run slightly above, others below our present position. I'm told that the gems formed in occasional pockets in the volcanic rock which were once filled with gas. An unusual combination of pressure and heat produced the Janus jewels.

'The gemstones themselves lie in a different sort of material from the mountain, like diamonds in the kimberlite of Terra and the Bronine rainbow craters which are mined on Evoria. That's what my engineers tell me, anyhow.'

Ignoring her possessive reference to him, Meevo made a curt gesture of acknowledgement. 'It is so. Similar examples of isolated gem formation lie within the Empire, though nothing so unusual as this.'

Something tickled Flinx's brain, and he found himself staring down into the dim recesses of the shaft. 'Someone's coming towards us,' he announced finally.

Rudenuaman turned to look, commented idly, 'Just a few of the natives. They're primitive types, but intelligent enough to make good menial workers. They have no tools, no civilization, and no language beyond a few grunts and imitated human words. They don't even wear minimal clothing. Their sole claim to rudimentary intelligence appears to be in the simple modifications they make in their cave-homes – rolling boulders in front to make a smaller entrance, digging deeper into the hillside, and so on. They do the heavy manual work for us, and they're careful with the jewels they uncover.

'We've simplified the drilling equipment for their use. Their fur is thick enough so that the cold inside the mountain doesn't seem to bother them, which is fortunate for us. Even with thermal suits it would be hard for humans and impossible for AAnn to work the gem deposits any more, considering how deep the shaft now runs into the mountain. If they mind the cold, they seem willing to risk it for the rewards we give them in return for each stone.'

'What do you reward them with?' Flinx wondered curiously. The bulky shapes were still coming slowly towards them. The hair on the back of his neck prickled and Pip stirred violently within the folds of the warm suit.

'Berries,' Meevo snapped in disgust. 'Berries and fruits, nuts and tubers. Root eaters!' he finished, with the disdain characteristic of all carnivores.

'They're vegetarians, then?'

'Not entirely,' Rudenuaman corrected. 'They're apparently quite able to digest meat, and they have the teeth and claws necessary for hunting, but they much prefer the fruits and berries our automatic harvester can gather for them.'

'Dirt grubbers,' the AAnn engineer muttered. He glanced at Rudenuaman. 'Excuse me from your play, but I have work to do.' He turned and lumbered back up the shaft.

By this time the four natives had come near enough for Flinx to discern individual characteristics. Each was larger than a big man and two or three times as broad – almost fat. How much of that bulk was composed of incredibly dense brown fur marked with black and white splotches he couldn't tell. In build and general appearance they were essentially ursinoid, though sporting a flat muzzle instead of a snout. It ended in a nearly invisible black nose that was almost comical on so massive a creature.

Short thick claws tipped the end of each of four seven-digited members, and the creatures appeared capable of moving on all fours or standing upright with equal ease. There was no tail. Ears were short, rounded, and set on top of the head. By far the most distinctive features were the tarsier-like eyes, large as plates, which glowed amber in the tunnel's fluorescent light. Huge black pupils like obsidian yolks floated in their centres.

'Nocturnal from the look of them, diurnal at the least,' was Sylzenzuzex's intrigued comment.

The natives noticed the new arrivals, and all rose on to their hind legs for a better look. When they stood upright they seemed to fill the whole tunnel. Flinx noted a slight curve at the back of their mouths, which formed a falsely comic, dolphinish grin on each massive face.

He was about to ask another question of Rudenuaman when something stirred violently within his suit-top. Flinx's frantic grab was too late to restrain Pip. The flying snake was out and streaking down the shaft towards the natives.

'Pip . . . wait, there's no . . . !'

He had started to say there was no reason to attack the furry giants. Nothing fearful or threatening had scratched his sensitive mind. If the minidrag were to set the group of huge natives on a rampage, it was doubtful any of them would get out of this tunnel alive.

Ignoring his master's call, Pip reached the nearest of the

152

creatures. On its hind legs, the enormous animal was nearly three metres tall and must have weighed at least half a ton. Great glowing eyes regarded the tiny apparition, whose venom was nearly always fatal.

Pip dived straight for the head. At the last second pleated wings beat the air as the minidrag braked – to land and curl lightly about the creature's shoulder. The monster eyed the minidrag dispassionately, then turned its dull gaze on Flinx, who gaped back at the giant in shock.

For the second time in his life, Flinx fainted . . .

The dream was new and very deep. He was floating in the middle of an endless black lake beneath an oppressively near night sky. So dark was it that he could see nothing, not even his own body . . . which might not have been there.

Against the ebony heavens four bright lights drifted. Tiny, dancing pinpoints of unwinking gold moved in unpredictable yet calculated patterns, like fireflies. They danced and jigged, darted and twitched not far from the eyes he didn't have, yet he saw them plainly.

Sometimes they danced about each other, and once all four of them performed some intricate weaving in and out, as complex and meaningful as it was quickly forgotten.

'He's back now,' the first firefly observed.

'Yes, he's back,' two of the others agreed simultaneously.

Flinx noted with interest that the last of the four fireflies was not the steady, unwavering light he had first thought. Unlike the others, it winked on and off erratically, like a lamp running on fluctuating current. When it winked off it disappeared completely, and when it was on it blazed brighter than any of the others.

'Did we frighten you?' the winker wondered.

A disembodied voice strangely like his own replied. 'I saw Pip . . .' the dream-voice started to say.

'I'm sorry we shouted at you,' the first firefly apologized.

'Sorry we shouted,' the other two chorused. 'We didn't mean to hurt you. We didn't mean to frighten you.'

'I saw Pip,' Flinx mused, 'settle around one of the native's shoulders. I've never ever seen Pip do that to a stranger before. Not to Mother Mastiff, not to Truzenzuzex, not to anyone.'

'Pip?' the third voice inquired.

'Oh,' the second firefly explained, 'he means the little hard mind.'

'Hard but tasty,' agreed the first one, 'like a *chunut*.'

'You thought the little hard mind meant to hurt us?' first voice asked.

'Yes, but instead he responded to you with an openness I've never seen before. So you must also broadcast on the emphatic level, only your thoughts are friendly thoughts.'

'If you say we must,' third firefly elucidated, 'then we must.'

'But only when we must,' fourth voice said sternly, blazing brighter than the other three before vanishing.

'Why does the fourth among you come and go like a fog?' Flinx's dream-voice murmured.

'Fourth? Oh,' first voice explained, 'that's Maybeso. That's his name – for this weektime, anyway. I am called Fluff.' Flinx got the impression the other two lights brightened slightly. 'These are Moam and Bluebright.' The fourth light blazed momentarily.

'They're mates,' it said, and then winked out once more.

'Gone again,' Flinx observed with disembodied detachment.

'That's Maybeso, remember?' reminded Fluff-voice. 'Sometimes he's not here. The rest of us are always here. We don't change our names, either, but Maybeso comes and goes and changes his name every weektime or so.'

'Where does Maybeso go when he goes?'

Bluebright replied openly, 'We don't know.'

'Where does he come from when he comes back, then?'

'Nobody knows,' Moam told him.

'Why does he change his name from weektime to weektime?'

'Ask him,' Moam and Bluebright suggested together.

Maybeso came back, his light brighter than any of theirs.

'Why do you change your name from weektime to weektime, and where do you go when you go, and where do you come from when you come back?' Flinx-voice wondered.

'Oh, there's no doubt about it,' Maybeso told him in a dream-singsong, and winked away again.

Fluff spoke in a confidential dream-whisper: 'Maybeso, we think, is a little mad. But he's a good fellow all the same.'

Flinx noted absently that he was beginning to sink beneath the surface of the black lake. Above him the four lights swirled and dipped curiously.

'You're the first who's talked to us,' Fluff-voice murmured.

'Come and talk to us more,' Moam requested with pleasure. 'It's fun to have someone to talk to. The little hard one listens but cannot talk. This is a fun new thing!'

Flinx's dream-voice bubbled up through the deepening oily liquid. 'Where should I come and talk to you?'

'At the end of the long water,' Moam told him.

'At the end of the long water,' confirmed Bluebright.

'At the far end of the long water,' added Fluff, who was rather more precise than the others.

'No doubt about it,' agreed Maybeso, winking on for barely a second.

About it, about it . . . the words were subsumed in gentle rippling currents produced by Flinx's slowly sinking body. Sinking, sinking, until he touched the bottom of the lake. His legs touched first, then his hips, then back, and finally his head.

There was something peculiar about this place, he thought. The sky had been blacker than the water, and the water grew lighter instead of darker as he sank. At the bottom it was so bright it hurt his eyes.

He opened them.

A glistening, almost metallic blue-green face dominated by two faceted gems was staring down at him with concern. Inhaling, he smelled coconut oil and orchids. Something tickled his left ear.

Looking for the source, he discovered Pip's small reptilian face lying on his chest. A long pointed tongue darted out and hit him several times on the cheek. Apparently satisfied as to his master's condition, the minidrag relaxed and slid off the pillow to coil itself comfortably nearby.

Pillow?

Taking a deep breath, Flinx smiled up at Sylzenzuzex. She backed away and he saw that they were in a small, neatly furnished room. Sunlight poured in through high windows.

'How are you feeling?' she inquired in the sharp clicks and whistles of symbospeech. He nodded and watched her slump gratefully on to a thranx sleeping-sitting platform

155

across the room.

'Thank the Hive. I thought you were dead.'

Flinx rested his head on a supporting hand. 'I didn't think that mattered much to you.'

'Oh, shut up!' she snapped with unexpected vehemence. He detected confusion and frustration in her voice as feelings and fact vied within her. 'There have been plenty of times when I would have cheerfully cut your throat, if I hadn't been under oath to protect it. Then there have been an equal number of other occasions when I almost wished you didn't wear your skeleton outside in.

'Like the time back on Terra when you saved my life, and the way you've stood up to that barbaric young female.' Flinx saw her antennae flicking nervously, the graceful curve of her ovipositors tightening uncertainly. 'You are the most maddening being I have ever met, Flinx-man!'

He sat up carefully, found that everything worked inside as well as out. 'What happened?' he asked, confused. 'No, wait . . . I do remember blacking out, but not why. Did something hit me?'

'Nobody laid a parcel hook on you. You collapsed when your pet charged one of the native workers. Fortunately, that manoeuvre seems to have been just a bluff. The native didn't know enough to be frightened.' Her expression turned puzzled. 'But why should that make you faint?'

'I don't know,' he answered evasively. 'Probably the shock of visualizing the rest of the natives rending us into pieces after Pip killed one of their number. When he didn't, the shock was magnified because Pip just doesn't take to strangers that way.' Flinx forced himself to appear indifferent. 'So Pip likes natural fur better than a thermal suit, and he snuggled down in one of the natives. That's probably what happened.'

'What does that prove?' Sylzenzuzex wondered.

'That I faint too easily.' Swinging his legs off the bed, he gave her a grim look. 'At least now we know why this world's Under Edict.'

'*Shhh!*' She nearly fell off her sleeping platform. 'Why . . . no, wait,' she admonished him. Several minutes passed during which she made a thorough inspection of the room, checking places Flinx would never have thought to inspect.

'It's clean,' she finally announced with satisfaction. 'I

expect they don't think we have anything to say that's worth listening to.'

'You're certain?' Flinx asked, abashed. 'I never thought of that.'

Sylzenzuzex looked offended. 'I told you I was training in Security. No, there is nothing in here to listen to you save me.'

'Okay, the reason this world has been placed Under Edict by the Church met us in the tunnel today. It's the natives . . . Rudenuaman's grunting, goblin-eyed manual labourers. They're the reason.'

She continued to stare at him for another minute, considered laughing, thought better of it when she saw how serious he was.

'Impossible,' she muttered finally. 'You have experienced a delusion of some sort. Surely the natives are nothing more than they appear to be – big, amiable, and dumb. They have not yet developed enough for the Church to isolate this world.'

'On the contrary,' he objected, 'they're a great deal more than they appear to be.'

She looked querulous. 'If that's true, then why do they perform heavy manual labour for long hours in freezing temperatures in exchange for a few miserable nuts and berries?'

Flinx's voice dropped disconsolately. 'I don't know that yet.' He glanced up. 'But I know this – they're natural telepaths.'

'A delusion,' she repeated firmly, 'a hallucination you experienced.'

'No.' His voice was firm, confident. 'I have a few slight talents of my own. I know the difference between a hallucination and mind-to-mind communication.'

'Have it your way,' Sylzenzuzex declared, sighing. 'For the sake of discussion let us temporarily assume it was not an illusion. That is still no reason for the Church to place a world Under Edict. A whole race of telepaths is only theory, but it would not be enough to exclude them from associate membership in the Commonwealth.'

'It's not just that,' Flinx explained earnestly. 'They're . . . well, more intelligent than they appear.'

'I doubt that,' she snorted, 'but even a race of intelligent telepaths would not be considered such a threat.'

'*Much* more intelligent.'

'I won't believe that until I see evidence to prove it,' she objected. 'If they represented any kind of serious threat to the Commonwelath . . .'

'Why else would the Church put this world Under Edict?'

'Flinx, they have no tools, no clothing, no spoken language – no civilization. They run around grubbing for roots and fruits, living in caves. If they're potentially as clever as you claim, why do they persist in dwelling in poverty?'

'That,' admitted Flinx, 'is a very good question.'

'Do you have a very good answer?'

'I do not. But I'm convinced I've found the reason for the Church's actions. What is the effect of putting a race Under Edict?'

'No contact with outside parties, space-going peoples,' she recited. 'Severest penalties for any infraction of the Edict. The race is free to develop in its own way.'

'Or free to stagnate,' Flinx muttered. 'The Commonwealth and the Church have aided plenty of primitive peoples, Why not the Ujurrians?'

'You set yourself up as arbiter of high Church policy,' she murmured, drawing away from him again.

'Not me!' he half shouted, slamming both hands noisily against the bedcovers. His hands moved rapidly as he talked. 'It's the Church Council that sets itself up as the manipulator of racial destinies. And if not the Church, then the Commonwealth government does. And if not the Commonwealth, then the great corporations and family companies. Then there is the AAnn Empire which sets itself above everything.' He was pacing angrily alongside the bed.

'My God, but I'm sick to death of organizations that think they have the right to rule on how others ought to develop!'

'What would you have in its place?' she challenged him. 'Anarchy?'

Flinx sat down heavily on the bed again, his head sinking between his hands. He was tired, tired, and much too young. 'How should I know? I only know that I'm getting damned sick of what passes for intelligence in this corner of creation.'

'I can't believe you're so innocent,' she said, more gently now. 'What else do you expect from mere mammals and insects? The Amalgamation was just the beginning of your race's and mine's emergence from long dark age. The Commonwealth and the United Church are only a few of your centuries old. What do you expect of it so soon – Nirvana? Utopia?' She shook her head, a gesture the thranx had acquired from mankind.

'Not for me or you to set ourselves up above the Church, which helped bring us out of those dark times.'

'The Church, the Church, your almighty Church!' he shouted. 'Why do you defend it so? You think it's composed of saints?'

'I never claimed it was perfect,' she responded, showing some heat herself. 'The Counsellors themselves would be the last to claim so. That's one of its virtues. Naturally it's not perfect – it would never claim to be.'

'That's what Tse-Mallory once said to me,' he murmured reflectively.

'What . . . who?'

'Someone I know who also left the Church, for reasons of his own.'

'Tse-Mallory, that name again,' she replied thoughtfully. 'He was that stingship mate of my uncle's you mentioned before. Bran Tse-Mallory?'

'Yes.'

'They talk of him as well as of Truzenzuzex at the Clan meetings.' She snapped herself back to the present – no use thinking wistfully about things she would probably never be able to experience again. 'Now that you've decided the universe is not perfect and that the instrumentalities of intelligence are somewhat less than all-knowing, what do you propose we do about it?'

'Have a talk with our friends-to-be, the Ujurrians.'

'And what are they going to do?' she smirked. 'Throw rocks at the Baron's shuttles when he returns? Or at the beamers that are surely stocked in plenty here?'

'Possibly,' Flinx conceded. 'But even if they can do nothing, I think we'll have a far better chance of surviving among them than there, than waiting for Rudenuaman to get tired of having us around. When that happens she'll dispose of us as casually as she would an old dress.' He let his mind wander, saw no reason to hide himself from Sylzenzuzex any more. 'There's only one guard outside the door.'

'How do you know . . . oh, you told me,' she answered herself. 'How extensive are your talents?'

'I haven't the vaguest notion,' he told her honestly. 'Sometimes I can't perceive a spider in a room. Other times . . .' He felt it better to keep a few secrets. 'Just take my word that there's only one guard outside. I guess our docility has convinced Rudenuaman we don't require close watching. As she said, there's nowhere for us to run to.'

'I'm not sure I disagree with her,' Sylzenzuzex murmured, her gaze going to the chill mountains outside. 'Though I must admit that if we do escape, she *may* leave us alone. We would be no more danger to her in the mountains than we are here.'

'I'm hoping she thinks so,' he admitted. 'The Baron wouldn't agree with her. We have to leave now.' Sliding off the bed, he walked to the door and knocked gently. The door slid aside and their guard eyed them carefully – from several paces away, Flinx noted.

He was a tall, thin human with a worn expression and hair turned too white too soon. As near as Flinx could tell, he was not an AAnn in human disguise.

'You interrupted my reading,' he informed Flinx sourly, indicating the small tape viewer that rested nearby. This reminded Flinx of another tape he wanted to read himself. Despite the anxiety surging inside him, he would have to wait until much later, if ever, to see that tape.

'What do you want?' It was clear that this man was well informed about their co-operation thus far. Flinx shouted with his mind, conjuring up a sensation of half-fear.

Pip shot out from under the pillows on the bed and was through the door before the man could put his viewer aside. A beamer came up, but instead of firing the man crossed both hands in front of his face. Flinx jumped through the opening and planted a foot in the other's solar plexus. Only closing lids kept his eyes from popping out of his face.

The guard hit the far wall with a loud *whump*, sat down, and leaned like a rag doll against the chair leg. This time the minidrag responded to Flinx's call. He settled tensely back on Flinx's shoulder, glaring down at the unconscious guard.

Sylzenzuzex came up hurriedly behind him 'Why didn't he shoot immediately? As a matter of fact . . .' She hesitated, and Flinx sensed her mind working.

'That's right. No one here recognized Pip as a dangerous animal. The only one I told was Rudenuaman's bodyguard. In all the rush she must have neglected to inform everyone else. We were trapped here without hope of escape, remember? The only others who knew were Challis and Mahnahmi. He's dead, and she's fled.'

Flinx gestured behind him. 'That's why I called Pip off and knocked him out myself. Everyone's still ignorant of Pip's full capabilities. Sooner or later, Linda will remember to tell her mistress. But by then we should be free. We'd better be – Rudenuaman won't give us a second chance.'

'What are we going to do now?'

'No one's seen us except a small corps of armed security personnel and a few people up at the mine. This is a good-sized installation. Act as if you know what you're doing, and we might walk out of here without being challenged.'

'You are crazy,' she muttered nervously, as they entered the lift. 'This may be a large base, but it's still a closed community. Everyone here must know everyone else.'

'You participate in a bureaucracy and still you don't understand,' Flinx observed sadly. 'Everyone in a complicated operation like this tends to stick pretty much to his own speciality. Each one interacts with people within that speciality. This is hardly a homogeneous little society here. Unless we encounter one of the guards who met us on landing, we ought to be able to move about freely.'

'Until our guard regains consciousness,' she reminded him. 'Then they'll come looking for us.'

'But not beyond the boundary of the base, I'll bet. Rudenuaman will be more irritated than angry. She'll assume the environment here will take care of us. And it will, if the Ujurrians don't help us.'

The lift car started downwards. 'What makes you think they will?'

'I got the impression that they're anxious to talk to me. If you have ten marooned thranx speaking only Low Thranx and an eleventh suddenly appears, wouldn't you want to talk to him?'

161

'Maybe for a while,' she conceded. 'Of course, after I'd heard everything he had to say I might want to eat him, too.'

'I don't think the Ujurrians will do that.' The lift reached ground level.

'What makes you so certain? Berries or not, they are omnivorous, remember. Suppose they're simply telepathic morons?'

'If I'm wrong about them, then we'll die a lot cleaner than at Rudenuaman's hands. I'm betting on two things – a dream, and the fact that I never before saw Pip fly at any being he didn't intend to attack.' Reaching down, he rubbed the back of Pip's head through the jumpsuit fabric.

'You were right, Syl, when you said he was flying towards greater warmth, but the warmth wasn't in the Ujurrian's fur.' The lift door slid aside and they strode boldly out into the deserted hall.

Leaving the structure they started walking between buildings, heading towards the lake. Several people passed them. Flinx didn't recognize any of them, and fortunately none of them recognized the two prisoners.

As they neared the outskirts of the base Flinx slowed, his senses alert for anything like an automatically defended perimeter. Sylzenzuzex searched for concealed alarms. They didn't find so much as a simple fence, Apparently there were no large carnivores in this valley, and the merchantwoman's opinion of the natives they already knew.

Once they reached the concealing trees, they accelerated their pace, moving as fast as Sylzenzuzex's injured leghand would permit. Despite the abnormally long day, the sun was low in the sky before they slowed. When the sun finally moved behind one of the towering snowy peaks, its warmth would dissipate quickly in the mountain air. Sylzenzuzex would be affected first, and most severely; but Flinx didn't doubt that he'd also be dangerously exposed in his thin jumpsuit.

He hoped their furry hosts could do something about that. If no one was waiting for them at the far end of the lake – the 'long water' of his dream – he was going to be very embarrassed. And very sorry.

At its lower end the lake narrowed to a small outlet, then

tumbled with the bright humour of all mountain streams down a gentle slope, dancing and falling with fluid choreography over rocks and broken logs and branches. Despite the density of the forest overhead, the thick heatherlike ground cover was lush here.

Flinx picked out small flowering plants with odd needle-like leaves and multiple centres. Minute furred creatures dug and twisted and scurried through this low-level jungle.

Sylzenzuzex sniffed disdainfully, her spicules whistling, as they watched a tiny thing with ten furry legs and miniature hooves dart down a hole in the far bank of the stream.

'Primitive world,' she commented. 'No insects.' She was shivering already. 'That's not surprising. This world is too cold for them – and me.'

Flinx began hunting through the trees and was rubbing his hands together. Occasionally he would reach into his jumpsuit to fondle Pip. The minidrag also came from a hothouse world. It had grown still in an instinctive effort to conserve energy and body heat.

'I'm not exactly at home here either, you know,' Flinx told her. Glancing worriedly upward, he saw that the sun had been half swallowed by a mountain with a backbone like a crippled dinosaur.

'We can freeze to death out here tonight, or go back and take our chances with that female,' Sylzenzuzex stammered. 'A wonderful choice you've given us.'

'I don't understand,' he muttered puzzledly. 'I was so certain. The voices were so clear.'

'Everything is clear in a dream,' she philosophized. 'It's the real world that never makes sense, that's fuzzy at the fringes. I'm still not sure that you're not a little fuzzy at the fringes, Flinx.'

'Ho, ho,' a voice boomed like a hammer hitting the bottom of a big metal pot. It was a real voice, not a telepathic whisper.

'Joke, I like jokes!'

Flinx's heart settled back to its normal beat as he and Sylzenzuzex whirled, to see an enormous wide shape waddle out from between two trees. There was little to distinguish one native from another physically.

Flinx, however, now knew to hunt for something less

163

obvious. It blinked brightly out at him, a strong, concentrated mental glow – like a firefly, he reminded himself.

'Hello, Fluff. You have a sense of humour, but don't, please, sneak up on us like that again.'

'Sense of humour,' the giant echoed. 'That mean I like to make jokes?' On hind legs he towered above them. 'Yes. What is better than making jokes? Except maybe building caves and eating and sleeping and making love.'

Flinx noticed that the broadly grinning mouth was moving.

'You're talking,' Sylzenzuzex observed simultaneously. She turned to Flinx. 'I thought you said they were telepathic?'

'Can do mind-talk too,' something said inside her head, making her jump.

'So that's telepathy,' she murmured at the new experience. 'It's kind of unnerving.'

'Why trouble with talking?' Flinx wondered.

'Is less efficient, but more fun,' Fluff husked.

'Lots more fun,' two voices mimicked. Moam and Bluebright appeared, shuffling towards the stream. Lowering to all fours, they began lapping the water.

'Why don't you talk like this to the people at the base?'

'Base? Big metal caves?'

Flinx nodded, was rewarded with a mental shrug.

'No one ask us to talk much. We see inside them that they like us to talk like this,' and he proceeded to produce a few grunted words and snorted phrases.

'It make them happy. We want everyone to be happy, So we talk like that.'

'I'm not sure I understand,' Flinx admitted, sitting down on a rock and shivering. A monstrous shape materialized at his shoulder, and Sylzenzuzex jumped half a metre into the air.

'No doubt about it,' thundered Maybeso. One paw cuddled two wrinkled objects while the other held a large plastic case. Flinx felt a warm thought flow over him like a bucket of hot water and then Maybeso was gone.

'What was that?' a gaping Sylzenzuzex wanted to know.

'Maybeso,' Flinx told her absently, examining what the mercurial Ujurrian had brought. 'Thermal suits – one for you and one for me.'

After climbing into the self-contained heated overclothing they spent a few luxurious moments defrosting before they began their inspection of the big case's contents.

'Food,' Sylzenzuzex noted. 'Two beamers . . .'

Flinx reached into the depths of the container, aware he was trembling. 'And this . . . even this.' He withdrew his hand, holding a small, slightly battered spool.

'How?' he asked Fluff, awed. 'How did he know?' Fluff's smile was genuine and went beyond the one frozen into his features.

'Maybeso plays his own games. Everything is a game to Maybeso, and he's very good at games. Better than any of the family, In some ways he's just like an overgrown cub.'

'Cub,' agreed Moam, 'but a big light.'

'Very big light,' Bluebright agreed, raising his head and licking water from his muzzle with a long tongue.

'It's fun to have someone who can talk back,' Fluff observed playfully. Then Flinx had the impression of a hurt frown. 'Others came but did not land, Maybeso saw them and says they did some strange things with constructs – with instruments like those at the metal caves. They got very excited, then went away.'

'The Church exploration party,' Flinx commented un-necessarily.

'We didn't understand why they went away,' a troubled Fluff said. 'We wished they would have come down and talked. We were sad and wanted to help them, because they were frightened of something.' Again the mental shrug. 'Though we could have been wrong.'

'I don't think you're wrong, Fluff. Something frightened them, all right.'

Sylzenzuzex paid no attention to him. She was staring at Fluff, her mandibles hanging limp. Flinx turned to her, asked, 'Now do you understand why this world was put Under Edict?'

'Under Edict,' Fluff repeated, savouring the sound of the spoken words. 'A general admonition embodying philo-sophical rationalizations which stem – '

'You're a fast learner, Fluff,' gulped Flinx.

'Oh sure,' the giant agreed with childish enthusiasm. 'Is fun. Let's play a game. You think of a concept or new word and we try to learn it, okay?'

'It wasn't a game to the exploration party which took readings here,' Sylzenzuzex announced suddenly. She looked over to Flinx. 'I see what you were trying to tell me.' To the giant: 'They didn't land because . . . because they were afraid of you, Fluff.'

'Afraid? Why be afraid of me?' He slapped his metres-wide torso with a paw that could have decapitated a man. 'We only live, eat, sleep, make love, build caves, and play games . . . and make jokes, of course. What to be afraid of?'

'Your potential, Fluff,' Flinx explained slowly. 'And yours, Moam, and Bluebright, and you too, Maybeso, wherever you are.'

'Someplace else,' Moam supplied helpfully.

'They saw your potential and ran like hell instead of coming down to help you. Put you Under Edict so no one else would come to help you, either. They hoped to consign you all to ignorance. You have incalculable potential, Fluff, but you don't seem to have much drive. By denying you that the Church saw they could – '

'No!' Sylzenzuzex shouted, agonized. 'I can't believe that. The Church wouldn't . . .'

'Why not?' snorted Flinx. 'Anyone can be afraid of the big kid down the block.'

'Is wrong to fear,' Fluff observed mournfully, 'and sad.'

'Right both times,' concurred Flinx. Suddenly aware his stomach demanded attention, he dug a large cube of processed meat and cheese from the plastic container, sat down on a rock. After removing the foil sealer, he took a huge bite out of it, then started searching the container for something suitable for Pip.

Sylzenzuzex joined him, but her inspection of the supplies was half-hearted at best. Her mind was a maelstrom, of conflicting, confusing, and destructive thoughts. The knowledge of what the Church had certainly done was shattering beliefs she'd held since pupahood. Each time another ideal came crashing down, it sent a painful stab through her.

Flinx had reached a decision. 'You wanted to talk, to play a concept and words game?'

'Yes, let's play,' Moam snuffled enthusiastically, ambling over.

'Let's talk,' agreed Bluebright.

Flinx looked grim, considered what he was about to do,

and was gratified to discover that it made him feel more satisfied than any decision he'd made in his entire life.

'You bet we'll talk . . .'

CHAPTER ELEVEN

'But not here,' Fluff put in.

'Definitely not here,' Bluebright echoed. 'Let's go to the cave.' Turning away from Flinx, he and Moam started off into the trees, matching each other stride for stride. Fluff waddled after them gesturing for Flinx and Sylzenzuzex to follow.

'*The* cave?' Flinx inquired later as he and the shaking thranx struggled to maintain the blistering pace. 'You all share the same cave?'

Fluff seemed surprised. 'Everyone shares the same cave.'

'You're all part of the same family, then?' Sylzenzuzex panted.

'Everyone same family.' The big native was obviously puzzled at these questions.

It occurred to Flinx that Fluff might have something other than immediate blood relationships in mind. A word with multiple meanings could be confusing to a human, to say nothing of an alien with a bare knowledge of the language.

'Are we of the same family, Fluff?' he asked slowly. Heavily furred brows wrinkled ponderously.

'Not sure yet,' their unassuming saviour finally told him. 'Let you know.'

Another hour of scrambling hectically over rocks and ditches, and Flinx found himself becoming winded. It was much worse for his companion, who finally settled to an exhausted halt in the middle of a clump of flowering growth.

'I'm sorry,' she murmured, 'I can't keep up. Tired and – cold.'

'Wait,' he instructed her, 'Fluff, wait for us!' Ahead, the three Ujurrians paused, looked back expectantly.

Flinx knelt and gently examined the broken leghand. Though Sylzenzuzex wasn't putting any pressure on it, the joint didn't seem to be healing properly.

'We're going to have to splint that break,' he muttered softly. She nodded agreement.

'Do at the cave,' Fluff advised, having retreated to join them.

'I'm sorry, Fluff,' Flinx explained, 'but she can't go any further unless we fix this break,' He considered, suggested, 'You three continue on – leave a trail of broken branches and we'll catch up with you later.'

'Foolish,' the native advised. He moved nearer, his huge bulk dwarfing the slim youth. Flinx noted that Pip hadn't moved. If his pet expressed no concern, then it sensed no threat behind those advancing luminous eyes.

Fluff studied the quaking Sylzenzuzex, asked curiously, 'What to do, Flinx-friend?'

'If you think it's foolish of us to follow your trail,' he told the Ujurrian carefully, alert for any indication of out-raged anger, 'you could let us ride.'

Bluebright scratched under his chin with a hind foot. 'What is ride?' he asked interestedly.

'Means to carry thems instead of gems,' a deep voice snorted with mild contempt at Bluebright's slowness. Flinx spun just in time to see the slightly phosphorescent form of Maybeso vanish into someplace else.

'Understand now,' Fluff bubbled with satisfaction. 'What do we do?'

'Just stand there,' Flinx instructed, wondering as he walked up next to that brown wall if this was going to turn out to be such a clever idea after all. The big ursine head swung to watch him. 'Now lie down on your stomach.'

Fluff promptly collapsed with a pneumatic *whump*. Tentatively placing one foot against his left flank, Flinx reached up and grabbed a double handful of coarse hair and pulled hard. When no protest was forthcoming, he pulled again, hard enough this time to swing himself up on the broad back.

'Okay, you can get on all fours again,' he told his jocular mount.

Fluff rose with hydraulic smoothness, his mind smiling. 'I see. This is a better idea.'

'A new fun thing,' Moam agreed. She and Bluebright ambled over to Sylzenzuzex and spent a minute arguing over who should have the privilege of trying this new experience first. Moam won the debate. She moved next to the watching thranx and lay down next to her.

Sylzenzuzex studied that muscular torso apprehensively, glanced across at Flinx. He nodded encouragement, and she climbed carefully on to Moam, dug her claws into the thick fur, and hung on firmly.

They discovered now how patiently the Ujurrians had walked before, to enable their two pitiful friends to keep up with them. If either Fluff or Moam noticed the weight on their backs it wasn't apparent, and the little group flew through the forest.

They had only one further mishap, when Flinx was nearly thrown. He barely managed to maintain his seat when Fluff rose without warning on to his two hind legs. He ran on like a biped to the manner born, and at a pace which no Terran bear could have duplicated. With seven limbs to hold on with, Sylzenzuzex kept her perch much more securely when Moam likewise rose to match Fluff's long two-legged stride.

It was impossible to tell how long or how far they had travelled when they descended into the last valley. From the beginning of the real run until the end, none of the ursinoids slackened their pace, though by then they were puffing slightly.

This third valley was dominated by the stream they'd run parallel to during their retreat. It broadened into another lake here, though one much smaller than that bordering the mining encampment now far behind them. A new variety of tree grew here among the quasievergreens. It had broad, yellow-brown leaves. Certain varieties, Flinx saw in the moonlight, held different kinds of berries, though these were scarce. Others boasted clusters of oval-shelled nuts, some big as coconuts.

'You eat those?' Flinx asked, pointing at the burdened branches.

'Yes,' Fluff informed him.

'And you also eat meat?'

169

'Only in snowtime,' his host explained quietly, 'when the *baiga* and *maginac* do not bloom. Meat is no fun, and more work. It runs away.'

They were moving towards a steep hillside now. In the soft moonlight Flinx saw that it was bare rock, devoid of talus. Several circles made dark stains against the grey granite.

Ujurrians of many sizes, including the first cubs they had seen, gambolled between the dark shoreline and the cave mouths.

'If one doesn't eat meat for variety,' Fluff went on, 'one begins to feel sick.'

'Why don't you like to eat meat?' Sylzenzuzex wondered.

Flinx prayed she wouldn't involve their impressionable hosts in some abstract spiritual dialogue.

Fluff spoke as if to children. 'Even the life of the *najac* or the six-legged ugly *coivet* is like a piece of the sun. When smothered, the warmth leaves it.'

'We do not like to make bright things dark,' Bluebright elaborated. 'We would rather make dark things bright. But,' he finished mournfully, 'we don't know how.'

They slowed to a walk, finally came to a complete stop outside the first of the caves. Flinx observed that the exterior of the entrance was composed of neatly piled boulders, chinked together with smaller rocks and pebbles in the absence of ferrocrete. Motioning for Fluff to lie down, he started to slide off the ursinoid's back.

A glance behind him showed a long glass spear of moonlight broken into pieces by the ripples and eddies on the lake. A look into the cave ahead revealed nothing but blackness.

'You said everyone shares the same cave, Fluff, but I see other openings in the mountainside.'

'Is all same cave,' the native explained.

'You mean they all connect inside the mountain somewhere?'

'Yes, all meet one another.' A warm mental smile came to him. 'Is all part of the game we play.'

'The game?' Sylzenzuzex echoed, chilled despite the fact her thermal suit was set on high. When Fluff didn't comment, she wondered aloud, 'Do you think we could build a fire?'

'Sure,' Moam said cheerfully. 'What is building a fire? Is like building a cave?'

Patiently, Flinx explained what was necessary, confident he would have to do so only once.

'We will go and gather the dead wood,' Moam and Bluebright volunteered, when he had finished his explanation.

'What is this game you play, the one involving your warren, Fluff?' Flinx inquired when the other two had departed.

Fluff ignored the question, urged them into the cave where he silently exchanged greetings with another huge native.

'This is Softsmooth, my mate,' he informed them in response to the question Flinx phrased in his mind. 'You ask about the game, Flinx-friend? . . . Our parents' parents' parents many times over-and-dead worried that one day the cold would stay forever, and many lights among the family would vanish.

'I wouldn't call this a heat wave right now,' Sylzenzuzex commented.

'The cold comes when the sun is smothered by the mountains,' Fluff explained. 'Our many-times parents felt it was becoming colder each year. It seemed to them that each year the sun grew smaller than the year before.'

Flinx nodded slowly. 'Your world has an elliptical orbit, Fluff, but it's not a regular orbit. According to the statistics I saw, it's swinging farther and farther away from your sun every century – though how your ancestors realized this I can't imagine.'

'Many new concepts,' a frowning Fluff murmured. 'Anyhows, our parents many times dead decided how to fix. Should move closer to sun in certain way.'

'They were talking about regularizing Ulru-Ujurr's orbit,' Flinx husked. 'But how did they *know*?'

'Have to ask ancestors,' Fluff shrugged. 'Very difficult to do.'

'I'll bet,' Sylzenzuzex agreed readily.

'Was a new way, though,' the big native went on. 'Diggers . . .'

'The people at the mine?'

'Yes. They make their own caves very warm. We asked them how we could make warm, too.'

171

'What did they suggest?' Flinx wondered.

Fluff appeared confused. 'They told us to dig big hole in the ground and then pull dirt in on top of ourselves. We tried and found it does make warm. But you can't move, and one gets bored that way. Also no light. We did not understand why they told us to do this way. They do not do for themselves. Why they tell us to do that, Flinx-friend?'

'That's the AAnn excuse for humour at work,' he replied with quiet fury.

'AAnn?' Fluff queried, Moam and Bluebright returned, each buried under enormous armloads of dead branches.

'Some of the people at the mine,' Flinx explained, 'the ones with – the ones with the cold minds.'

'Ah, the cold minds,' Fluff echoed in recognition. 'We did not see how such cold ones could give us knowledge on how to become warm. But we tried anyway.'

Flinx couldn't look at the amiable native. 'How . . . how many of the experimenters died?'

'Experimenters?'

'The ones who tried burying themselves?'

'Oh, Flinx-friend worries wrongly. No one died,' Fluff assured him, feeling relaxation in the human's mind at these words.

'You see, we buried Maybeso . . .'

'Here is wood,' Moam said.

'Do you need more?' asked Bluebright.

'I think this is enough to last us at least a week,' Flinx told them. As he spoke Sylzenzuzex was arranging some of the broken wood in a triangular stack, delicate truhands making a sculpture out of twigs and thin trunks.

Flinx eased himself up against the wall of the cave, feeling the coolness of the stone through the thermal suit. 'How did your parents many times dead think you could regula – move closer to the sun?'

'By playing the game,' Fluff told him again. 'Game and making cave home is one.'

'Digging caves is supposed to bring your world nearer its sun?' Flinx muttered, not sure he had heard correctly.

But Fluff signalled assent. 'Is part of pattern of game.'

'Pattern? What kind of pattern?'

'Is hard to explain,' Fluff conceded languidly.

Flinx hesitated, voiced a sudden thought, 'Fluff, how

172

long have your people been playing the game of digging cave patterns?'

'How long?'

'How many of your days?'

'Days.' Fluff decided it was time to consult with the others. He called Bluebright over, and Moam came with Bluebright. Softsmooth joined them and for a brief moment Maybeso winked into existence to add his comment.

Eventually Fluff turned back to Flinx, spoke with confidence as he named a figure. A large figure. Exceedingly so.

'Are you certain of your numerology?' Flinx finally asked slowly.

Fluff indicated the affirmative, 'Number is correct. Learned counting system at the mine.'

Sylzenzuzex eyed Flinx speculatively as he turned away, leaned back against the wall and stared at the dark cold roof above. She paused prior to starting the fire. 'How long?'

There was a long pause before he seemed to come back from a far place, to glance across at her. 'According to what Fluff says, they've been playing this game of digging interconnecting tunnels for just under fourteen thousand Terran years. This whole section of the continent must be honeycombed with them. No telling how deep they run, either.'

'What is honey?' wondered Moam.

'What is comb?' Bluebright inquired.

'How far is deep?' Fluff wanted to know.

Flinx replied with another question. 'How long before this pattern is supposed to be finished, Fluff?'

The Ujurrian paused, his mind working busily. 'Not too long. Twelve thousand more of your years.'

'Give or take a few hundred,' Flinx gulped dully.

But Fluff eyed him reprovingly. 'No . . . exactly.' Great glowing guileless eyes stared back into Flinx's own.

'And what's supposed to happen when this pattern is complete, when the game is finished?'

'Two things,' explained Fluff pleasantly. 'We move a certain ways closer to the warm, and we start looking for a new game.'

'I see.' He muttered half to himself. 'And Rudenuaman thought these people were primitive because they spent all their time digging caves.'

173

Sylzenzuzex hadn't moved to light the fire. Her face was a mask of uncertainty. 'But how can digging a few caves change a planet's orbit?'

'A *few* caves? I don't know, Syl,' he murmured softly. 'I doubt if anyone does. Maybe the completed pattern produces a large enough alteration in the planetary crust to create a catastrophe fold sufficient to stress space the right amount at the right moment. If I knew more catastrophe math – and if we had the use of the biggest Church computer – I could check it.

'Or maybe the tunnels are intended to tap the heat at the planet's core power, or a combination of it and the fold . . . we need some brilliant mathematicians and physicists to answer it.'

Sylzenzuzex eyed Fluff warily. 'Can you explain what's supposed to happen, Fluff, and how?'

The bulky ursinoid gave her a mourful look, a simple task with those manifold-souled eyes. 'Is sad, but do not have the terms for.'

It was quiet in the cave then until the pile of dry wood coughed into life. Several small flames appeared at once, and in seconds the fire was blazing enthusiastically, Sylzenzuzex responded with a long, low whistling sigh of appreciation and settled close to the conforting heat.

'Is warm!' Moam uttered in surprise.

Bluebright stuck a paw close to the flames, drew it back hastily, '*Very* warm,' he confirmed.

'We can teach you – hell, we've already taught you – how to make all the fires like this you want. I'm not saying you should abandon your game, but if you're interested Sylzenzuzex and I can show you how to ensure your warmth during aphelion a lot sooner than twelve thousand years from now.'

'Is easier,' Fluff conceded, indicating the fire.

'And fun,' added Moam.

'Listen, Fluff,' Flinx began energetically, 'why do your people work so long and hard for the cold minds and the others at the mine?'

'For the berries and nuts they bring us from far places,' Softsmooth supplied from a little alcove cut into the cave wall.

'From far places,' Bluebright finished.

174

'Why not travel there and get them for yourselves?'

'Too far,' Fluff explained, 'and too hard, Maybeso says.'

Flinx leaned away from the wall, spoke in earnest tones, 'Don't you understand, Fluff? I'm trying to show you that the people at the mine are exploiting you. They're working you as hard as you're willing, at tremendous profit to themselves, and in return they're paying you off with only enough nuts and berries to keep you working for them.'

'What is profit?' asked Moam.

'What is paying off?' Bluebright wanted to know.

Flinx started to reply, then realized he didn't have the time. Not for an explanation of modern economics, the ratio of work to value produced, and a hundred other concepts it would be necessary to detail before he could explain those two simple terms to these people.

Leaning back again, he stared out the cave mouth past the flicker of the fire. A smattering of strange stars had risen above the rim of the mountains hugging the far side of the lake. For hours he remained deep in thought, while his hosts relaxed in polite silence and waited for him to speak again. They recognized his concern and concentration and stayed respectfully out of his thoughts.

Once he moved to help Sylzenzuzex resplint her broken joint with a stronger piece of wood. Then he returned to his place and his thoughts. After a while the stars were replaced by others, and they sank in their turn.

He was still sitting there, thinking, when he heard a sound like that made by a warehouse door mounted on old creaky hinges. Fluff yawned a second time and rolled over, opening saucerish eyes at him.

In a little while, the sun was pouring into the cave, and still Flinx hadn't offered so much as a good morning. They were all watching him curiously. Even Sylzenzuzex maintained a respectful silence, sensing that something important was forming beneath that unkempt red hair.

It was Fluff who broke the endless quiet. 'Last night, Flinx-friend, your mind make a steady noise like much water falling. Today it is like the ground after water has fallen and frozen – a sameness piled high and white and clean.'

Sylzenzuzex was sitting on her haunches. With truhands and her one good foothand she was cleaning her abdomen, ovipositors, great compound eyes, and antennae.

175

'Fluff,' Flinx said easily, as if no time had passed since they had last conversed, as if the long night had been but the pause of a minute, 'how would you and your people like to start a new game?'

'Start a new game,' repeated Fluff solemnly. 'This is a big thing, Flinx-friend.'

'It is,' admitted Flinx, 'It's called civilization.'

Sylzenzuzex stopped in mid-preen and cocked her head sharply at him, though there was far less certainty in her voice when she spoke her objections: 'Flinx, you can't. You know now why the Church placed this world Under Edict. We can't, no matter how we may feel personally about Fluff and Moam and the rest of these people, contravene the decision of the Council.'

'Who says so?' Flinx shot back, 'Besides, we don't know that the Edict was declared by the Council. A few bureaucrats in the right place could have made their own little godlike decision to consign the Ujurrians to ignorance. I'm sorry, Syl, but while I admit the Church is responsible for some good works, it's still an organization composed of humanx beings. Like all beings, their allegiance is first to themselves and second to everyone else. Would the Church disband if they could be convinced it was in the Commonwealth's best interests? I doubt it.'

'Whereas you, Philip Lynx, are concerned first with everyone else,' she countered.

Frowning, he started pacing the warming floor of the cave. 'I honestly don't know, Syl. I don't even know who I am, much less what I am.' His tone strengthened, 'But I do know that in these people I see an innocence and kindness that I've never encountered on any humanx world.' He stopped abruptly, stared out at the stars the morning sun made on the lake.

'I may be a young fool, a narrow-minded idealist – call it anything you like, but I think I know what I want to be now. If they'll have me, that is. For the first time in my life, I know.'

'What's that?' she asked.

'A teacher.' He faced the patient Ujurrians. 'I want to teach you, Fluff. And you Moam, and you, Bluebright and Softsmooth, and even Maybeso, wherever you are.'

'Here,' a voice grumbled from outside. Maybeso was

176

lying on the low heatherlike growth before the cave entrance, rolling and stretching with pleasure.

'I want to teach all of you this new game.'

'A big thing,' Fluff repeated slowly. 'This is not for us alone to decide.'

'Others must be told,' Bluebright agreed.

It took some time for everyone to be told. To be exact, it took eleven days, four hours, and a small basket of minutes and seconds. Then they had to wait another eleven days, four hours, and some minutes for everyone to answer.

But it took very little time for each individual to decide.

On the twenty-third day after the question was asked, Maybeso appeared outside the cave. Flinx and Sylzenzuzex were sitting by the lakeshore with Fluff, Moam, and Bluebright. They didn't notice the new arrival.

At that moment, Flinx was holding a long tough vine with sharp shards of bone attached to one end. While the others of their small group watched, he was teaching Fluff how to fish. Fluff looked delighted as he brought in the fourth catch of the day, a rounded silvery organism that looked like a cross between a blowfish and a trout.

Swimmers, the Ujurrians explained, had smaller lights than *najacs* and other land prey. Therefore fishing was a smaller evil than hunting.

'This too is part of the new game?' Moam inquired, duplicating the vine and bone hook arrangement perfectly on her first try.

'It is,' Flinx admitted.

'That's good,' Bluebright observed.

'I hope everyone agrees.'

Sylzenzuzex downed another clutch of berries. The sugar content was satisfactory, and the freshness enlivened her diet.

Miffed, Maybeso vanished from before the cave and reappeared next to her. She nearly fell off the smooth granite she'd been crouched on.

'Everyone has answered,' Maybeso announced. 'Most everybody says yes. We play the new game now.'

'Fourteen thousand years of digging, down the excretory canal,' Sylzenzuzex commented, climbing to her feet again and brushing at her abdomen. 'I hope you know what you're doing, Flinx.'

'Not to worry,' Maybeso snorted at her. 'Only here do we play new game, now. Other places on backsides of the world will continue with old game. If new game is not fun,' he paused slightly, 'we go back to old game.' He turned a forceful gaze on Flinx. 'Forever,' he added.

Flinx shifted uncomfortably as the enigmatic Ujurrian vanished. Several weeks ago he had been so sure of himself, fired with a messianic zeal he had never previously experienced. Now the first real doubts were beginning to gnaw at his confidence. He turned away from the stares around him – the ursinoids were well equipped for staring.

'Is good,' was all Fluff murmured. 'How do we begin the game, Flinx?'

He indicated the perfect hook-and-line arrangements everyone had completed. 'Fire was a start. This is a start. Now I want everyone who works for the people at the mine to come here to learn with us – at night-time, so the cold minds will not become suspicious. That would be,' he hesitated only briefly, 'bad for the game.'

'But when will we sleep?' Moam wanted to know.

'I won't talk too long,' replied Flinx hopefully. 'It's necessary. Maybe,' he added without much confidence, 'we can accomplish the first part of the game without making any light places dark. Ours or anyone else's.'

'Is good,' declared Fluff. 'We will tell the others at the mine.'

Sylzenzuzex sidled close to him as the ursinoids dispersed.

'Teach them something basic about civilization while we help ourselves,' he murmured. 'Once they get rid of the people at the mine, they'll have a start at obtaining all the nuts and berries they want . . .'

CHAPTER TWELVE

'I hope,' Teleen auz Rudenuaman ventured, 'that the Baron concludes his hunt soon. We're running low on a number of synthetics and supplements for the food synthesizers, and we're nearly out of stock on several other unduplicatable items.'

'There is no need to worry about the Baron,' Meevo FFGW assured her from beneath his stiff human face.

There really wasn't any reason for concern, she insisted to herself, turning to look out the newly replaced pink window panels. On the mountain above, the miners worked steadily, efficiently as always.

The Baron had made several journeys through Commonwealth territory before. Nevertheless, she couldn't help experiencing a pang of concern every time one of her ships carried any of the disguised reptilians. She might survive, via a web of confusing explanations, if a Commonwealth patrol ship ever intercepted one of those missions and discovered the AAnn on board.

But she would lose an irreplaceable business associate. Not all of the AAnn aristocracy were as understanding of human motivations or as business-minded as Riidi WW.

The office communit buzzed for attention. Meevo rose and answered the call. Turning from the vista of forest and mountain, she saw his flexible humanoid mask twist repeatedly, a sign that incomprehensible reptilian contortions were occurring beneath.

'Said what . . . what happened?' The AAnn's thick voice rose. Teleen leaned closer. 'What is going on, Meevo?'

Slowly the AAnn engineer replaced the communit receiver. 'That . . . was Chargis at the mine. The escaped human and thranx have returned alive. He reports that there are many natives with them, and that the newcomers have joined with those working the mine in armed revolt.'

'No, no . . .' She felt faint as his words overpowered her. 'The natives, in arms . . . that's impossible.' Her voice rose to a scream as she regained control of herself. 'Impossible! They don't know the difference between a power drill and a beamer. Why would they want to revolt, anyway? What do they want . . . more nuts and berries? This is insane!' Her face elongated suddenly, dangerously. 'No, wait – you said the human and thranx had returned with them?'

'So Chargis insists.'

'But that's impossible, too. They should have died weeks ago from exposure. Somehow,' she concluded inescapably, 'they must have succeeded in communicating with the natives.'

'I would say that is understatement,' the engineer declared. 'I was told the natives possessed no language, no means of communicating abstract concepts among themselves – let alone with outsiders.'

'We have overlooked something, Meevo.'

'As a nye, I say that is so,' the engineer concurred. 'But it will not matter in the end. It is one thing to teach a savage how to fire a weapon and another to explain the tactics of warfare to it.'

'Where did they get weapons, anyway?' Teleen wondered, staring up the mountainside once more. The distant structures showed no sign of the conflict evidently taking place within.

'Chargis said that they overwhelmed the guard and broke into the mill armoury,' Meevo explained. 'There was only one guard, as there are none here who would steal weapons. Chargis went on to say that the natives were clumsy and undisciplined in breaking in, and that the human and thranx tried hard to quiet them.' He grinned viciously. 'They may have unleashed something they cannot control. Chargis said . . .' The engineer hesitated.

'Go on,' Teleen prompted, determined to listen to it all, 'what else did Chargis say?'

'He said that the natives gave him the impression that they regarded this all as . . . a game.'

'A game,' she repeated slowly. 'Let them continue to think that, even as they are dying. Contact all personnel on base,' she ordered. 'Have them abandon all buildings except those here, centred around Administration. We have hand

180

beamers and laser cannon big enough to knock a military shuttle out of the sky. We'll just relax here, holding communications, food processing, this structure, and the power station until the Baron returns.

'After we've incinerated some of their number,' she continued casually, as though she were speaking of pruning weeds, 'the game may lose interest for them. If not, the shuttles will end it quickly enough.' She glanced back at him. 'Also have Chargis gather some good marksmen into two groups. They can use the two big groundcars and keep our friendly workers bottled up where they are. Mind the shooting, though; I don't want anything damaged within the mine buildings unless it's absolutely unavoidable. That equipment is expensive. Barring that, they can have target practice on any natives they find outside.'

She added, in a half-mutter, 'But under no circumstances are they to kill the human youth or the thranx female. I want both of them healthy and undamaged.'

She shook her head, disgusted, as the engineer moved to relay her orders, 'Damned inconvenient. We're going to have to import and train a whole new clutch of manual labourers . . .'

Everything, Flinx thought furiously, had gone smoothly and according to plan – at the start. Then he had watched helplessly as months of planning amd instruction were cast aside, submerged in the uncontrollable pleasure the Ujurians took in breaking into the armoury to get at the toys which made things vanish. Not even Fluff could calm them.

'They're enjoying themselves. Flinx,' Sylzenzuzex explained, trying to reassure him. 'Can you blame them? This game is much more exciting than anything they've ever played before.'

'I wonder if they'll still think so when some of their lights are put out,' he muttered angrily, 'Will they think my game is still fun after they've seen some of their friends lying on the ground with their insides burnt out by Rudenuaman's beamers?' He turned away, speechless with anger at himself and at the Ujurrians.

'I wanted to take over the mine silently, by surprise, without killing anyone,' he finally grumbled. 'With all the

181

noise they made breaking into the armoury, I'm sure th
remainder of the building staff heard and reported below.
she's smart, and she is, Rudenuaman will place her remair
ing people on round-the-clock alert and wait for us to com
to her.'

He grew aware of Fluff standing nearby, looked deep int
those expectant eyes. 'I'm afraid your people are going t
have to kill now, Fluff.'

The ursinoid looked back at him unwaveringly, 'Is unde
stood, Flinx-friend. Is a serious game we play, this civil
zation.'

'Yes,' Flinx murmured, 'it always has been. I'd hoped t
avoid old mistakes, but . . .'

His voice died away and he sat on the floor, starin
morosely at the metal surface between his knees. A coo
leathery face rubbed up against his – Pip. What he didn
expect was the gentle pressure below the back of his neck
where his b-thorax would have been had he been thranx

Looking back and up he saw faceted eyes gazing int
his. 'Now you can only do the best you can do,' Sylzenzuze
murmured softly. The delicate truhand moved gentl
massaging his back. 'You have begun this thing. If you don
help finish it, that female down there will.'

He felt a little better at that, but only a little.

A sharp crack like tearing metal foil sounded clearly
Flinx was on his feet, running in the direction of the sounc
which was followed soon by a second. From a transparer
panel running the length of an access corridor they wer
able to peer out and down the gentle slope on the right sid
of the large building. It was devoid of growth, which ha
been cleared off for a distance of twenty metres from the sid
of the structure.

Across the clearing, near the edge of the forest, they coul
see the hovering shapes of two groundcars. The same car
Flinx noted, which had met their shuttle upon its arriv
here so many weeks ago.

Each car mounted a small laser cannon near its fron
Even as they watched, a thin red beam jumped from the en
of one such weapon to the rocky slope ahead and abov
There were several small shafts there, sunk into the cliffsid

Soon the clean rock was scarred by three black ellipsoid
modest splotches of destruction where brush had bee

crisped and the lighter silicate rocks fused to glass.

From somewhere at the upper end of the mine shaft a blue line from a hand beamer flashed down to strike the exterior of the groundcar. The car's screen was more than strong enough to absorb and dissipate such tiny bursts of energy.

Unexpectedly, the two cars turned and moved rapidly back downslope towards the main installation. Their muted hum penetrated into the corridor where Flinx and the others watched silently as the cars, floating smoothly a metre above the surface on thick cushions of air, turned and stopped just out of beamer range.

A moment later the familiar bulk of Bluebright came churning around the corner towards them. Pulling up sharply, he let his words spill out in between steam-engine pants: 'They have killed Ay, Bee, and Cee,' he gasped, his enormous eyes wider than usual.

'How did it happen?' Flinx asked quietly. 'I *told* everyone that they wouldn't fire into these buildings. They won't risk damaging their equipment because they're not yet convinced we pose a serious threat to them.'

Fluff took over the explanation, having already communicated silently and rapidly with Bluebright. 'Ay, Bee, and Cee went outside the metal caves.'

'But *why*?' Flinx half asked, half cried.

'They thought they had created a new idea,' Fluff explained slowly. Flinx showed no comprehension, so the ursinoid continued. 'These past many days you have told us over and over that this game you call civilization should be played according to common sense, logic, reason. From what Bluebright tells me, Ay, Bee, and Cee decided among themselves that if this was so the cold minds and the others would see that it was reason and logic to co-operate with us, since we have taken their mine from them.

'They went out without weapons to talk logic and reason to those in the machines. But,' and Fluff's voice grew hurt at the wonder of it, 'those did not even listen to Ay, Bee, and Cee. They killed them without even listening. How can this thing be?' The shaggy head peered puzzledly down at Flinx. 'Are not the cold minds and the ones like you down there also civilized? Yet they did this thing without talking. Is this the reason you speak of?'

Flinx and Sylzenzuzex had yet to see one of the jovial

ursinoids angry. Fluff appeared close to it, though it really wasn't anger. It was frustration and lack of understanding.

Flinx tried to explain. 'There are those who don't play the game fair, Fluff. Those who cheat.'

'What is cheating?' wondered Fluff.

Flinx endeavoured to explain.

'I see,' Fluff announced solemnly when the youth had finished. 'This is a remarkable concept. I would not have believed it possible. The others must be told. It explains much of the game.'

Turning, he and Bluebright left Flinx and Sylzenzuzex alone in the corridor.

'How long,' she asked, staring out the window panel towards the distant complex, 'do you think they will sit down there before growing impatient and coming up after us?'

'Probably until the shuttles return. If we haven't resolved this before then – no, we *must* finish this before the Baron comes back . . . We have nothing but hand beamers here. They have at least two surface-to-space, gimbal-mounted laser cannons down by the landing strip, in addition to the smaller ones mounted on the groundcars. Possibly more. We can't fight that kind of weaponry. I hope Fluff and Bluebright can get that through their family's hairy skulls.' He moved up alongside her to stare out the panel.

'I'm sure the two big guns are directed towards us right now. If we tried a mass retreat they'd incinerate the lot of us, just like Ay, Bee and Cee. We're going to have to – '

A high-pitched scream suddenly floated shockingly down the corridor. It rose from mid-tenor to the high, wavering shriek of the utterly terrified . . . then stopped. It was undeniably human.

The second scream was not. It came from an AAnn. Then came more screams of both varieties.

Pip was fluttering nervously above Flinx's shoulder and cold perspiration had started flowing from beneath the crop of red hair.

'Now what?' he muttered uneasily, as they started off in the direction of the screams. Every so often another scream would be heard, followed at regular intervals by an answering sound from the opposite camp.

In one respect they were all alike – short and intense.

They must have heard two dozen before encountering Moam and Bluebright. 'What happened?' he demanded. 'What were those screams?'

'Lights,' began Moam.

'Going out,' Bluebright finished.

Flinx discovered he was trembling. There was blood on Moam's naturally grinning mouth. Both broad, flat muzzles were stained with it. There were small groups of workers and guards who had been unsuccessful in their attempt to flee the captured mine.

'You've killed the prisoners,' was all he could stutter.

'Oh yes,' Moam admitted with blood-curdling cheerfulness. 'We not sure for a while, but Fluff explained to us and family. Cold minds and people down there,' then gesturing in the direction of the main base, 'cheat. We think we understand now what is to cheat. It means not playing the game by the rules, yes?'

'Yes, but these aren't my rules,' he whispered dazedly, 'not my rules.'

'But is okay with us,' Bluebright offered. 'We understand these rules not yours, Flinx-friend. Not good rules. But cold minds make up new rules, we play that way okay too.'

The Ujurrians waddled off down the corridor.

Flinx sank to his knees, leaned up against the wall. 'Game, it's still all a game to them.' Suddenly he looked at Sylzenzuzex and shuddered. 'Goddamn it, I didn't want it to happen like this.'

'You are she who rides the *grizel*,' Sylzenzuzex said without anger. 'You have wakened it. Now you must ride it.'

'You don't see,' he muttered disconsolately. 'I wanted Fluff and Moam and Bluebright and all the rest of them to be spared all our mistakes. I want them to become the great thing they can – and not,' he finished bitterly, 'just a smarter version of us.'

Sylzenzuzex moved nearer. 'You still hold the *grizel* by its tails, Flinx. You haven't been thrown yet. It is not you who taught them to kill – remember, they do hunt meat.'

'Only when they have to,' he reminded her. 'Still,' and he showed signs of relaxing some, 'this may be a time when they have to. Yes, a snowtime hunt, to live. The rules have been altered, but we still have rules. They just need to be defined further.'

'That's right, Flinx, you tell them when it's all right to kill and when it's not.'

He looked at her oddly, but if there was anything hidden beneath the surface of her words he couldn't sense it. 'That's the one thing I never wanted to do, even by proxy.'

'What made you think you'd ever have the opportunity?'

'Something . . . that happened not so long ago,' he said cryptically. 'Now it's been forced on me anyway. I've been shoved into the one position I vowed I'd never hold.'

'I don't know what you're rambling on about, Flinx,' she finally declared, 'but either you ride the *grizel* or it tramples you.'

Flinx looked up the corridor to where Moam and Bluebright had turned the corner. 'I wonder who's going to ride whom?'

The answer came several days later. There had been no assault from below, as he'd guessed, although the two groundcars pranced daily right next to the walls of the mine structures, daring anyone to show a fuzzy head.

Fluff woke them in the small office Flinx and Sylzenzuzex had chosen for sleeping quarters. 'We have made a backtrap,' he told them brightly, 'and we are going to catch the groundcars now.'

'Backtrap . . . wait, what . . . ?' Flinx fought for awareness, rubbing frantically at his eyes still rich with sleep. Vaguely he seemed to recall Fluff or Softsmooth or someone telling him about a backtrap, but he couldn't form a picture of it.

'You can't stop a groundcar with a . . .' he started to protest, but Fluff was already urging him to follow.

'Hurry now, Flinx-friend,' he insisted, listening to something beyond the range of normal hearing, 'is started.'

He led them to the mill supervisor's office, a curving transparent dome set in the southernmost end of the building.

'There,' Fluff said, pointing.

Flinx saw several of the ursinoids running on all fours over exposed, bare ground. They were racing for the upper slopes, near the place where the main shaft entered the mountain. Still well behind, Flinx could make out the two groundcars following.

'What are they doing out there!' Flinx yelled, leaning against the transparent polyplexalloy. He looked helplessly at Fluff. 'I told you no one was to go outside the buildings.'

Fluff was unperturbed. 'Is part of new game. Watch.'

Unable to do anything else, Flinx turned his attention back to the incipient slaughter.

Moving at tremendous speed, the three ursinoids passed the near end of the building, below Flinx's present position. Fast as they were, though, they couldn't outrun the ground-cars. First one burst, then another jumped from the muzzles of the laser cannon. One hit just back of the trailing runner, impelling him to even greater speed. The other struck between the front-runners, leaving molten rock behind.

The three runners, Flinx saw, would never make the open doorway at the upper end of the mill. The groundcars suddenly seemed to double their speed. When they fired again, they would be almost on top of the retreating Ujurrians.

He visualized three more of the innocents he had interfered with turned to ash against the grey stone of the mountainside.

At that point the ground vanished beneath the ground-cars.

There was a violent crash, the whine of protesting machinery, as the two vehicles were unable to compensate fast enough for the unexpected change in the surface. Still moving forward, both abruptly dipped downward and smashed at high speed into the far wall of the huge pit.

Flinx and Sylzenzuzex gaped silently at the enormous rift which had unexpectedly appeared in the ground.

'Backtrap,' Fluff noted with satisfaction. 'I remembered what you tell us about how the little machines work, Flinx-friend.' Battered humans and AAnn – the latter's surgical disguises now knocked all askew – were fighting to get control of themselves within the wreckage of the two cars.

A mob of furry behemoths was pouring from the mine buildings towards the pits. Flinx could make out the narrow ledges of solid earth and rock that ran like a spiderweb across the rift. They formed safe pathways across which the three decoy runners had retreated. By the same token, they were far too narrow to provide adequate support for the ground-cars. The surface against which their air jets pushed had been suddenly pulled away.

Hundreds of thin saplings now lined the edges of the pit.

These had been used to support the heavy cover or twigs, leaves, and earth, all carefully prepared to give the appearance of solid ground.

New screams and the flash of blue hand beamers lit the pit as the ursinoids poured in. Flinx saw a three-hundred-kilo adolescent male pick up a squirming AAnn and treat its head like the stopper of a bottle. He turned away from the carnage, sick.

'Why is Flinx-friend troubled?' Fluff wanted to know. 'We play game with their rules now. Is fair, is not?'

'Ride the *grizel*,' Sylzenzuzex warned him in High Thranx.

By the head, not the tail, something echoed inside him. He forced himself to turn back and watch the end of the brief fight.

As soon as it became clear to the observers down below what had happened, a red beam the thickness of a man's body reached upward from a small tower at the base's far end. It passed unbroken through several sections of forest, cutting down trees like a lineal scythe and leaving the stumps smoking, until it impinged on the mountainside to the left of the pit. A flare of intense light was followed by a dull explosion.

'Get everyone back inside, Fluff,' Flinx yelled. But an order wasn't necessary. Their work concluded, the ursinoids who had assaulted the pit were already running, dodging, scampering playfully back into the mine.

Flinx thought he saw movement far below as the top of the tower started to swivel towards him, but apparently calmer heads prevailed. The mill itself was still out of bounds for destructive weaponry. Rudenuaman had no reason yet to raze the mountainside, to turn the complex mine and mill into a larger duplicate of the small slag-lined crater which now bubbled and smoked where the heavy laser had struck. Much as she might regret the loss of the two groundcars and their crews, she was not yet desperate.

So no avenging light came to destroy the building. The simple natives were to be permitted their one useless victory. Undoubtedly, Flinx thought with irony, Rudenuaman would attribute the brilliant tactic to him, never imagining that the huge dull beasts of burden had conceived and executed the rout entirely by themselves.

'I wonder,' he said to Sylzenzuzex over a meal of nuts and

berries and captured packaged food, 'if there's any point to continuing this. I've never really felt as if I were in control of things. Maybe . . . maybe it would be better to run back to the caves. I can still teach from there – we both can – and we have a lot of life left in us.'

'You're still in control, Flinx,' Sylzenzuzex told him. She tapped one truhand against the table in a pattern few human ears would have recognized. 'The Ujurrians want you to be. But you go ahead, Flinx. You tell them all,' and she waved a hand to take in the whole mine, 'that they should go back to their caves and resume their original game. You tell them that. But they won't forget what they've learned. They never forget.'

'O'Morion knows how much knowledge they've acquired from this mine already,' Flinx mumbled, picking at his food.

'They'll go back to digging their cave pattern, but they'll retain that knowledge,' she went on. 'You'll leave them with the game rules Rudenuaman's butchers have set. If they ever *do* show any initiative of their own, after we've gone . . .' She made a thranx shrug. 'Don't blame yourself for what's happened. The Ujurrians are no angels.' Whistling thranx laughter forced her to pause a moment. 'You can't play both God and the Devil to them, Flinx. You didn't introduce these beings to killing, but we'd better make certain we don't teach them to enjoy it,

'Moping and moaning about your own mistakes isn't going to help us or them. You've put your truleg in your masticatory orifice. You can pull it out or suffocate on it, but you can't ignore it.' She downed a handful of sweet red-orange berries the size of walnuts.

'We not enjoy killing,' a voice boomed. They both jumped. The Ujurrians moved with a stealth and quietness that was startling in creatures so massive. Fluff stood in the doorway on four legs, filling it completely.

'Why not?' Sylzenzuzex asked. 'Why shouldn't we worry about it?'

'No fun,' explained Fluff concisely, dismissing the entire idea as something too absurd to be worthy of discussion. 'Kill meat when necessary. Kill cold minds when necessary. Unless,' and beacon-eyes shone on the room's other occupant, 'Flinx say otherwise.'

Flinx shook his head slowly, 'Never, Fluff.'

'I think you say that. Is time to finish this part of game.' He gestured with a paw. 'You come too?'

'I don't know what you have planned this time, Fluff, but yes,' Flinx concurred, 'we come too.'

'Fun,' the giant Ujurrian thundered, in a fashion indicating something less than general amusement was about to ensue.

'I don't want any of the buildings down there damaged, if it can be avoided,' Flinx instructed the ursinoid as he led him and Sylzenzuzex down corridors and stairways. 'They're filled with knowledge – game rules. Mechanical training manuals, records, certainly a complete geology library. If we're going to be marooned on this world for the rest of our lives, Fluff, I'm going to need every scrap of that material in order to teach you properly.'

'Is understood,' Fluff grunted. 'Part of game not to damage buildings' insides. Will tell family. Not to worry.'

'Not to worry,' Flinx mimicked, thinking of the alert and armed personnel awaiting them at the base of the mountain. Thinking also of the two atmosphere-piercing laser cannon set to swivel freely in the small tower.

Fluff led them downward, down through the several floors of mill and mine, down to the single storage level below ground. Down past rooms and chambers and corridors walled with patiently waiting, snoozing, playful Ujurrians. Down to where the lowest floor itself had been ripped up. There they halted.

Moam was waiting for them, and Bluebright and Softsmooth and a dimly glimpsed flickering something that might have been Maybeso, or might have been an illusion caused by a trick of the faint overhead lighting.

Instead of stopping before a solid ferrocrete barrier, they found three enormous tunnels leading off into total darkness. Light from the room penetrated those down-sloping shafts only slightly, but Flinx thought he could detect additional branch tunnels breaking off from the three principal ones further on.

'Surprise, yes?' Fluff asked expectantly.

'Yes,' was all a bewildered Flinx could reply.

'Each tunnel,' the ursinoid continued, 'come up under one part of several metal caves below, in quiet place where cold minds are not.'

'You can tell where the floors aren't guarded?' Sylzen-zuzex murmured in amazement.

'Can sense,' Moam explained. 'Is easy.'

'Is good idea, Flinx-friend?' a worried Fluff wondered. 'Is okay part of game, or try something else?'

'No, is okay part of game, Fluff,' Flinx admitted finally. He turned to face the endless sea of great-eyed animals. 'Pay attention, now.'

A massive stirring and rolling shivered through the massed bodies.

'Those who break into the power station must shut everything off. Push every little knob and switch to the – '

'Know what means *off*,' Bluebright told him confidently.

'I probably should leave you alone, you've managed fine without my help,' Flinx muttered. 'Still, its important. This will darken everything except for the tower housing the two big cannon. They'll be independently powered, as will the shuttlecraft hangar beneath the landing strip. Those of you who get into the cannon tower will have to – '

'Am sorry, Flinx-friend,' a doleful Fluff interrupted. 'Cannot do.'

'Why not?'

'Floors not like this,' the ursinoid explained, eyes glowing in the indirect lighting. He indicated the broken ferrocrete lying around. 'Are thick metal. Cannot dig through.'

Flinx's spirits sank. 'Then this whole attack will have to be called off until we can think of something that will eliminate that tower. They can destroy all of us, even if they have to melt the entire remaining installation to do so. If Rudenuaman were to slip away and reach the tower, I don't think she'd hesitate to give the order. At that point she'd have nothing further to lose.'

'Not mean to make you worry, Flinx-friend,' comforted Bluebright.

'Nothing to worry about,' Moam added.

'Have something else to take care of tower,' explained Fluff.

'But you . . .' Flinx stopped himself, went on quietly, 'no, if you say you do, then you must.'

'What about the three who got themselves killed?' Sylzenzuzex whispered. 'They thought they had something too. This time there are many more lives at stake.'

Flinx shook his head slowly. 'Ay, Bee and Cee were playing by different rules, Syl. It's time for us to trust our lives to these. They've risked theirs often enough on our say-so. But just in case . . .'

He turned to Fluff. 'There is one thing I must do even if this fails and we all end up dead. I want to come up through the floor of the big living house, Fluff. There is something in there that I need the use of.'

'In this tunnel,' Fluff told him, indicating the shaft at far left. 'Are ready, then?'

Flinx nodded. The huge Ujurrian turned and shouted mental instructions. They were accompanied by a nonverbal emotional command.

A soft, threatening rumble responded . . . a hair-curling sound as dozens, hundreds of massive shapes bestirred themselves in long lines reaching back into the far places of the mine.

Then they were moving down the tunnels. Flinx and Sylzenzuzex hugged close to Fluff, each with a hand tight in his fur. Sylzenzuzex's night vision was far better than Flinx's, but the tunnel was too black even for her acute senses.

If the Ujurrians' activities had been detected, Flinx reflected, they might never re-emerge into the light. They could be trapped and killed here with little effort.

'One question,' Sylzenzuzex asked.

Flinx's mind was elsewhere when he responded: 'What?'

'How did they excavate these tunnels? The ground here is rock-laden and the tunnels seem quite extensive.'

'They've been digging tunnels for fourteen thousand years, Syl.' Flinx found he was moving with more and more confidence as nothing appeared to deal death from above them. 'I imagine they've become pretty good at it . . .'

Teleen auz Rudenuaman panted desperately, nearly out of breath, as she limped along the floor. The sounds of heavy fighting sounded outside and below her.

A massive brown shape appeared at the top of the stair-well which she had just exited. Turning, she fired her beamer in its direction. It disappeared, though she was unable to tell whether she'd hit it or not.

She had been relaxing in her living quarters when the attack had come – not from the distant mine, but from under her feet. Simultaneously, hundreds of enormous, angry monsters had exploded out of the sublevels of every building, that is, except for the cannon tower. She'd barely had time to give the order for those powerful weapons to swing around and beam every structure except the one she was in when they had been destroyed.

A peculiar violent beam no thicker than her thumb had jumped the gap between the uppermost floor of the far-off mine and the tower's base. Where it had touched there was now only a deep horizontal scar in the earth. It had been so quick that she'd neither seen nor heard any explosion.

One moment the tower had been there – three storeys of armour housing the big guns – and the next she'd heard a loud hissing sound like a hot ember being dropped in water. When she turned to look, the tower was gone.

Now there was no place to run to, nothing left to bargain with. Her badly outmatched personnel – human, thranx and AAnn alike – had been submerged by a brown avalanche.

She'd tried to make for the underground shuttle hangar in hopes of hiding there until the Baron's return, but the lower floors of this building were also blocked by swarms of lemur-lensed behemoths. The ground outside was alive with them.

It made no sense! There had been perhaps half a hundred of the slow-moving natives living in the immediate vicinity of the mine. Surveys had revealed a few hundred more inhabiting caves outside the vicinity.

Now there were thousands of them, of all sizes, over-running the installation, overrunning her thoughts. The crash of overturned furniture and shattered glassalloy sounded below. There was no way out. She could only retreat upwards.

Limping to another stairwell, she started up to her apart-ment-office on the top floor. The battle was all but over when the cannon tower had been eliminated. Meevo confirmed that when he reported the power station taken. Those were the last words she heard from the reptilian engineer.

With the station, the power to communications and the lifts had gone. It was hard for her to mount the stairwell, with her bad leg. Her jumpsuit was torn, the carefully applied makeup covering her facial scars badly smudged. She would meet death in her own quarters, unpanicked to the end, showing the true self-confidence of a Rudenuaman.

She slowed at the top of the stairs. Her quarters were at the far end of the hall, but there was a light shining from inside the chamber nearst the stairwell. Moving cautiously, she slid the broken door a little further back, peered inside.

The light was the kind that might come from a small appliance. There were many such self-powered devices on the base – but what would anyone be doing with one here and now, when he should have a beamer in his fist?

Holding her own tightly, she tiptoed into the chamber.

These quarters had not been lived in since the demise of their former occupant. The light was coming from a far corner. It was generated by a portable viewer. A small, slight figure was hunched intently before it, oblivious to all else.

She waited, and in a short while the figure leaned back with a sigh, reaching out to switch the machine off. Fury and despondency alternated in her thoughts, to be replaced at last by a cold, calm sense of resignation.

'I ought to have guessed,' she muttered.

The figure jerked in surprise, spun about.

'Why aren't you decently dead, like you're supposed to be?'

Flinx hesitated, replied without the hint of a smile, 'It wasn't destined to be part of the game.'

'You're joking with me . . . even now. I should have killed you the same time I finished Challis. But no,' she said bitterly, 'I had to keep you around as an amusement.'

'Are you sure that's the only reason?' he inquired, so gently that she was momentarily taken aback.

'You play word games with me, too.' She raised the muzzle of the beamer. 'I only regret I haven't got time to kill you slowly. You haven't even left me that.' She shrugged tiredly. 'The price one pays for undersight, as my aunt would say, corruption be on her spirit. I am curious, though – how did you mange to tame and train these creatures?'

Flinx looked at her pityingly. 'You still don't understand anything, do you?'

'Only,' she replied, her finger tightening on the beamer's trigger, 'that this comes several months too late.'

'Wait!' he shouted pleadingly, 'if you'll give me one min –'

The finger convulsed. At the same time someone doused

her eyes with liquid fire. She screamed, and the beam passed just to the right of Flinx to obliterate the viewer nearby.

'Don't rub!' he started to yell, rushing around the chair he'd been sitting in – already too late. At the moment of contact she'd dropped the beamer and begun rubbing instinctively at the awful pain in her face. She was on the floor now, rolling over and over.

The distance between them was no longer great, but by the time he reached her she was unconscious and stiff. Thirty seconds later she was dead.

'You never did take the time to listen, Teleen,' he murmured, kneeling numbly by the doubled-over corpse. Nervously flicking his long toungue in and out, Pip settled softly on Flinx's shoulder. The minidrag was taut with anger.

'Your life was too rushed. Mine's been too rushed, also.'

Something moved in the doorway. Looking up, Flinx saw a wheezing Sylzenzuzex standing there, favouring her splinted leghand. One truhand had a firm grip on a thranx-sized beamer.

'I see you found her,' she observed, her breath coming through the spicules of her b-thorax in long whistles. 'Softsmooth tells me that the last bits of resistance are almost cleaned out.' Her compound eyes regarded him questioningly as he looked back down at the body.

'I didn't find her. She found me. But before I could make her listen, Pip intervened. I suppose he had to; she would have killed me.' Unexpectedly, he glanced at her and smiled.

'You should see yourself, Syl. You look like a throwback from Hivehom's pre-tranquillity days. Like a warrior who has just concluded a successful brood raid on a neighbouring hive. A wonderful advertisement for the compassionate understanding of the Church.'

She didn't respond to the jibe. There was something in his voice . . . 'That's not like you, Flinx.' She studied him as he turned back to stare at the corpse, trying to remember everything she knew of human emotion. It seemed to her that his interest in this woman, who for a few *tams of vackel* had worked willingly with the sworn enemies of humanx kind, was abnormal.

Sylzenzuzex was not her uncle's equal when it came to intuitive deduction, but neither was she stupid. 'You know

something more about this human female than you have
said.'

'I must have known her before,' he whispered, 'though I
don't remember her at all. According to the time intervals
given on the tape that's not too surprising.' He gestured
limply at the chamber behind him. 'This was Challis's apart-
ment.' His hand returned to indicate the corpse. For a
moment his eyes seemed nearly as deep as Moam's. 'This
was my sister.'

Not until the following afternoon, after the bodies had been
efficiently buried by the Ujurrians, did Sylzenzuzex insist on
hearing about everything that had been recorded on the
stolen tape.

'I was an orphan, Syl, raised on Moth by a human
woman named Mother Mastiff. The information I found
said that I'd been born to a professional Lynx named Rud,
in Allahabad on Terra. The records also said I was a second
child, though they didn't give details. Those facts were to be
found on the tape Challis stole, the tape I didn't read until
last night.

'My mother also had an elder sister. My mother's husband
who according to the tape was not my father, gave that
elder sister a position in his commercial firm. After he died,
under still unexplained circumstances, the sister took control
of the company and built it into a considerable business
empire.

'It seems my mother and her sister were never the best of
friends. Some of the details of what amounted to my
mother's captivity, and that's what it reads like, are . . .' He
had to stop for a moment.

'It's easy to see how a mind like Challis's would be
attracted to details like that. My mother died soon after her
husband. A number of unexplained incidents followed. No
one could be certain, but it was theorized they might be
attributable in some way to her male nephew. So . . . I was
disposed of. A small sale in so large a commercial concern,'
he added viciously.

'It amused the elder sister, Rashalleila, to keep the girl
niece around. The sister's name was Nuaman. The niece –
my sister – was called Teleen. She became a mirror image of
her aunt, took the company from her, and merged her

mother's name with her aunt's. Symbospeeched it. Teleen of Rud and Nuaman . . . Teleen auz Rudenuaman.

'As for me – I was long forgotten by everyone. Challis's researchers were interested in the part about my causing some "unexplained incidents", as they were called. He never troubled to make any other connections from the information.'

They walked on in silence, past the long gouge in the earth where the cannon tower had stood. Fluff, Moam, Bluebright, and Softsmooth trailed behind. They came upon a small building set alongside the landing field. Earlier, one of the Ujurrians had discovered that it led down to the extensive shuttlecraft hangar. The hangar held complete repair and construction facilities for shuttlecraft, as would be necessary on an isolated world like this. There was also an extensive machine shop and an enormous technical library on all aspects of Commonwealth KK ship maintenance. It would make a very useful branch of the Ujurrian school Flinx was planning to set up.

'I didn't have time to ask last night, Fluff,' Flinx began, as they passed the end of the scar, 'how did you manage that?'

'Was fun,' the big ursinoid responded brightly. 'Was Moam's idea mostly. Also a young She named Mask. While others dug tunnels, they two read much that was in books at the mine.'

'Made some changes in cold minds' cave digger,' Moam supplied.

'The press drill,' murmured Sylzenzuzex, 'they must have modified the press drill. But how?'

'Change here, add this,' explained Moam. 'Was fun.'

'I wonder if *modified* is quite the word for turning a harmless tool into a completely new kind of weapon,' Flinx mused. He looked skyward. 'Maybe we'll let Moam and Mask and their friends play with the library and machine shop below. But first we have some other modifications that have to be carried out in a hurry . . .'

The big freighter came out of KK drive just inside the orbit of Ulru-Ujurr's second satellite, moving nearer on short bursts from its immensely powerful spacespanning engine. The freighter entered a low orbit around the vast blue-brown world, remaining directly above the only installation on its surface.

'Honoured One, there is no response,' the disguised AAnn operating the ship's communicator reported.

'Try again,' a deep voice commanded.

The operator did so, finally looked up helplessly. 'There is no response on any of the closed-signal frequencies. But there is something else – something very peculiar.'

'Explain,' the Baron directed curtly. His mind was spinning.

'There is evidence of all kinds of subatmospheric broadcasting, but none on any frequencies I can tap into. And none of it is directed at us, despite my repeated calls.'

A man named Josephson, who was a very important executive in Rudenuaman Enterprises, moved next to the Baron. 'What's going on down there? This isn't like Madam Rudenuaman.'

'It is not like many things,' observed the Baron cautiously. He turned his attention to another of the control pod operatives. 'What is the cloud cover like above the base?'

'Clear and with little wind, sir,' the atmospheric meteorologist reported quickly. 'A typical Ujurrian autumn day.'

The Baron hissed softly, 'Josephson-sir, come with me please.'

'Where are we going?' the confused executive wanted to know, even as he followed the Baron down the corridor leading to the far end of the command blister.

'Here.' The Baron hit a switch and the door slid back. 'I require maximum resolution,' he instructed the on-duty technician.

'At once, Honoured One,' the disguised reptilian acknowledged as he hurried to make the necessary adjustments to the surface scope. Sitting down alongside the tech, the Baron punched the requisite co-ordinates into the scope computer himself.

Then he remained motionless for several minutes, staring through the viewer. Eventually he moved aside, gestured that Josephson should take his place. The human did so, adjusting the focus slightly for his eyes. He gave a verbal and physical start.

'What do you see?' the Baron inquired.

'The base is gone, and there's something in its place.'

'Then I may not be mad,' the Baron observed. 'What do you see?'

'Well, the landing strip is still there, but something like a small city is climbing from the lakeshore up into the mountains. Knowing the terrain, I'd say several of the unfinished structures are a couple of hundred metres high.' His voice faded with astonishment.

'What does this suggest to you?' the Baron asked.

Josephson looked up from the scope, shaking his head slowly.

'It suggests,' the Baron hissed tightly, 'that the structures may be built deeply into the mountains. By whom or how deeply we will not know, unless we go down to see for ourselves.'

'Wouldn't advise that,' a new voice boomed.

Josephson gave a cry and stumbled out of the chair, pressing himself back against the console. The technician and the Baron whirled, both reaching simultaneously for their sidearms.

An apparition stood solidly in the centre of the room. It was a good three metres tall, standing on its hind legs, and its bulk nearly dented the deck. Huge yellow eyes glared balefully down at them.

'Wouldn't advise it,' the apparition repeated. 'Get lost.'

The Baron's hand beamer was aimed – but now there was nothing to shoot at.

'Hallucinations,' Josephson suggested shakily, after his voice returned.

The Baron said nothing, walked to the place where the creature had stood. He knelt in a way no human could, hunting for something on the floor. 'A very hirsute hallucination,' he commented, examining several thick, coarse hairs. His mind was churning furiously.

'You know I've never been outside the main installation,' Josephson declared. 'What was it?'

'An Ujurrian primitive,' the Baron explained thoughtfully, rubbing the hairs between false-skinned fingers.

'What . . . what was it talking about?'

Disgust was evident in the Baron's voice. 'There are times when I wonder how you humans ever achieved half of what you have.'

'Now, look,' the executive began angrily, 'there's no need to get abusive.'

'No,' the Baron admitted. After all, they were still within Commonwealth territory. 'There is no reason to get abusive. I apologize, Josephson-sir.' Turning, they left the room and the wide-eyed technician.

'Where are we going now?'

'To do what the creature said.'

'Just a minute,' Josephson eyed the unblinking AAnn aristocrat firmly. 'If the Madam is in trouble down there . . .'

'Sssisssttt . . . use your brain, warm-blood,' the Baron snorted. 'Where there was a small base there is now a rapidly growing city. Where there used to be a single welcoming signal there is now a multitude of peculiar local communications. From a few clusters of cave-dwelling natives, there comes a teleport who advises us curtly not to land. Who advises us curtly – in your vernacular I might add, Josephson-sir – to make haste elsewhere.

'I think it reasonable, considering the evidence, for us to comply quickly. I act according to realities and not emotions, Josephson-sir. That is why I will always be one who gives orders and you will always be one who takes them.' He hurried his pace, pushing past the man and leaving him standing, to gape down the corridor after him.

As directed by the Baron, the freighter left Ulru-Ujurr's vicinity at maximum velocity. Resting in his sumptuous cabin, the Baron pondered what had taken place during his absence. Something of considerable importance, with unknowable implications for the future.

Of one thing he was certain: Madam Rudenuaman and the enterprise they had collaborated on no longer existed. But there could be a host of reasons why.

That the natives were more than ignorant savages now seemed certain . . . but how much more certain he could not say. A single genius among them could have been mnemonically instructed to deliver what had been, after all, an extremely brief message. A new experimental device could have projected him aboard the freighter.

The burgeoning city below could be the product of the Church, the Commonwealth, a business competitor, or an alien interloper. This section of the Arm was still mostly unexplored; anything could be setting itself up on an isolated, unvisited world like Ulru-Ujurr.

He had done well by the venture. There were a number of small stones still in his possession, which he could ration out slowly to the Commonwealth over the years. His status at the Emperor's court had risen considerably, though the Imperial psychotechnicians' scheme of implanting suicidal impulse-plays into the Janus jewels and then selling them to important humans and thranx would now have to be abandoned.

That was too bad, for the programme had been very successful. Yet this could have been worse. Whatever had wiped out the installation and Madam Rudenuaman could also have taken him, had he not gone in pursuit of the human child.

A pity the way she happened to encounter that human patrol vessel, forcing him to abandon any hope of eliminating her. Almost as if she'd known what she was doing. But it did not matter much, he knew. Let her rave about Ulru-Ujurr to any who might be credulous enough to listen – for now that world was no concern of his.

In the future, given the inevitable triumph of the Empire, he could return with an Imperial fleet, instead of skulking about in disguise like this and in the forced company of despised mammals and insects. Then he might re-establish control, nay, sovereignty over that enigmatic world, holding all the glory and profits to be gained therefrom for himself and the house of WW.

Maybe so, he mused pleasurably, maybe so.

He did not hear the voice that echoed in response from the depths of Someplace Else. A voice that echoed ... maybe not!

The day dawned bright and warm. Sylzenzuzex found she could walk about freely with only the flimsiest covering.

She had developed a special rapport with the shy adolescent female called Mask, who had turned out to be a wonderful guide to the history and unexpectedly complex interrelationships of the Ujurrians. So Sylzenzuzex was revelling in her study of a subject dear to her heart.

Perhaps some day it would form the basis for a monograph, or even a full dissertation, one important enough to win reinstatement in the Church for her. Although the discovery that the Church had indeed been responsible for quarantining these people continued to cause her to question that organization's standards, and her own future participation in it.

She left her quarters in the building, intending to mention yesterday's revelations to Flinx. But he did not seem to be anywhere around, nor was he at the landing strip school, nor at any of the factory centres ringing the old mine. One of the ursinoids finally directed her to a place at the far end of the valley, where she had once fled Rudenuaman's grasp. After a fair climb up a steep bluff, she found him sitting cross-legged on a ledge consorting with a local insect no larger than his finger. It was enamelled green and ochre, with yellow-spotted wings.

Pip was darting through the nearby bushes, worrying an exasperated, sinuous mammal half his size.

From here one could look back down the full length of the valley, see the azure lake cradled between snow-capped peaks, and watch the steady progress of construction along the south shore.

When Flinx finally turned to her, he wore an expression so sorrowful it shocked her.

'What's the matter . . . why so sad?' she inquired.

'So who's sad?'

She shook her valentine-shaped head slowly. When he didn't respond, she gestured towards the lake valley.

'I don't know what you have to be disappointed about. Your charges seem to have taken to your game of civilization with plenty of enthusiasm. Is it the ship Maybeso boarded? Whatever he told them must have been effective. They haven't come back, and there's been no sign of another ship in the months since.'

By way of reply he pointed towards the north shore of the lake. A vast metal superstructure was rising there. It was nearly as long as the lake itself.

'Something about the ship?'

He shook his head. 'No . . . about the reason behind it. Syl, I've only accomplished half of what I set out to do. I know that my mother's dead, but I still don't know who my father was or what happened to him.' He stared hard at her. 'And I want to know, Syl. Maybe he's long dead, too,

202

or alive and even a worse human animal than my sister turned out to be; but *I want to know*. I *will* know!' he finished with sudden vehemence.

'How does that connect with the ship?'

Now he cracked a wan smile. 'Why do you think the Ujurrians are building a ship?'

'I don't know . . . for fun, to explore . . . why?'

'It's my present from them – Moam's little surprise. He knows I want to go looking for my father, so they're doing their best to help me look. I told them they couldn't construct a KK-drive ship here . . . that it had to be done clear of a planet's gravity. You know what he said? "We fix . . . too much trouble other way."'

'He located an Ujurrian – skinniest one I ever saw – who thinks only in mathematical terms. She's so weird – her name-translation came out as "Integrator" – she can almost understand Maybeso. Moam set her the problem. Two weeks ago she cracked the problem of landing in a gravity well on KK-drive. Commonwealth scientists have been trying to solve that puzzle for a couple of hundred years.'

He sighed. 'All to help me find my father. Syl . . . what happens if the Ujurrians don't find the rest of the cosmos, our civilization, to their liking? What if they decide to "play" with it? *What have we unleashed?*'

She sat back on trulegs and foothands and pondered. Long minutes passed. The gem-encrusted bug flew away.

'If nothing else,' she told him finally, staring down at the ship, 'a way to go home. You worry overmuch, Flinx. I don't think our civilization will hold much of interest for these creatures. It's *you* they're interested in. Remember what Maybeso said . . . if this new game bores them, they'll go back to their old one.'

Flinx considered this, appeared to brighten. Then abruptly he rose, brushed the dust from his legs. 'I suppose you're right, Syl. I can't do any good worrying about it. When they finish the ship, it *will* be time to go home. I need Mother Mastiff's acerbity, and I need to lose myself again, for a while.' He glanced up at her oddly. 'Will you help?'

Sylzenzuzex turned great, glowing multifaceted eyes on Pip, watched as the minidrag folded pleated wings to dive down a burrow after the retreating mammal. Sounds of scuffling came from below.

'It promises to be intriguing . . . from a purely scientific point of view, of course,' she murmured.

'Of course,' Flinx acknowledged, properly straight-faced.

A narrow reptilian head popped out of the burrow and a pointed tongue flicked rapidly in their direction. Pip stared smugly back at them, a Cheshire cat with scales . . .

Coming Soon

THE END OF THE MATTER
by Alan Dean Foster

'A moment, young man.' The technician was nearly seventy. The President was, however, a good deal older. 'There is, of course, no way of stopping, turning, or destroying a collapsar?'

Remembering to whom he was talking, the physicist kept any sign of condescension from his voice. 'Hardly, sir. Anything we could throw at it, whether a million SCCAM projectiles or another star, would simply be sucked in. The more we tried to destroy it, the larger it would become, though we wouldn't notice its growth, since it would still be only a point in space. Furthermore, we already know from measurements sent back by the first drone that this wanderer consists of much more than a single collapsed star. Much more. Perhaps several hundred suns.' He shrugged. 'Some of my colleagues believe that because of the wanderer's speed and theoretical mass, it may be an object only guessed at by recent mathematics: a collaxar. A collapsed galaxy, sir, instead of a single star.'

. . . And the collapsar was heading towards the Commonwealth. Three planets were in its path; three and a half billion lives were threatened.

Flinx was to become involved in the fate of those three planets. He was also to become involved with the Qwarm . . .

Every instinct, everything in him, warned Flinx against entering the blackness inside. That was countered, as usual, by his relentless curiosity. He slipped through the slight opening. A dim light shone in a near corner, near mountainous heaps of extruded plastic casings. Treading softly, with a dim shape fluttering nervously overhead, he moved towards the light.

Suddenly he could sense unease, even fear. Marshalled against it was a frightening coolness. Both were far from here and moving rapidly away from him. From the lighted region he was approaching he detected nothing. Very slowly, he peered around a last, four-metre-high yellow case.

Six bodies filled the space his astonished gaze encountered. Six! They lay draped over crates, contorted on the metal floor, and bunched beneath overturned casings. Four were women, two men. All were clad in the by now too-familiar black. Several showed naked skulls, their caps missing. Copious amounts of blood lent murderous highlights to the devastated scene. Several of the smaller crates were shattered. It must have taken some unknown, awesome force to crack those seamless containers.

In a few hours, Flinx knew, some warehouse supervisor would arrive to open up, and get the shock of his or her life.

There were only dead Qwarm here, no sign of any other intruders. Flinx couldn't conceive of anyone or anything that would attack, let alone destroy, such a large number of professional assassins. He stiffened. A hint of a far-off mental scream had touched him, alerted him once more to something that continued to move away from this place. Whatever it was, he considered, it might not continue to move *away*.

Once again Flinx looked back at the crumpled, silent bodies, some of which were partially dismembered. Again he noted the cracked plastic casings strewn casually about. Some great force had been at work here, for reasons Flinx could not imagine. That distant mental shriek continued to echo in his mind as he found himself backing away slowly from the nightmarish scene. Darkness closed tight around him once more.

Something touched his shoulder.

THE TAR-AIYM KRANG
by Alan Dean Foster

The Tar-Aiym had been dead for perhaps a million years
Once they had fought against and then ruled the galaxy. But
now they had vanished, leaving only the legend of their final
artifact — the lost Krang

Nobody knew what the Krang might be, but everyone wanted
it. Until it was found . . .

For the Krang had a purpose. The Krang had power and a will
of its own.

NEW ENGLISH LIBRARY